the Irish Daughter

BOOKS BY DAISY O'SHEA

EMERALD ISLES SERIES
The Irish Key
The Irish Child
The Irish Family Secret

DAISY O'SHEA

Bookouture

Published by Bookouture in 2025

An imprint of Storyfire Ltd.
Carmelite House
50 Victoria Embankment
London EC4Y 0DZ

www.bookouture.com

The authorised representative in the EEA is Hachette Ireland
8 Castlecourt Centre
Dublin 15 D15 XTP3
Ireland
(email: info@hbgi.ie)

Copyright © Daisy O'Shea, 2025

Daisy O'Shea has asserted her right to be identified as the author of this work.

All rights reserved. No part of this publication may be reproduced, stored in any retrieval system, or transmitted, in any form or by any means, electronic, mechanical, photocopying, recording or otherwise, without the prior written permission of the publishers.

ISBN: 978-1-83618-904-6
eBook ISBN: 978-1-83618-902-2

This book is a work of fiction. Names, characters, businesses, organizations, places and events other than those clearly in the public domain, are either the product of the author's imagination or are used fictitiously. Any resemblance to actual persons, living or dead, events or locales is entirely coincidental.

PROLOGUE

ESTHER, 1957

Esther stood at the hospital door for a moment, her hand on her breast, her heart beating so hard it brought a flush to her cheeks. Today, finally, she would bring her baby home. She closed her eyes briefly, then steeled herself to step through. She was instantly engulfed by the overwhelming fumes of bleach and carbolic soap – the scent of death, her father had called it. And sure, hadn't he died there? Brought in for a small operation to remove a gangrenous toe, he had passed under the anaesthetic. She hadn't grieved for him, and neither had her mother, who had just one year of relative peace before taking herself off to join him; a heart attack while she was, ironically, on her knees saying the rosary.

Esther had long wondered whether she had accepted Adrian's proposal simply to escape the rigid discipline imposed by the Sisters of Mercy in Skibbereen. Their charitable act – taking in the young orphan – had been greeted with sighs of relief from Esther's distant relatives. God forbid they should be landed with another mouth to feed when times were hard enough already. But that cold discipline during her formative years had knotted her hands and knees with pain that would remain with her for the rest of her life. There had been times during those barren years when she had prayed for the Lord to bring pestilence down upon her distant family, who had palmed off the burden of an orphaned child.

When her youngest daughter, Hannah, contracted the polio, Esther wondered, in some dark recess of her mind, whether the Lord was, in fact, quietly castigating her for her own ungenerous thoughts. Adrian, whose soul was rooted in the ever-turning life cycle of the farm, told her not to be so daft. It was nature at its most unforgiving. Sometimes cows got sick and died, too. There was no rhyme nor reason, no bigger plan.

Her husband was a dour presence at the best of times: working all hours, coming in from the fields to eat and sleep, barely a civil word spoken. This wasn't the marriage she had imagined when he had brought her home as his bride, seated in the cart behind a donkey, trotting up a boreen glistening with dew-drenched primroses. But religion had been instilled in her from birth, and she quietly retained her own faith despite his cynicism, so she had prayed daily, hourly, for Hannah to live and come home, and now her prayers had been answered.

This would only be her second visit to the hospital since Hannah had been taken away from her by the men in the ambulance, too sick to complain about being lifted from her mother's arms. *No, she couldn't come with the child. Polio was highly contagious. The hospital was floundering under the weight of sick and dying children.*

The first visit had been a disaster. When the epidemic had been contained, Esther was advised that she could come in and view Hannah through the tiny square window in the ward door. This she had done, waving madly to get Hannah's attention.

Hannah, a shrunken waif packed tightly under starched sheets, was smaller than Esther recalled. She had held her arms out and screamed herself hoarse for her mama, and Esther had stood there outside the ward, tears streaming over her forced smile, unable to go in and provide the comfort her child needed. She'd been advised that it wasn't in Hannah's best interests for her to come again, not until Hannah was well enough to be brought home. It was difficult enough already. Further visits would only upset the fragile order maintained by vigilant and overworked nursing staff.

So, for nearly seven months she had driven the donkey cart daily to the priest's house to use the only telephone in Roone Bay, to be provided with brief news of Hannah's condition. *The paralysis had crept up her body. Her legs, her arms, her throat, but she was still breathing, thank the Lord.* The disease had stopped its cruel passage before paralysing the muscles that kept her heart beating. Once she was able to suck water from a sponge, and swallow, apparently the prognosis was good. She would survive. But no one could foresee how permanent the damage would be, and recovery from the disease was known to be slow, counted in months rather than weeks.

Eventually she was able to eat gruel. Then she began to recover the use of her arms. *And her legs?* Esther asked anxiously. No. Her legs remained paralysed. She would, God willing, learn to walk again with aids, but the perfect child Esther recalled, her sunny-natured, inquisitive, beautiful little girl, would struggle to the end of her days.

Esther went through the motions of the daily routines of providing for her family, while her thoughts travelled the long journey into Cork city hospital and her sick child. Adrian rolled his eyes to the unforgiving heavens and wished the matter settled, one way or the other, so that they could get on with their lives. He muttered under his breath that it would have been better if Hannah had died, wasn't life hard enough already? And weren't weans easy come by, arriving screaming into the world too often, to further stretch the family's meagre resources?

Today Esther had come to bring Hannah home, but she was

secretly terrified. The hospital staff were thrilled by Hannah's progress, but Esther was exhausted by the months of worry, and now the time had come to bring Hannah home, she wondered how she would ever cope with a child who could barely stand unaided, let alone walk.

The austere long ward, with its neat rows of iron bedsteads was quieter now. Some of the beds were empty, and the remaining children were quiet, subdued, simply waiting to see what life would throw at them. Esther walked slowly to the bed where Hannah had lain. It was empty, pristine, its corners regimented as though no child had ever been there.

She stood, stunned for a moment, until a nurse padded over in soft shoes that made small squeaking noises on the lino. 'Can I help you, ma'am?'

'My daughter. Hannah Barry. Where is my daughter? She's gone.'

Her voice rose on each word, almost ending on a shriek, but the nurse put a comforting hand on her shoulder and said softly, 'Mrs Barry, your daughter is down here. Come – I'll take you.'

Her panic subsided as she followed the young nurse back down the length of the ward. Of course. Why had she supposed Hannah would still be in the same bed?

'Here we are, so,' the nurse said, checking the name on the clipboard hanging on the end of the bed. The little girl stared at Esther curiously but with a total lack of recognition.

'Hannah, sweetheart, your mam has come to take you home.' She cast a sidelong grimace towards Esther, visibly trying to stem her own threatening tears, and whispered, 'So sad; the little girl in the next bed died last night. She just stopped breathing. So unexpected, after we thought she was doing so well, too. Well, she's gone to a better place. This disease is so cruel. I'm glad I'm not the one who has to tell her parents.'

'You must know all the children like they're your own,'

Esther said through a haze of mental turmoil. Was it possible for a mother to not recognise her own child?

'I'm sure I will, in time. I've only been in this ward for a couple of days. All the poor children. I don't think I could have coped, working here during the worst of it. Have you brought clothes for her?'

'I have,' Esther said. Her head was so filled with white noise, she wasn't sure if she had spoken out loud.

'Right, so. I'll get Hannah dressed, and you can watch how I manage the callipers. She walks well enough with two sticks and a little help, but you'll need to be carrying her around for a while yet. You'll be bringing her back in every few months for a check-up, and the callipers will be changed as she grows out of them.'

She reached to pull back the covers. 'Come on then, sweetheart. Your mama is going to take you home.'

By the time the bus pulled into Roone Bay, Esther was frazzled. The little girl had cried and screamed as she was taken out of the hospital, beating at her with clenched fists crying *mama, mama*, over and over. Other women on the bus, seeing the child's callipers, had crossed themselves and exchanged sympathetic gazes with Esther before leaving her to cope with the understandably distressed child, who had eventually, to everyone's relief, fallen asleep from pure exhaustion.

In Roone Bay, Adrian was waiting for her with the donkey cart. 'Guess you got her, then,' he said, reaching to take the child so that Esther could climb up onto the seat.

As he glanced down at the sleeping child, her face still blotchy from crying, he froze. 'Esther,' he enunciated slowly. 'What in God's name have you done?'

1

HANNAH

I feel kind of special, sitting in the passenger seat of Noel's big car. It smells of leather and oil, and I can almost see my reflection in the polished walnut dashboard. I reach out and touch it carefully. I barely know Noel, our local millionaire, or *big nob* as they say here, yet when Dad passed, he was there, on the doorstep, offering his help. I'm not normally one to accept help, but I'm grateful to not be driving the donkey cart all the way to Bantry. It's bad enough to be a figure of fun in Roone Bay, now that cars have become the norm, but to drive further is to be stared at by strangers.

'Beautiful, isn't she?' Noel says, tapping the dashboard and throwing me a sidelong glance, somehow sensing my silent awe. 'I could get a more modern car, but I've grown quite fond of this one. It's expensive on fuel, but it's not as if I drive far these days. Don't have much reason to, in fact.'

'It's lovely,' I agree.

As he drives, he chatters on about this and that, presumably to put me at my ease. I've seldom been in a car at all, and while I'm as excited as a child on an outing, I'm a little uneasy about the summons from the solicitor in Bantry to sort out my father's affairs.

The solicitor has an office above a grocery shop. We follow his secretary up a narrow set of creaking wooden stairs, and she leads us into a small, cluttered, dark room.

Lorcan Byrne, grey-haired, bent with age, rises to greet us. His face seems pale, as if he's spent too many years indoors, but his eyes are bright and alert. 'Hannah,' he says, shaking my hand. 'I'm sorry to be meeting you on this matter. Do accept my condolences. Do call me Lorcan. Come on in. Take a seat. Noel, thank you for being Hannah's chauffeur for the day.'

'No problem,' Noel says.

And to me: 'Do you mind me talking in front of Noel? I'm about to impart personal information that you might wish to keep to yourself.'

'I can wait downstairs,' Noel offers.

I give a nervous laugh. I can't imagine he'd have anything to tell me about my father that I don't already know. 'I'm happy for Noel to stay.'

'Okay,' he says doubtfully.

He pats a pile of papers and squares them exactly in line with the wooden edge of his desk as he mentally searches for words. 'Right. We keep track of death notices in the local papers, which is how I became aware that your father had passed. Are you au fait with the terms of his will?'

'I didn't know he'd even made one,' I admit. 'Not until you sent me that letter asking me to call in and see you about it. Mam said if I stayed to look after Dad, the farm would be passed down to me. I'm the youngest, but I'm the only child of his left at home. The only one in Ireland, actually.'

The solicitor looks down at his hands. 'It's not so simple, I'm afraid.'

I feel the first stirring of concern in my gut. Maybe it was naïve of me, but I'd always known I would inherit the farm, and my plans for it had been several years in the making. My oldest brother, Mark, who was supposed to take over the farm, had walked out years back, and we had never heard from him again. Everyone in Roone Bay had seen my father lose the plot and turn to drink after Mam died. It had been a matter of local debate in the last few years as to whether his body would give up the fight against alcohol poisoning, or if he would get himself run over as he staggered along the road to Roone Bay each day.

In the end, it had been the former.

'It occurred to me,' Lorcan says, 'that maybe after Mark left, your father might have made a new will. Might you go home and check your father's papers?'

He sounds hopeful, but I shake my head. 'I didn't find any papers at all. I looked.'

He continues, 'I've asked around, but I've discovered nothing so far. In all honesty, if there was a new will, I suspect someone would have contacted you by now. And what about the deeds to the farm? Were they signed over to you at any time?'

I grimace and shrug. 'I searched the house after Dad died, but as I said, I found nothing. I wondered if there even were any deeds, because the farm has been in the family for generations. When I got your letter, I wondered if you had them.'

'There were deeds – I saw them. I offered to keep them safe, but your father took them home with him.' His lips purse with concern. 'Are you sure you've looked everywhere?'

'There were just birth certificates, in a pot on the dresser.'

There's a long pause. It seems to me that Lorcan is trying to form words he knows I won't want to hear. 'The thing is,' he says finally, 'the farm is legally bequeathed to your brother Mark, with the proviso that he lives there and works the farm for a minimum of ten years.'

I'm too stunned to speak.

Noel raises his brows at me in question. 'Do you mind me interfering?'

I numbly shake my head.

'So, what if Mark doesn't come back and manage the farm?'

'It's to be sold and the proceeds split between him and his siblings.'

Noel turns to me. 'How many siblings are there?'

'Six, including me,' I say blankly.

'It's a small farm, very run-down, so a six-way split wouldn't provide a lot for each of you,' he muses. 'But maybe it would be enough for you to buy a small house in the town.'

The words are flowing around me while I'm mentally floating somewhere else, numbed by Lorcan's revelation. The farm has been my home all my life, almost thirty years; the last ten spent caring for my father's needs. I thought I would inherit the farm. I was led to believe I would. I actually can't imagine living anywhere else. But it never once occurred to me to check the legality of Mam's promise.

How naïve.

Noel sighs and turns back to Lorcan. 'Do Hannah's brothers and sisters know their father has passed?'

'I sent letters to all of them,' I interrupt, 'but didn't get any response.'

'I sent Mark a letter advising him of the terms of the will,' Lorcan says, 'but thought I would approach the other siblings after I'd spoken to him and ascertained his intentions. He has yet to make contact with me, also.'

'Maybe they'll all see reason and let you inherit,' Noel suggests hopefully.

I don't believe that for a moment. I ask Lorcan, 'But if you haven't told my other sisters and brothers, why are you telling me?'

He looks down at his hands. 'It's slightly unprofessional, but although they might eventually benefit from the inheritance, they aren't directly going to suffer for lack of it. I'm afraid there's more, and it's not good news,' he adds softly.

I don't see how it can be worse. If I don't inherit the farm, my hopes of marrying Cathal slip so far down the scales of possibility as to be almost negligible. I swallow hard, trying not to panic. I'm almost sure I'm pregnant, and while I was expecting to be married, I was almost ecstatic. But now? My stomach lurches with what it will mean to be an unmarried mother in the small community of Roone Bay. I grow light-headed and feel my cheeks burn as my future suddenly feels like it's spiralling out of control.

Noel reaches over, takes my hand and squeezes it, aware of my stunned panic, but not at all aware of its full implications. But whatever I imagined Lorcan was going to say, the words he actually utters don't make any sense at all.

'Hannah, I'm really sorry, but you're specifically excluded from the inheritance...'

In that moment I realise just how much my father had hated me – and for how long.

'What?' Noel exclaims sharply. 'Why?'

Lorcan takes a long breath and fixes his gaze on me. 'Because apparently Hannah is not his biological child.'

For a long moment I'm blinded by a fog of incomprehension, then clarity drops firmly into place. If I am not his own offspring, no wonder my father hated the sight of me. Another man's child. A cuckoo in his nest. 'Did my mother... Was my mother having an affair?'

Lorcan shakes his head. 'That I don't know. But—'

'But my father's name is on my birth certificate!'

'As is your mother's,' Lorcan says, 'but—'

'So, there's no proof that she's *not* his daughter,' Noel interrupts. 'Especially if she has a birth certificate to say she is.' He turns to me with a slight smile. 'So, if there's no proof that you're *not* your father's daughter, only his wording on the will, you could lay a claim against a share of the property for being unjustly excluded, especially as you were the only child who stayed to care for both of your parents when the others all left.'

'That's true,' Lorcan says. 'But if you challenge the will, which specifically excludes you, it's a matter for the courts, and there's also the problem of the missing deeds.'

'Might Dad have given them to Mark?'

'I don't know. I think it's unlikely, because he knew Mark was emigrating, so it wouldn't have been a wise thing to do. But I have no idea what he did with them,' Lorcan admits.

I curl my lip. 'I'd get short shrift from the courts if they think I'm my mother's bastard from an affair.'

The solicitor nods as he addresses his answer to me. 'Although times are changing, that is, unfortunately, still the case. As Noel says, you can contest the will on the basis that your own life has been on hold for many years while caring full-time for your father, which is commendable, but I'm afraid there's no simple answer as to what the courts might decide. And if you instigate legal proceedings, you need to bear in mind that the inheritance might be eaten up in fees if it becomes contentious. And there is one other thing I need to mention, off the record.'

Noel and I stare at him in silence.

'Your father told me that you are not your mother's child, either. He said you were adopted. I don't know if that's true as it contradicts your birth certificate, but that's what he told me.'

'That can't be right,' Noel says, as taken aback as me.

Lorcan shrugs. 'It provided substance to his decision to cut Hannah from his will. Even if it's not morally acceptable, I was obliged to write the will he wanted. I tried to talk him out of it at the time, but you know your father... He was, ah, insistent.'

I can imagine. Dad had a temper on him, and if anyone argued, he'd dig his heels in like a mule.

I have the sense that I've floated out of reality. I wonder if the whole strange tale is some kind of joke. Can it even be true? But, somehow, I believe it. A lifetime of feeling *different* suddenly falls into place. If it's true, I can see that Dad hadn't wanted another man's child to inherit *his* farm. I wonder, now, if he hadn't hated *me*, exactly, but just hated the fact that I wasn't his own child. But he'd shown no compassion for the child who was blameless in the deception.

My confusion morphs into anger. 'Dad wasn't able to love me but was selfish enough to withhold that information from me as long as I was useful, looking after Mam, then himself after she died. And then he was prepared to abandon me all over again, after his death. I wonder if my brothers and sisters knew, all along.'

'I doubt it,' Noel soothes. 'They would never have been able to keep such a secret all these years.'

'But my birth certificate states that they were my parents!'

'That, of course, is the big mystery,' Lorcan agrees. 'You can contest the will, of course, and might in the end be able to claim your share on the basis of the birth certificate. But I doubt a judge would award you the farm in its entirety. What your father told me is not provable, and my word doesn't alter the fact. The assumption for the exclusion, of course, would be that you are the result of an indiscretion on your mother's part.'

'And the courts are ruled by men and the church,' I say bitterly.

'I'm sorry to have been the bearer of such news, but I believed it was my moral duty to advise you. I felt it was incumbent upon me to let you know the truth of the matter,' he adds a little self-consciously.

He glances at his watch, bringing the meeting to a close. 'I'm afraid I'm going to have to let you go. I have another appointment. If you do decide to take action, it will be on the basis of contesting your father's will on the strength of your birth certificate. I don't intend to mention to anyone else what your father told me in confidence.'

Which presumably means he would totally deny ever having told me what Dad said.

Noel obviously comes to the same conclusion. He reaches for Lorcan's hand, and they do a manly handclasp. 'Thank you for your, ah, thoughtfulness in fully explaining the situation. We understand that you didn't have to.'

Lorcan nods and gives me a brief smile of condolence as he shakes my hand. 'I wish you well, Hannah. I really do.'

I leave, still numbed. I don't think Lorcan is lying – I mean, why would he? But if I was adopted, where are the papers? Why did my parents pass me off as their real daughter? And if I'm not Hannah Barry, where is she? She must have truly existed for there to be a birth certificate in that name.

How does one process a revelation like this?

On the way back to Roone Bay, I stare at the countryside as it flashes past. Even the question of the inheritance pales into insignificance beside the empty page of my identity. I've never seen a strong family likeness between me and my siblings, and now I understand why: I take after my unknown parents. Who are they? Are they local? Are they even still alive? Have they been aware, all this time? Would they speak up if they knew I was being made homeless? Until I know the truth, I will forever be looking at strangers in the street, wondering, *Are you my mother? Are you my father?*

2

HANNAH, A FEW WEEKS EARLIER

It was a bleak winter's day when Dad finally passed.

When I found him, still and cold, my first feeling was, selfishly, excitement. I would no longer be dictated to by a disenchanted man who thought a daughter of less value than a son. Cathal and I could now marry. I would have my chance at life, despite him. I would no longer be lonely.

I used to wonder why people were scared of Dad, until I saw him brandish a shotgun at the newly appointed Father O'Donnell, who was introducing himself to the community. Dad was out of his head with the drink, spittle running down his chin as he screamed, *Take your god and to hell with you! Get out! I don't want preaching leeches on my land.* The priest, who knew little Irish, got the message. He turned tail and ran, his robes flapping like crow's wings as Dad fired. Thankfully the force of the blast sent Dad flailing backward through the door, his shot flying into the uncaring wind.

Father O'Donnell never came back to the farm while Dad was alive, afraid, perhaps, that he'd find his god sooner than he would have liked. Yet he knew I was there, alone with Dad, who was losing his hold on sanity. The wonder of it was, I was never afraid for myself. Dad had never laid a violent hand on me. He mostly ignored me. Maybe that was worse.

When Cathal proposed, he hadn't exactly been the romantic suitor. He'd been honest. It would be a union of convenience. He'd always hankered after a place of his own, and I needed a man to run the farm.

Mam apparently married Dad for love, but I wonder, now, if she was disappointed in how it turned out. Yet it was my intolerant father who fell down and didn't pick himself up again when she died. It only occurs to me, now they're both gone, that Mam was the strong one. She believed in God's everlasting grace. But had she sometimes wondered what life might have been like if she hadn't married a poor farmer? If she did, she never voiced dissatisfaction, not even when she was dying. She would say, *Thank the good Lord we're not living in the days of the famine.* I used to wonder how she could say that, when the same good Lord hadn't had a care to all those poor souls who starved to death. She attributed everything good in the world to God and everything bad to our own actions.

As choices went, I thought Cathal a fairly good option. He had youth on his side. He was tall and strong and incredibly good-looking, and I imagined him fathering beautiful babies. It didn't take me long to see the benefits, and I tacitly agreed that it would be in both our interests to marry. There was something satisfying about making a rational decision about my future.

I thought Dad would be pleased. His own sons had abandoned him, and he'd never thought to see me married. Now he'd have a son-in-law to take over the running of the farm and give him grandchildren to breathe new life into the old house. But when I told him, he gave a roar of disapproval. *I'll be damned if that langer will ever inherit this farm!* Maybe he didn't like the thought of a man other than his own son running the farm when he was gone.

Cathal suggested that he should come up and explain to

Dad the benefits, and although I was dubious, I thought maybe Dad would listen to him when he wouldn't listen to me. When Cathal came visiting, however, Dad reached for his shotgun, and Cathal made an undignified and hasty exit. Not quite the romantic moment I'd hoped for.

'Why, Dad?' I asked later, stunned by his aggression. 'What did you expect? I'm the only one left. I'm not exactly able to run the farm myself. And I'm not inundated with suitors.'

His glance raked me from my face to my callipers. He didn't need to say anything for me to know that he understood why. He'd called me a cripple on too many occasions to count. But I didn't get polio to spite him, and of all his children, I was the only one who stayed. It was horrible of him to hate me for something I couldn't help.

'Is it the family name?' I pressed. 'Do you want Cathal to change his name to Barry? I could ask him.'

Dad sneered and cast me a sidelong look. 'You're a romantic fool. Of course it's not the name. In fact, it's not even—' Then he stopped short and stated, while stone-cold sober, 'That scrounging langer is never going to inherit my farm. You might as well get that straight, so.'

He grabbed his threadbare jacket and disappeared out into the barn. I knew better than to follow. It was always his way of avoiding dialogue. I was angry but didn't say what was in my mind: he was happy enough for me to keep his house and cook his dinners, but he'd rather I died an old maid than had a chance at happiness.

No, Cathal and I weren't in love. Honesty and loyalty surely have a far more lasting value than the ephemeral and somewhat idealistic notion of love that I'd read in fiction. My parents had apparently started their marriage deeply in love, but if so, it had faded under the weight of life's unforgiving pressure. In my lifetime, I never saw evidence of anything other than their commitment to stick by the vows they made under oath.

According to Mam, Dad had been handsome and gentle and kind when she fell in love with him, if that's even possible. Cynicism tells me he probably said what Mam needed to hear when he was courting, and once the knot was tied, he didn't need to make the same effort. I never saw him provide her with so much as a bunch of primroses, though they nestle freely in the field ditches. When she was dying, I can only guess that her mind invented twisted memories of lost love. She begged me to look after him, because he could not look after himself, and I promised I would, and I did. More fool me.

We didn't have a phone, so the day Dad died, I went up to the upper paddock to bring the donkey down. I remember that the view was stunning that morning. There was a faint hint of salt on the air. The sky was endless blue, the hilltops standing stark and bleak. The ever-present Atlantic drifted serenely below, uncaring of all our human foibles. There, where the rugged rocks perch on our isolated hillside, where the winding boreens, threaded with ribbons of grass, are lost in the rolling landscape, it was as though nothing had changed for a thousand years.

But I breathed in the scent of a new beginning.

As I imparted the news of my father's passing to the priest, Father O'Donnell, I didn't pretend to grieve and nor did he.

'So, what will you do now, Hannah?'

I flushed slightly. 'Cathal Carrol has asked for my hand.'

A worried look flashed over his brow. 'Are you going to accept? Isn't it too soon?'

'Suitors aren't exactly queueing at my door,' I said. 'It's no secret that he wants the farm, and I want children.'

'Well,' he said doubtfully. 'I suppose that's a good reason to marry. But I heard no whispers about a marriage?'

'It's been a while. Dad didn't want Cathal to inherit his farm, for some reason. He saw him off with a shotgun when he came visiting.'

'I have first-hand experience,' the priest said dryly. 'Well, you did your duty by your parents, that no one can deny. But' – he put his hands on my shoulders and caught my gaze – 'are you sure, though? Cathal's no farmer, when all's said and done.'

'He's prepared to learn.'

'Well, don't act too hastily. You're young yet, and there's a life waiting if you go out and seek it. You could stay with Aine in London for a while. Go and see a bit of the world before making a decision you can't undo.'

My sister had repeatedly asked me to go to London and live with her, but I can't imagine living in a city, bound in by all that brick and concrete. I love living amongst the fields and the mountains, with the sea just over the horizon. Anyway, it was too late to back out. Cathal offered me a future that I once thought out of reach, and I was committed far more than the priest could guess. Cathal and I were adult enough to make this decision in the cold light of practicality. We wouldn't be setting out with a false rosy glow in our eyes. At least he never made me feel gauche and clumsy. Despite ours being a union of mutual convenience, he had lifted my spirits, given me hope. I was dreaming of the weight of his secret child in my arms.

'I'll send up the undertaker,' Father O'Donnell had said, interrupting my musing. He meant well, I know. He'd said his piece and didn't try further to make me reconsider my options.

'Thank you, Father. There's no need for a lying-in. I don't know who would come.'

'Have the lying-in, girl. Get your dad ready. I'll get the undertakers to bring up a casket and spread the word, and Mickey Hoolihan's boys can help get him down to the table. People will pay their respects – don't you worry about that, now. They knew him before he was lost to the drink. People know how it was for you. You've been a good daughter. Loyal. More than he deserved, may God forgive him.' He crosses himself fervently. 'Now, you go on and prepare him. I'll arrange the removal and come on up to the house in a while. We can pray together that he finds peace – and maybe finds God, too.'

'Thank you, Father.'

'So, a brief word to Him upstairs for your father's soul.'

I dutifully smiled at his godly humour, bowed my head with him and prayed, because in a small community one had to be seen to be doing the right thing; though, if I didn't, I suspect he'd understand. I wasn't supposed to feel bitter, but there were times I couldn't stop myself from wishing I'd received even the slightest token of affection from my dad. The polio stealing my legs wasn't my fault after all. Later, of course, I found out the true reason for his dislike of me, but during the lying-in and the funeral, I was still planning a new life for myself, not realising that it had already veered well out of control.

On the way back to the farm, people waved as I passed. I was an anachronism on my little donkey cart, a landmark in the scenery. They all knew my story, as the priest said, and the grapevine would be humming with news of Dad's passing.

At the farm, I unharnessed the cart, and Old Grey ambled happily back up into the paddock.

I summoned up my courage and set the water heating. I washed Dad, and shaved and dressed him. He would have been mortified to know that his daughter had performed those personal and intimate acts to make him presentable for the lying-in. When that was done, I set to with baking. Father O'Donnell was right. Observance to tradition is what binds a small community. Dad would be sent off in style because he and Mam had once been part of the community. I had a flash of amusement. If anything would wake Dad from the dead, it would be knowing the priest was in his house, standing over him, praying for his soul.

Then I wrote letters to my distant siblings, letting them know Dad had passed. I doubted that any would come back for his funeral, any more than they had come back for Mam's. Well, not unless they were looking for a slice of the inheritance, of course. It was too far, too costly, and the ties that bound them had long rotted away.

Mickey Hoolihan's boys, from the farm up the road, helped the undertaker to manhandle Dad's coffin down the stairs and into the kitchen, and it turned out that Father O'Donnell was right about the wake. It seemed as if all of Roone Bay had come to see Dad off, as was the custom. That, or they came to gawp at me and the ancient run-down house that might have come out of the dark ages. Even Noel O'Donovan from the Big House came, bringing his housekeeper, Mrs Weddows, who had been Mam's friend before their lives took different turns. I'd said hello in passing to Noel, but we'd never really spoken. He brought crates of wine and porter, probably knowing I couldn't afford them. I tried to thank him, but he brushed it off with a wave of his hand. 'Sorry for your troubles,' he said and gave me a kiss on the cheek.

I wondered which troubles he meant, because Dad dying was probably the least of them. 'Thank you,' I murmured.

'If you need help getting to Aine in England, or selling the farm, come and see me. I mean it. Anything at all. It's not a bother.'

I flushed at his kindness and his implied charity.

Mrs Weddows brought a plate of fresh bread. The scent wafted up from under the cloth, bringing tears of nostalgia to my eyes. It was the scent of our kitchen when I'd been a child.

'Sorry for your troubles,' she echoed, seeing the tears, probably mistaking them for grief. She planted a kiss on my cheek. 'Your mam was a saint,' she said, 'and you' – she stepped back and nodded as if she had made a decision – 'well, to be sure, don't you have her kindness in you?'

I found a watery smile. 'I'm no saint.'

I remembered her being a no-nonsense kind of woman, and this was evident as she added, somewhat more quietly, 'Your mam would be proud, so. Now your father has passed, you need to be thinking about yourself. You go out and find yourself a life. It's about time.'

'Thank you,' I said again, blushing as she bustled on.

Mickey Hoolihan took my hands in both of his. He was uneducated like Dad and had inherited similar scrubby acres. Unlike Dad, he'd brought his farm into the new era and made it work. But he had two sons who stayed, and one in America who sent him fat cheques, from what I'd heard. 'Sorry for your loss, Hannah. I'll come and talk to you about the land when things have had time to settle.'

I nodded. As well as managing his own acres, Mickey had been renting Dad's fields for several years; that's where the money came from that paid for the drink that killed Dad. I wonder if Mickey ever thought of that. But they were my fields now, and Cathal and I would need to take them back if we were to keep our own cows.

Finally, the priest called us to prayer, and we gathered around Dad, who was lying on a trestle in the living room. I'd done a good job. He was looking more presentable in death than he had in the last few years of his life, and the anecdotes that were recalled as people sent him on his way spoke of a bright-eyed prankster, always in the thick of trouble. For the first time I got a hint of the youth my mother had fallen in love with. But I viewed his body dispassionately. If he'd had any love in him at all, he'd used it all up before I was born. And why had everyone come when it was too late? Dad had been troubled when he was alive; surely his troubles were all over now.

As Father O'Donnell brought his eulogy to an end, Cathal

sidled up behind me and whispered in my ear, 'Dunna he ever talk a load o' gobshite?'

'Shush!' I whispered back, barely containing a snort of laughter. Our contract was supposed to be a secret, but Cathal placed a proprietary hand on my shoulder, which surely wouldn't go unnoticed.

I glanced at him over my shoulder to see his expression sly with our secret agreement. Clean-shaven, wearing a three-piece tweed suit, probably borrowed, I thought he could have been a model if he'd had the mind. His twinkling blue eyes were filled with mischief. He was truly a magnet for the female eye, with his nose straight as a blade, his prominent cheekbones, dark eyelashes and thick, unruly hair. My whole being sang when he winked back at me. I knew he only wanted the farm, but I told myself it was enough.

I recalled that Cathal had courted my sister Aine when he'd been a callow youth, tall and gangly with just a hint of his blossoming charisma. Even then, Aine had been vibrant and passionate in a way that made the auld ones mutter that she was a bold one and would come to a bad end. They were wrong; she was just destined for other things.

Father O'Donnell finished his eulogy, which held hints of a sermon on the ills of drink. There was a swift marking of crosses over breasts, and Cathal cleared his throat. 'Sorry for your loss, Hannah. I'd best be taking the family on now, having paid our respects, so.'

I lost count of the number of people who paid their respects. It was kind of obligatory to be seen doing so, even though they had avoided Dad for a long while. I amused myself with the thought that some people came just to make sure he was gone. He could be loud and angry under the influence, and had caused more than one roola-boola in town through his drunken antics. At the wake, I didn't see anyone express true sadness at his demise; they were wallowing in memories, laughing over the theft of a chicken or a window smashed by a stone. I doubt they laughed then, when times were so hard.

I sensed that Father O'Donnell was enjoying himself, having Dad finally at the unremitting mercy of his prayers. It's just as well he had no idea just how far Cathal and I had progressed in our plans, or he might have wanted to read me a sermon, too.

When the last of the mourners had gone, I looked at Dad's almost serene expression, one he never betrayed while he was alive, and wished I'd known the man Mam said she'd married.

3

HANNAH

It's a good month after my disturbing meeting with Lorcan Byrne, the solicitor in Bantry, when the half-door bangs back on its hinges, startling me to my feet. A stranger walks straight into the kitchen without asking. I'm too shocked to even think about being scared. I have a vague feeling that I should know him, but I can't think where from. He's tall, built thick around the shoulders, with a strong, clean-shaven jawline and big hands. He's well dressed, in a dark suit, a long overcoat and a black felt hat with a turned-up brim, the sort I've seen in magazines in the library.

His gaze sweeps the room, then lands squarely on me. 'You wrote that Dad died.' Seeing my confusion, he adds, 'I'm Mark.'

'Oh!' Understanding floods in as I vaguely recognise my older brother. It's years since he left, and I didn't know him well then, there being so many years between us, but now I see the resemblance to Dad. 'I didn't recognise you!'

'Nor me you. You were a skinny runt when I left. You've put a bit of weight on.'

Well, of course I had. My older brothers and sisters are distant strangers; they were already drifting away into new lives while Aine and I were busy morphing into teenagers. We both came into the world as afterthought or accident, years after Mam thought her childbearing days were over. My siblings had left Ireland one after the other as I was growing up, and Mam had sadly never seen any of them return. Our family was whittled away a year at a time, as fledglings fly the nest; it was the natural course of events for poor families like ours.

Mam used to chant a backward counting rhyme when I was little: *There were seven in the bed and the little one said, roll over, roll over. They all rolled over and one fell out... There were six in the bed, and the little one said, roll over, roll over...* I think it was said with pathos, but I thought it funny at the time, being the littlest one in the family. *What happens when the last one goes?* I asked Mam. *Oh, they all come back, one by one,* she had answered with a laugh. But they hadn't, and perhaps it was no more than she expected.

Mark was the last to follow in the footsteps of his younger brothers, and his unexpected exit had been a betrayal too huge for Dad to cope with. He was supposed to be Dad's successor, take over the farm, marry, and fill the old house with another generation of Barrys. He wasn't supposed to abandon his birthright. That's when Dad rented the fields out and took openly to the drink, because Mark stole the future from him.

Mark left Aine and me, his two youngest sisters, to mind our parents when Mam was sick and Dad was losing his way. Aine, two years my senior, was never going to stay in Roone Bay. She was too vibrant – a waste of space, Dad said, because she would rather be dancing than helping with the chores. She had no intention of getting hitched to a Roone Bay culchie – her words. She wanted to go places, find herself a different life. She did, after Mam died, leaving me to care for Dad, who made no attempt to disguise his disdain. After all, who was going to marry someone like me?

'I'm so sorry – you're too late for the funeral,' I say. 'Dad is already buried. I can show you the grave, down at the cemetery, right beside—'

'I didn't come to weep at his graveside,' he interrupts sharply. 'I came for what's mine.'

'I didn't realise you'd left anything behind.' I'm somewhat taken aback by his aggressive bluntness. I'd cleaned out the bedrooms and either washed the bedding, or thrown it out. There are no personal items remaining in the ancient farmhouse from any of my siblings, save for the worn boots Aine had left behind when she stalked away in her new heeled shoes. Those I'd left where they were, as if having her boots there meant part of her was still with me. It's not as if I could wear them, after all.

'Not stuff,' he says arrogantly. 'The farm. It's mine. Dad left it me.'

For a moment, I had forgotten about the will. Blood rushes from my head along with all my hopes that Mark would be reasonable. 'Well, theoretically, he did, but Mam said if I stayed to look after Dad, I would inherit the farm. Dad never said anything different... It's been over ten years. I was hoping we could talk about it.'

'Talk about what?' He pulls some papers out of an inner pocket, flashes them at me, and stuffs them back. 'Dad's will, signed and witnessed, leaving the farm to me. Nothing to talk about, is there?'

'I thought you might honour Mam's wishes.'

He stabs his chest with a finger. 'I'm the oldest. It was always mine.' He glances down at my callipers. 'And what would you be doing with a farm, anyway. You can't manage it at all.'

'I'm going to marry. My husband will work the farm.'

He sneers. 'Oh, you had it all arranged nicely for yourself, then? Sorry to burst your bubble.'

I flush. 'You never came back. I thought you didn't want to live here.'

'Of course I don't. I left because I hated the damn place, and that hasn't changed.' His eyes scour the basic room, which is both living area and kitchen, the same now as when it had been built, well over a hundred years ago. 'I'm going to sell it. Someone will want the fields, anyway. The house is a hovel. Dad let the whole place go to the dogs. My wife wouldn't live in this pigsty, not for a minute.'

'You're married?'

'With four children.'

'Mam never knew. She always wondered.'

'Mam never had a thought that wasn't put there by Dad. She should have left him years back.'

I'm shocked into silence at his coldness, his lack of compassion and also his seeming lack of understanding. In Ireland women didn't leave their husbands. Marriage was a vow for life, for better or worse.

He paces for a moment, his derogatory expression making me unexpectedly ashamed of the house I'd grown up in.

'I need the money,' he says, kicking the leg of the table. 'When I was broke, I made a table and a few chairs like Granddad did back in the day and discovered a market for them. If American-Irish think buying rough timber furniture takes them back to their roots, I'm not going to argue. I wouldn't want them in my home, but they sell well. With an injection of cash, my business would really take off. I'll be able to find better premises, hire some labour. Dad owes me that, for all the years I wallowed in these bloody bogs.'

Bitterness seeps into my mind. 'Dad owes it to you, who walked away? And what about me? I looked after Mam while she was dying. Then I looked after Dad all these years while he was drinking himself into his grave because you left and broke his heart!'

'He didn't have one to break,' he mutters. 'He never gave a damn about anything except the land.' He glares at me. 'You saw the will Dad wrote, then?'

'The solicitor told me there was one. I didn't read it,' I say honestly.

I'm wondering whether he will admit the bit about his siblings sharing the value if he doesn't live here, or the fact that I'm not Dad's natural daughter. I wonder if he thinks, as I did, initially, that our mother had been having an affair.

He turns away, not quite hiding sly amusement; the action providing answer enough. 'Well, anyway, I'm going to sell the place, and I can't sell it with you still living here. You'll have to find somewhere to go. Perhaps your husband-to-be can find you a place with his family.'

I don't doubt this man is my brother. The resemblance to Dad is clear: in his stance, his blunt arrogance, in the faded grey of his eyes. I don't see any hint of Mam's tired kindness. He plonks himself down on Dad's chair, and I almost laugh. A moment ago, I had been imagining that when he turned up, we'd have an adult conversation about the inheritance. I'd thought that, somehow, we could work it out.

'You could go to London,' Mark suggests. 'Aine went there, didn't she? You two were always close.'

'I could come to America and live with you,' I snap.

I'm pleased to see panic fleetingly strike the arrogance from his face. 'You can't come back with me,' he says heavily. 'My wife wouldn't...'

'Wouldn't what? Want a cripple in the house?'

He flushes faintly and I realise that's the truth. He wouldn't want a dependent younger sister any more than I'd want to live with a brother who hasn't an ounce of compassion in him. Through our conversation I hear the rushing of sea on pebbles inside my head. I put my hand on the table to steady myself, wondering if I'm going to pass out.

Dad had signed the farm away to Mark many years ago and never told me. I wonder if Mark has the deeds in his pocket as well as a copy of the will. I'm dumbfounded by the cruelty of that act. Dad had accepted my care all these years, knowing he was leaving me with nothing, not even his thanks.

Mark stalks to the dresser and hauls down the old salt jar that contains the few rolled-up birth certificates. He rifles through them. 'So, what have you done with the deeds?' he asks. 'They were in here.'

So, he doesn't have the deeds. That pleases me.

'I've never seen any deeds. I searched over the house for papers after Dad died and found nothing.'

He glares. 'If you've hidden them away, it won't help you, anyway. The will is clear.' He paces to the press, opens the door as if expecting the deeds to be conveniently sitting there, then slams it in disgust. 'Okay. The solicitor can sort it out. It's been owned by our family for generations. I'm the oldest son, and I have the will signed by Dad. He'll want these, I guess.' He stuffs the birth certificates in his pocket.

I leap up. 'One of those is mine!'

He pulls them out, riffles through them and throws mine onto the table. 'You can have it, for all the good it will do.'

'But—'

'You'd better start thinking about where to go, but you can stay in the house until it's sold.'

'That's generous,' I say sarcastically.

He nods, as if I mean it. 'Isn't there someone in the town who will take you in? To look after children or something?'

He's not trying to be helpful. He wants to pluck me out and dispose of me, like an unwelcome bug in his dinner. 'Who would ask me to mind their children? I can't walk far, and I don't drive.'

He sees my point, and his frown deepens. 'Anyway, you'll need to find somewhere.'

'If you're the head of this family, how about you make arrangements for my well-being?' I suggest icily.

'Not my problem,' he says. 'You're not a child. Sort it out yourself.'

I don't know where the words come from, but a burst of anger rises from somewhere deep within. 'I'll contest the will. With my long history of caring for our parents, I might be awarded ownership. At worst, we might end up with half each.'

He scowls. 'I'd advise against it. But if you want to make a fool of yourself, go ahead. I promise, all you'll do is make yourself a laughing stock in the townland.'

I feel a rush of gratitude towards Lorcan Byrne. He didn't have to tell me about the will, but forewarned is, as they say, forearmed. It's obvious that Mark intends to try to sell the farm and keep the proceeds for himself. That's useful to know. Though I'd hesitate to call it blackmail, knowing the terms of the will gives me a card to play against him when the time comes. But for now, I play ignorant. 'I'm not going to let you walk in and just take the farm. I'm owed something for all the years I've spent here.' I limp over to the door and grab my coat from its hook.

'Where are you going?'

'To hitch up the donkey cart.'

He seems genuinely shocked. 'Jeez! This place!'

I look back. 'Will you be staying here?'

'Not on your life. I'll stay at the hotel. But you can give me a lift down to my car.'

'Go down the way you came up, on your own two feet,' I snap. I'm pleased to see that the hems of his trousers have a muddy tideline and his towny shoes are sodden.

But that small victory doesn't touch the despair that sits like a brick on my heart. I can't afford to take action against Mark, and I'm frightened to tell Cathal about the will, because his proposal is based solely upon him acquiring my family's land by marrying me. And if our brief indiscretion means I'm pregnant, as I suspect, then my past and my future have all tumbled into a dark place from which I can see no hope of climbing free. Cathal was keen to get me in the family way, but even now being an unmarried mother in Ireland isn't an enticing prospect.

4

HANNAH

After Mark leaves me reeling, I limp up to the field to bring Old Grey down for the drive into town. At the upper paddock, I lean on the gate for a moment, taking the weight from my legs. When I was a child, the callipers created sores that bled, but once I stopped growing, they created hard ridges around my thighs where they dug in. Prolonged activity makes me so tired. The effort of dragging my dead legs with the weight of iron is exhausting. I think of Aine, dancing away in London, and sigh. I don't know what it feels like to dance. Light as air, maybe, like flying.

The mountain behind the farm is softened by a thin layer of fog, through which a pale sun is fighting, lending a mystical promise to the day. Any other time I'd let the scene seep into my soul, cleanse it of discontent. But presently I feel betrayed, uncertain. At Dad's funeral, Noel O'Donovan offered to help, and I can't think of a time I've needed help more than now. Even if all he can offer me is a shoulder to cry on, right now, I'd accept.

Old Grey seems put out at being disturbed from his solitude. Maybe the old donkey knows it's just two days since we went to the weekly market to sell the eggs, and he wasn't expecting to be disturbed. He, too, is getting long in the tooth. I lead him down to the barn and harness him to the cart. By the time I've finished, I don't have to worry about meeting Mark in the boreen; he'll be long gone.

But as I'm about to clamber awkwardly onto the bench seat, I experience a prickling between my shoulder blades. I swivel to find old Turlough standing in the yard, watching me. His faithful old dog is sitting beside him, leaning against his legs – a large, shaggy mutt he collected somewhere along his travels. An eccentric figure, the locals are protective of him; a sporadic visitor who turns up when the wind changes. He lives on the road, tramping around West Cork and Kerry, up into Connemara and even further, some say, but he was born here, in Roone Bay. He's a weird mix of old stories, gentle humour and confused comprehension. Mam told me something happened that stopped him from growing up right, or settling, but I wonder if he was simply born different. He's as much part of the landscape as the streams that come and go with the weather.

Mam said he'd been a friend of Dad's father, Granddad Conor, back in the day. It's rumoured that the pair of them had run messages for the rebel band that roamed these mountains during the War of Independence. I imagine the two youths, little more than schoolboys, used by the rebels as go-betweens, darting across the hills and streams, perhaps thinking it a fine game. But somewhere along the way Turlough had mislaid himself and forgotten how to come back into the community. I've said hello while passing him on the road, and sometimes he's made himself at home in our farm, but there's no harm in him, and stories are just stories.

I raise my crop in greeting as I walk Old Grey over to the ditch. 'Turlough. Top of the morning to ye. Will ye come in?'

He shakes his head. 'Heard your da passed.'

'He's been buried this month gone.'

'Ah, sure, I know it. I paid my respects.' He pauses and I wait him out while Old Grey rips at some leaves on the bank. 'I heard one of his lads was back from America.'

'That would be Mark. Dad left the farm to him,' I add, trying to keep my expression neutral.

'Ah. Thought it were that one. He's come back to work the land?'

His face betrays the echo of surprise, which fades as I tell him, 'No, he just wants the value of it.'

'Ah. And what about ye? Will he give ye a home?'

I shake my head. 'But no more would I want to go to America.'

'Wondered if it was that,' he says knowingly. He tips his head in the direction of the farm just up the valley from ours. 'Well, ye'd best be speaking to young Mickey, then. He'll have the knowing of it.'

'I will,' I say.

I'll tell Mickey about Mark wanting to put the farm up for sale. Maybe he'd like to offer for the land first, being that its adjacent to his own. If there's any rent outstanding, I could do with it, too, but it's not in me to ask.

'You can stay in the barn,' I say. 'There are eggs to be taken and water on the hob indoors.'

'You're a good girrul, Hannah. I'll be seeing ye.'

He hovers for a moment as if there's something more he wants to say, but he shakes his head and turns away. I might come back and find a cup washed on the drainer and some eggs gone. That's fine by me.

I wonder if the stories about him are true. I have every admiration for those men who risked their lives in search of Ireland's freedom from the English overlords. They conducted their guerrilla warfare on little more than prayers and stolen guns.

Granddad and Turlough might have been children at the time, but war makes children grow up quickly – or not grow up at all.

I click my tongue and Old Grey walks on.

When I look back, Turlough is gone. It was like a visitation from a spectre that had been dragged reluctantly from the past to impart something important to those he left behind. I'm left with the feeling that he wanted to say something further but for some reason lost the courage.

5

HANNAH

The boreen has got worse year after year, washed out by the heavy winter rain. Old Grey steps naturally from one side to the other, avoiding potholes that have become more like crevasses. Dad used to bring buckets of stones from the field to fill the holes, but that was before Mam died, before Mark left and Dad lost the will to do anything at all.

I sit on the high bench of the sturdy cart and see the landscape anew. Maybe I'm viewing it through the strangeness of an unknown future that has arrived suddenly and devastatingly. I thought I was the last of the Barrys, here on our ancient farm, and that I would be staying here, mother to a new line of farming folk, albeit with a different name, but now it seems not.

I think back on the last couple of months, of the plans I'd made for the future; plans that were so long in the dreaming and that might now have been shot to pieces. I didn't tell Cathal I might be pregnant, maybe because I wasn't certain, or maybe because I already had doubts about the wisdom of my actions. Now I am certain, I'm still hesitant to tell him. Maybe he will do the honourable thing and marry me despite everything, but I truly don't think he will. I want – maybe need – a husband, but he wants land. I don't want to tell him the truth about Dad's will yet, partially because I don't want the fairy tale to end but also because, well, things might change. I suspect I can claim part of the inheritance, because according to my birth certificate I *am* Hannah Barry, and there's nothing except my father's comment to say otherwise. Surely the law will see that my loyalty to my parents and my continued occupancy of the property provides a right of inheritance. No, the strangely unsettling conundrum is that if I'm not Hannah Barry, who am I? If I was adopted as the solicitor suggested, where are the papers?

A flash of movement ahead interrupts my dark musing. For a moment, I think it's Mark, coming back up the boreen for some reason, but as we draw closer, I realise it's a stranger picking his way carefully up towards the farm. It's a rare enough occurrence. I don't want to splash past, so pull Old Grey to a halt and wait.

As he draws nearer, I realise he's my age or maybe a little older. He's neat and slim, medium height, his hair trimmed short. His boots are laced up over his ankles, with the hems of his trousers tucked in. His hands are stuffed in the pockets of a tweed jacket that's shaped in at the waist and cut longer in the body than would be usual around here. I guess whoever it is has left his car down below rather than risk driving up the rutted boreen, with its deep drains either side, which are presently tumbling with murky water draining down from the sodden mountains.

For a moment, he doesn't see me, he's so busy avoiding the potholes, then he glances up, startled to find himself face to face with a donkey, and involuntarily steps backward into a deep puddle. His features break into a laugh that lights his whole face. 'Oh, goodness. There go my only decent trousers. Hello. I hope I'm not trespassing?'

I can't help laughing with him. There's something uniquely

compelling about his open amusement that draws me in to share the moment.

'It's not the trespassing that you should be worried about but potholes!'

'I think I got that,' he says. 'I'm looking for Adrian Barry. I was told he had a farm up here somewhere.'

Now he's close, I see fine lines around his eyes, and his accent tells me he's English. A stranger is strange enough but an Englishman? I didn't know Dad had any connection at all with the English. In fact, he hated them with a passion; the whole devil's brood, to use his term. I'd grown up imagining those strange creatures across the water to be somehow horrific in appearance, but age taught me to pay no mind to Dad's ranting. And Aine's letters from England are filled with – what would Father O'Donnell call it? – *joie de vivre*. She has never a bad word to say about the English and, in fact, has mentioned several little kindnesses, not least those of Mrs Clancy, her landlady, a war widow, who took her in when she was desperate.

'Adrian Barry was my father,' I say. 'I'm afraid you're too late. He passed recently.'

He's still for a moment, then sighs. 'He's dead? So, the young man below sent me on a wild goose chase, then.'

'That was probably Mark, my brother. I should apologise for him; sure, he's not going to do it for himself.'

A slight narrowing of the eyes suggests he's picked up on the nuance, but he shrugs. 'It's no matter, then. I'm sorry for your loss. But how peculiarly irritating to have missed your father. If only I'd been able to visit a year ago, as I had planned...'

I give a spontaneous chuckle. 'If you had, he would likely have seen you off with his shotgun. He had no love for the English.'

He echoes my amusement. 'Perhaps I'm lucky after all, then.'

I should drive on, but there's something wholesome and attractive about him, not least his ability to laugh at himself, and I have the strangest urge to not let him turn away so quickly. 'Might I be able to help?'

'You might, if he passed down any stories about his father's time with the IRA; that would be Conor Barry, I was told.'

'Now, why would an Englishman be asking about that, I wonder? Anyway, I'm afraid I can't tell you anything. Mam said Granddad Conor put his memories in a box and closed the lid. That was long before I was born. I never heard any stories of back in those days, not from him, anyway.'

'And your mother, is she around?'

'She's been gone many's the year.'

'Oh, I'm sorry. Well, I'd best head back down to the road. Unless you have brothers or sisters who might know more?' he asks hopefully.

'You already met my oldest brother,' I say with a grimace. 'The others are all gone, to America and Australia mostly, and I've a sister in London. She's a professional dancer now.' His gaze flicks automatically to my callipers, so I add with irritation, 'No, I don't dance.'

To my surprise, he doesn't look away in embarrassment. The callipers are the first thing people notice about me, of course. Not my face, which Mam used to say is pretty as sunshine, or my voice, which she said was given to me by the larks – it certainly didn't come from her – but the thick shoes locked to the metal-and-strap contraptions that look like some kind of torture instrument. I hate the ugliness of them. I'm probably the only woman in Ireland who regrets the disappearance of thick homespun skirts that drag the ground.

'Polio?' he asks.

'When I was three.'

'Ah, what a dreadful thing for a little child to experience. But you got off lightly, from what I've seen.'

I frown. 'Did I?'

'I'm a doctor in England. I've been treating people who contracted polio during the epidemic of the fifties, like you. Older people, the ones who survived. Luckily, since the vaccinations, I haven't had to deal with little children who contracted it. That must have been awful. The children wouldn't have had a clue what was happening to them; the pain, the fear, being taken away to hospital for months...'

'True,' I agree, somewhat sourly.

He smiles as if I've made a joke. It reaches his pale grey eyes, deepening the natural crow's feet. 'Well, you must be pleased that children today won't have to suffer as you've suffered. And one has to look on the bright side. Truly, you know it could have been worse.'

I really hate people saying that to me, but somehow from a doctor it doesn't sound trite. 'You're right. I could have died, be in a wheelchair, or permanently hospitalised. But' – I tap the crop against my metal brace – 'this isn't what I would have chosen for my life. It was hard when I was little, to have the hills taken from me and watch my sister dance.'

He doesn't give time to my self-pity. 'Life has a way of changing the best-laid plans. It's probably made you a stronger character.'

It's easy to say, I think. 'So, why are you here, delving into a past that the English are trying hard to sweep under the rug?'

'I, ah...' He hesitates awkwardly.

'Spit it out,' I advise.

'My granddad was a Temporary Constable,' he admits. 'A Black and Tan you would have called them. He was stationed down here, in Roone Bay. He and another man, Billy Devon, disappeared in 1920.'

A black cloud drifts overhead, darkening the day significantly. I feel the first splashes of what's likely to be a heavy downpour. The Englishman looks uncomfortable, and it's not hard to see why. Even now, the words Black and Tan make some of the old ones spit over their shoulder. 'You shouldn't be after telling people that,' I advise softly.

'I know the history, but my granddad was a good man; kind and conscientious, according to my great-gran. She would have said that about her son, I suppose, but I believe her. It's a sad enough story. He was dragged off to war as a young man, survived the trenches for over a year and was in an institution for a while when he got back. Traumatised, I guess. It was hard times in England when he was released, no work to be had, so he came to Ireland thinking he was going to do good, only he disappeared. His mother, my great-gran, never saw him again. My father was about three at the time. He never met his father at all.'

'And now you're looking to find out what happened?'

'That's about the sum of it.'

I grimace slightly. 'That's sad enough, so. But there's a lot of bad feeling still. The English shouldn't have been over here in the first place.'

'I know he was probably shot by the IRA. There were bad things done on both sides during the uprising.'

'It's called the War of Independence here,' I warn.

He nods, taking the hint. 'I should have remembered that. I've read a fair bit about Irish history, as you can imagine, but it's different actually being here. I feel like a pariah, with my English accent.'

'There are still those who hate the English, but most have moved on. There are plenty of English living here now. And Germans,' I add. 'They live for today, not for the past.'

'I was hoping people would be kinder if I told them Granddad's mother was from Kerry.'

'Which made him part Irish, so. But he still shouldn't have been with the Black and Tans. Is she still alive, your great-grandmother?' He shakes his head. 'So, maybe you should seek out her kin instead of delving into your granddad's disappearance. Even if he was, ah, executed by the IRA, no one's going to tell you the facts.'

'I'm not looking for blame or reparation. It's just that I made my great-grandmother a promise, you see. I said I'd try to find where her son – my granddad – is buried and lay a wreath. That's all.'

I'm silent for a moment. I grew up with tales of the Black and Tans and the atrocities they committed. The hushed fireside anecdotes suggest they were all villains drawn from English prisons, sent to Ireland to wreak havoc. I don't think that's entirely true, but I never thought of any of them as being good people, having mothers and sons who would grieve for them.

'I can't really help,' I say finally, wishing I could. He seems like a decent man, educated and kind, and I think with amusement that there haven't been many like that around here.

'Sorry I bothered you. I'll be going, then. Thank you for your help. I'm Justin Sanders, by the way.'

He grasps the side of the cart for balance and holds his hand up. I take it briefly, thinking, *How formal are these English!* I was no help at all, in truth, but for some reason decide that at least one person in Roone Bay should be nice to him, despite his granddad's past. 'My name is called Hannah. I hope you find what you're looking for.'

'I might have done just that,' he says, casting me a strangely intimate glance.

I feel heat trickle into my cheeks, then have another thought. 'Well, you might speak to Turlough. He was my granddad's friend, back in the day. He was up at the farm a few moments ago. He might still be there. You can go on up and call out, if you like.'

'How will I know which is your house?'

'It's the only one up this boreen.'

'Turlough what? Has he another name?'

I shrug. 'If he has, I don't know it. Everyone knows him as Turlough. But if he doesn't want to be found, you won't find him. He might be gone by now. He isn't like us. He walks the hills, beds down wherever.'

'He won't shoot me, though?'

I laugh. 'He's a gentle soul. He's more likely to cry over a dead pigeon than cause a fight. He doesn't much live in the real world, though. I don't know if he'll even be lucid. Some days he's better than others. But if anyone knows about your granddad, I suspect he will.'

'Thank you.'

'Now, I'd best be off.'

I click my tongue, and Old Grey plods on down the hill.

As we round the corner, I glance back. The Englishman is still standing there, watching. It's a good job he can't see my blush as I'm caught looking. He raises a hand and waves as I move out of sight. He's probably astounded at the sight of a girl driving a donkey cart, like something out of the past. There's something elegant and calm in his speech and manner that's a total contrast to Cathal's earthy arrogance. Is the man a fool, though, to come to Ireland asking about a granddad who was a Black and Tan? Does he not realise that resentment for hundreds of years of repression is still smouldering in the breasts of Ireland's citizens? Justin seems nice but maybe a little naïve to think that anyone will talk to him about that particular episode of the past.

It's hard to imagine English soldiers masquerading as police, prowling the West Cork farmlands with their guns, seeking those who had the gall to rebel against the English crown. But now that past is swept firmly under the carpet, overlaid by determinedly cheerful memories of a country childhood blessed by happiness despite being poor. Who wants to revisit the truth of the past? I'm a little cynical, but survival paints decency over foul deeds, and a generation later the fiction becomes fact, passed down with true patriotism to grandchildren. If you believed the stories, all the granddads in West Cork were heroes, though in truth, there were many who had gone into their homes and barricaded the doors so as not to be involved. No one speaks the truth of the matter. It's an unwritten law. But what kind of man would have become a Black and Tan? They were vicious thugs given free rein to murder and rape and pillage, like the soldiers of old. I don't think a decent man would have volunteered for that service.

I decide to firmly put Justin's quest out of my mind, but for some reason it won't be ousted. I feel drawn to him in an indefinable way, as if we are unified by our individual quests: him seeking his granddad's past, me seeking mine. But a trickle of self-derision underscores this thought. Do I see this unlikely encounter with an English doctor as something more than incidental? Is my attraction towards him because I see in him the possibility of a saviour, someone who will lift me from what is almost certainly an untenable position and carry me away to safety? Am I so weak that I need saving?

6

JACK, 1918

Jack had arrived at the training camp on Salisbury Plain with a group of lads who were tall and thin like himself, more suited to the school uniforms most of them had recently shed. Their hair was shaved short, and they were issued with uniforms that made them feel more like soldiers. Some allowed the fine growth of beard to linger, despite regulations, providing a slender mask to disguise the fear that was clearly written on each face. Jack wasn't into pretending. He had no illusions. He viewed these men-boys with something akin to sorrow. Many would march off to war and simply disappear into statistical mist, their youthful dreams shot to smithereens.

The long rows of hastily constructed wooden huts had been their home for a few short months while they drilled back and forth on the dusty chalk hills of southern England. Training was hurried, desperate. They quickly learned to march in formation, shoot a rifle. They yelled furiously as they thrust forward with their bayonets, the front knee bent so that the full force of the impact would come from the central body and take the enemy in the guts. It was academic, of course; the straw bales had been passively waiting to be impaled.

They had arrived at the camp as innocent children and left ostensibly as grown men, ready for battle. In that short time, they had developed a desperate camaraderie, joking, laughing, drinking and learning to choke on the cigarettes none had smoked before. But smoking made them feel older, and it was something to do with hands that might otherwise have been shaking. They knew that most of them would not see home again. The figures in the newspapers spoke for themselves. None spoke out loud of the fear that lay deep in the heart, along with the guilty prayer that it would be some other lad who would end up hanging on the barbed wire on the Western Front. But there was a strangely buoyant undercurrent as these new soldiers left for France. Many of them had never been abroad before, never even been on a boat, and that alone lent the added exhilaration of a new life experience. It had been impossible for the youths, with their planned lives still ahead of them, to imagine dying.

But die they had, in droves. Here, on the bleak Western Front, where blackened stumps of trees clawed for help amidst the carnage of war, all that endured from the training was that when the sergeant screamed an order, men jumped to obey.

Crouching with his back to the rough earth wall in the trench, his once-pristine boots buried in a foot of muddy water, Jack didn't recognise any of the faces around him. Faces came and went. It was better to never learn names. Darkness was approaching. The shrieking zing of the occasional bullet pierced the almost uncanny silence. They were waiting for the order that would send them over the top once again.

Another push had been ordered. Jack forgot, now, how many times he had waited, clenched with fear, for the order that would send him from this world into the next. So far, he'd been lucky. He seen comrades drop around him, some with stunned surprise on their faces in death, some with expressions of agony written on their features; but he was still alive and strangely unharmed.

Did God have a plan? If so, it was hard to see.

He had attended church regularly as a child, as a youth, and had gladly sung hymns that rose through the vaulted roof of their quaint village church, praising God on high for his kindness and bounty. He had truly believed and had felt emotionally privileged to be part of the loving community he'd been brought up in. But here and now, amidst the carnage of war, it was hard to believe that God even existed. He was, no doubt about it, in a hell designed and enacted by humans.

Darkness fell slowly, like a blanket drawn over the sky. It was a clear night. The smiling moon and twinkling stars were dreadful in their beauty; for if he could see the harsh outlines of the ruined landscape, the enemy could see him. Around him the men stilled with equally bleak awareness. One man started to recite the Lord's Prayer, and others joined in. The men's voices droned in a whisper along the trench.

'Shut that noise!' the sergeant hissed, and deathly silence fell.

'Ready, ready, ready,' was muttered, passed down the line.

'Stand your ground...'

'NOW GO! FOR GOD AND FOR ENGLAND! GO! GO! GO!'

The soldiers ran at the wall, leaped up and dived over the top as if desperation alone would take them through the killing zone. Bullets flashed across the night sky like a stream of deadly hornets. The air was filled with the buzzing of their tiny wings.

Jack didn't move.

Something inside him drifted away.

He stared up. The sky was beautiful. Like fireflies – or sparks from the bonfire on Guy Fawkes Night. He heard the crackle of the flames, felt the warmth of his father's protective hand around his. 'Look but don't touch,' his father said, crouching to be at his level. 'You might burn yourself.'

Then he was briefly back in the trench in France, confused to find the crouching sergeant pointing his handgun at him, screaming at him to get up and run, or be shot like a dog for disobeying a direct order. He was vaguely aware that something was wrong with this image. The sergeant was just a boy and shouldn't be playing with guns.

There was a sound in his head, and he realised that he was in church, but someone was pressing two adjacent keys on the organ. He could hear the push and pull of the bellows, and the long discordant wail went on and on. He wished it would just stop and let him sleep. He was so tired.

7

HANNAH

The threatening thundercloud overhead sparkles with lightning, followed by thunderclaps that reverberate over the hills. The following downpour is sudden and violent. I hope the Englishman has had the sense to duck into the farmhouse or barn and wait it out. Maybe he'll be lucky and find Turlough has done the same. But it's too late for me to turn back. My coat had lost any pretence of being waterproof a long while back, and I'm soaked through within minutes. The rutted boreen, already pitted with puddles, is soon running with a network of rivulets. I hunch my head between my shoulders as Old Grey plods stolidly along. I know from experience that there's no hurrying him. As I watch the donkey's sturdy, greying head nod with each step, I wonder what I will do with him. I can't just abandon him. But who will want a shook old donkey in this new age?

I don't want to cope with all this uncertainty. I'd rather slip back into the non-life I was living before. I'm fighting despondency, and a surge of anger flares in my chest. I didn't ask for this upheaval, and I want my life, my old life back. Tears stream down my face, mingling with the rain that's dripping down from my hair.

I struggle up the steps to Noel's house and lean on the bell.

Mrs Weddows opens the door, her mouth open to give out when she takes in the state of me. 'Sakes, girrul, you're soaked to the skin!'

I sway briefly and clutch the rail. When I speak, my voice is dull. 'Mrs Weddows, I don't know what to do.'

She stands back. 'For God's sake, come on in before ye die of the cold!'

I stand inside the door, worried about my sodden boots on the posh carpet, but she ushers me through to a living room where a warm peat fire smoulders. 'Sit ye there, and I'll tell himself that you're here,' she says.

I slump by the fire, and exhaustion takes over. When I open my eyes, I have a blanket tucked around me, and Noel is sitting opposite, his gentle face filled with concern. 'What's happened, Hannah? Take your time.'

Tears gather and, despite my determination, overspill. I take a deep breath and swipe them angrily from my face. 'Old Grey,' I say on a hiccup. 'He's outside...'

'I've taken care of him. Out with it, when you're ready.'

Noel's wife, Caitlin, comes in with a tray. 'Tea,' she says. 'It'll warm the heart of you. Go on – put your hands around the mug.'

'Thank you,' I say, and tears rise again. The truth is, I'm unused to kindness.

Noels takes his wife's hand as she stands beside him, her face creased with worry. I love that they found each other after a lifetime apart, each thinking the other dead. It's a fairy tale come true. For a fleeting moment, I wonder if my own problems might work out after all, like theirs did, but the odds are against it.

I take a deep breath and tell them.

There's a silence while the couple take in my news, then Caitlin says, 'Ah, yes, Grace told me an Irish-American had booked in. I didn't realise he was your brother. So, he's back to claim what's his, is he, after walking out on it all those years ago? What a langer!' She grins. 'Should I kick him out of the hotel?'

I give a wet chuckle. 'Not at all – he'd only come up to the house and bother me. It's just, well... I don't know what to do. I know what's in the will, of course. I was hoping we could discuss it amicably, but he's made it clear he doesn't want to share the inheritance with me or any of our – his – siblings. And there's the matter of the deeds. If he hasn't got them, where are they?'

'Well, child,' Caitlin says, patting the back of Noel's hand with her free one, 'you came to the right place. Noel will sort it out.'

'I will?' Noel asks, but his face betrays love and amusement. He ponders for a moment. 'Right. Well, this isn't the dark ages. He can't simply throw you out if you have nowhere to go, so don't worry about that. He's chancing his luck. I don't know what we can do, but let me have a think.'

'But you will stay here tonight,' Caitlin says firmly. 'You're wet through, and you'll have no fire lit, above.'

'I'd like to go home,' I hiccup.

I suddenly realise my home isn't mine after all, and my eyes flood again.

Caitlin comes over and gives me a one-armed hug. 'Stay here tonight, *a chara*. Jane will dry your clothes, and we'll see what the morning brings. Things always look less bad in the morning. Everyone in Roone Bay is worried about you, girleen. It will all be sorted, you'll see.'

Everyone is worried about me? Strange to hear that said,

after all these years of feeling isolated. But people here don't intrude on family matters, and Dad, who'd always scorned charity, had actively discouraged interference.

I sleep uneasily. I've never slept on a sprung mattress; it feels dangerously unstable when I turn over. And the warmth in the room has me throwing off the covers. It's strangely unsettling to be in the Big House, like a regular guest. I must have slept, though, because when I rise, I find my clothes freshly laundered on a chair beside the door, put there presumably by Mrs Weddows. I dress hurriedly, feeling like an intruder. Noel and Caitlin are salt-of-the-earth Irish, with no airs or graces, but I feel uncomfortable surrounded by their wealth.

I slip downstairs nervously, but Mrs Weddows is waiting for me. 'Come on through to the kitchen, girl. I have breakfast laid.'

I follow down a wide, curving staircase to a large kitchen warmed by an enormous range. Noel is sitting at the table in tattered clothes and well-used slippers, his feet stretched to the warmth. Three dogs are huddled as close as they can get to the range, including a huge Irish wolfhound. We've never had dogs at the farm. Dad had no time for them, and as the enormous dog rises to check me out, I back away nervously.

'Don't mind Lanky,' Noel says. 'She's a real dote. She came by one day looking for a home and decided to stay – like all the others. Show her the back of your hand.'

Lanky sniffs, gives a brief lick and lies back down, yawning, betraying a long jaw filled with lethal white teeth.

'There, the kiss of approval,' Noel says. 'She knows you now. Sit and help yourself.'

I'm sure I look a right gawk as I survey the table, with its packets of cereal, bread, jam, croissants and tub of butter, at a loss to know how to behave. Guessing my dilemma, Noel picks up a croissant, splits it open with his thumbs and lathers the inside with butter and jam.

Mrs Weddows dumps a large metal pot of tea on the table and pushes a plate in my direction. 'Eat your fill, girrul,' she says. 'Problems are best faced on a full stomach.'

'So, my challenge for today,' Noel muses as I tuck in, 'is to talk to Andy Coakley – he's my solicitor – and ask for his advice. Lorcan Byrne asked if your father had made another will that supersedes the one Mark has. I think that's the avenue we need to go down first. I'll get Andy onto it. Though, if he did, we might have heard about it after Adrian died. Andy will get word around, anyway, that's he's looking for Adrian Barry's will. There's no harm in spreading the word in the community.'

Dealings with solicitors are supposed to be secret, I think, but in a small town like Roone Bay, it wouldn't surprise me to find that Mark's arrival has made the grapevine buzz with news of an inheritance issue.

I flush and look down at my plate. 'I can't afford a solicitor.'

'Sure, don't you be worrying about the cost, girrul,' Mrs Weddows says sharply. 'Noel will see you sorted.'

'Righty-ho,' Noel says. 'I've just had my orders given.' He leans forward, and in a hushed whisper, says, 'Have you any idea what it's like for me with two women in the house? I'm a sorely tried man, it's true.'

But the twinkle in his eye makes me smile despite myself. A simple *thanks* seems inadequate for such generosity. I know he can afford to be generous, but feeling obliged to accept it is humiliating. 'I, ah, appreciate that,' I say in a small voice.

Mrs Weddows hitches her fists onto her hips. 'Now, don't ye go speaking my words around, but sure haven't ye been a dutiful daughter? More than yer da deserved, as God's my witness! And there's none would say different. Sure, ye need the house. What is that Mark Barry thinking of, to abandon ye all these years, then come in and think to steal it from under ye? Sure, there's no justice in that.'

Noel is openly grinning now. 'Well, I couldn't have said it better myself. Leave it with me for now. Once we know what's what, we can decide what to do. It might be that we can just persuade Mark to sell the property and divvy the proceeds without it going too far down the legal money pit. Sure, it will be enough to buy a small house in town, which might suit ye better.'

'And you can stay here until it's sorted,' Mrs Weddows says.

'I'd rather be in my own house,' I say diffidently.

'Well, sure you would,' Noel agrees. 'But if Mark comes bothering, just come straight back here. I'll get word to him myself that we're looking out for you. Sure, he won't be doing himself any favours to spread what he's about, anyway.'

'Thank you.'

'Will you be sad to lose the farm?' Noel asks after a moment.

'A small house would be better than nothing, but' – I flush faintly – 'Cathal Carrol and I have an understanding... to work the farm, you see.'

Both Noel and Mrs Weddows stare at me speechlessly.

'I know he wants the inheritance,' I admit, 'but I could do worse. He's strong from the blacksmithing work and is prepared to learn. And,' I add in a small voice, seeing how the information is being taken, 'I want to be married and have children.'

I don't need to say *like any normal woman*, but Mrs Weddows understands. 'Oh, my dear,' she says, a catch in her voice, 'of course you want to get married and have children, but—'

Noel clears his throat loudly, and she stops herself midsentence. 'Let's see what we can find out about the will, and everything else will take its natural course, eh?'

Mrs Weddows nods. 'Her being up there with just a donkey

cart and not even a telephone, though. Well, a body might worry for her, especially now, with himself acting up like the spit of his father, with no care to his own kin.'

'You don't have a *phone?*' Noel asks, clearly surprised. 'I'll have one put in today.'

'No, you mustn't... I do well enough without. I can't—'

'I won't sleep unless you have a phone. Do an old man a favour, girrul, it's not a bother. Right, I'll sort that now, and then I'll call Andy. I'll let you know what happens, eh?'

'Is there anything I should do?'

'Not really. But when you go back up to the farm, have a look around, see if those deeds have been hidden away in some secret place, like where Adrian kept his stash of poitín,' he adds with a wink. 'But don't you let Mark push you out. There's no rushing where inheritances are concerned. If you and Mark don't come to an amicable agreement, it might go on for years.'

He makes it sound like this is a good thing.

'Mark is set to dig his heels in.'

'If he's got his nob on straight, he won't instigate anything with the solicitor too soon. If he does, you'll both end up with nothing.'

'Maybe he's not that daft,' I say doubtfully, 'but he doesn't want to share. He wants it all. He said he can manage without the deeds, but I think he's up there now, taking the place apart looking for them. I don't see why Dad would have hidden them anywhere, though. If they were in the salt pot on the dresser for all those years, why aren't they there now?'

'So, maybe a solicitor has them. Maybe your dad did make a new will after all. That would be interesting.' He looks me in the eye. 'But, girrul, stay here today until the telephone is installed. Jane is right to be worried with you being up there alone and Mark in a lather about the inheritance.'

I shake my head. 'Thank you so much, but I need to go

home,' I say. 'It doesn't feel right being here. I appreciate what you're doing, but...'

'I understand. You just want to be in your own space. Well, I'm still having the telephone installed. For my own benefit, you understand? So I don't have to drive up that track if I need to speak to you.'

The blatant lie makes me smile. 'Thank you, then. So, where will I find Old Grey?'

'Give me five minutes, and I'll bring him out to you,' Noel says.

Old Grey stands like a statue while I clamber onto the seat. Whether he's being patient or has fallen asleep on his feet, too old to fight the reins, I'm not sure. There were times when Mam took us to the market and he would simply stop and refuse to move until he was good and ready. At those times she threatened to turn him into sausages, but she never lashed out at him with the crop, as I'd seen Mark do. And nor do I. I click my tongue to set him moving.

I find myself thinking about Justin's granddad, Jack, who came to Ireland and disappeared. I've seen the black-and-white images of the war, the almost unimaginable carnage. I doubt anyone survived the experience mentally unscathed. For Jack to have survived that, only to be transported instantly to another battlefield, albeit without the trenches and bombs, was surely not advisable. If he did something bad, sure, the IRA would have held a field hearing and possibly executed him. Someone in Roone Bay must know the truth, but prising that information from lips that have been sealed for sixty years will be nigh on impossible.

8

JACK, 1920

In the aftermath of the war, Jack had been sent home from France under an undistinguished cloud and spent many months in an institution for brain-damaged soldiers while the powers that be were trying to work out what to do with him. He was well aware he had narrowly escaped being shot for cowardice, and when he was offered a chance to redeem himself in Ireland as a Temporary Constable, it suited him to take it. He had never wanted to be anything other than a policeman, like his father, but the war, with its conscription of ever-younger young men, had ripped his dreams away before they materialised. He was lucky to have not just survived but come home physically undamaged. As for his mind, well, the horrific images embedded there could never be removed and would no doubt trouble him to the end of his days. He was old-school, like his father, however. Despite being plagued with nightmares, there was no reason to distress his family by talking about them.

His Irish mother, when he wrote to tell her he had 'volunteered' to go to Ireland, seemed relieved. He would have a hard time of it in a small village in England with the label *coward* hanging over his head. When so many people had lost loved ones, she knew it would be difficult for the community to accept that he was basically a good man and hadn't intended to let anyone down. *War isn't where a man earns glory,* she wrote back, *it is where he survives or dies.* She said she was glad her son hadn't tried to be a hero. *Trust in God and the Irish, son – they will surely see you're a decent man. You did nothing wrong, and there are worse fates than going to the old country. Rosie and little Walter will be waiting for you when hearts have cooled...*

Jack later had deep misgivings about going to Ireland. In hindsight, it bore all the hallmarks of a bad decision. He was well educated and read the newspapers voraciously, analysing and rationalising beyond what was written, as his father had taught him. His mother, being Irish, had also provided him with a somewhat different slant than that printed. Ireland, he concluded, contrary to government statements, was on the brink of true civil war.

After the Easter Uprising of 1916, a temporary peace had been negotiated between the Irish and the English while the world war was in full swing, but once it was over, Irish nationalism had soared into open aggression.

They simply wanted to rule their own country.

But there was resentment on both sides of the Irish Sea. In trying to dampen the smouldering Irish fire, the English government had not insisted on conscription in Ireland, which fanned the anger of the English, whose husbands and sons had been marched off to war, to return broken, or not return at all.

Many Irishmen had chosen to enlist, through moral rectitude or even because they needed the income, and thousands of Irish had died abroad. Unlike the English, however, those who survived were not greeted as returning heroes by their countrymen. Under the roiling cloud of rebellion, they were seen as traitors to Ireland's cause.

Bad feeling bred below the surface during the fighting, but once the war was over, nationalist fervour flowered openly in

Ireland. Reading between the lines in her letters, Jack could see that his own mother was torn. Her deep integrity and fiery temper were confused by events beyond her understanding. In her eyes, her son – being half Irish himself – would be the ideal person to bring sense to the situation.

Jack, however, was well aware that he would have little power to influence anyone in Ireland. He wasn't going as an auxiliary officer; they would be drawn from England's moneyed classes, just as they had in the army. Despite his intellect, he would be going as a foot soldier, a copper on the beat, doing whatever he was commanded to do, as he had in the army. He had no misconceptions: those at the bottom of the pile carried the blame when things went wrong, while their superiors received medals when the operations were a success.

That was true in all walks of life.

It was late in 1920 when Jack was shipped over to Dublin with several hundred men, and night temperatures were bitter. A few volunteers had accepted the offer in preference to jail, but most were working-class men, there for the income. The postwar depression meant work was scarce and pay minimal. They had families to feed, and more than three shillings a week had been encouragement enough to bring men flocking to recruit.

Like him, most of the Temporary Constables had been soldiers through conscription, not choice, and had survived more through luck than expertise. But even when limbs were left intact, war left scars buried in the mind, and many young men found slipping back into normal society more difficult than going to war in the first place; lost innocence cannot be regained. Many of his fellow Temporary Constables were little more than children, albeit jaded beyond their years; others were working-class men trying to support their families, but some resented that the Irish had not been conscripted as they had, and thought of this appointment as an opportunity to teach the bloody Irish a lesson.

Jack was pleased to learn that his own circumstances had not been broadcast; not out of respect for himself, he'd been told curtly, but to maintain order. Being branded an alive coward wasn't so noble as being bravely dead. No one wanted to work with someone discredited for cowardice in the trenches. Jack couldn't argue with that. But when shots were threading overhead like a giant storm of angry wasps, he'd entered a dazed, mindless state where nothing mattered. He hadn't heard the commands through the noise that filled his mind. But to the brass, he'd disobeyed a direct order from a superior and was lucky not to have been summarily shot. The war, by then, was on its last gasp, and the officers were not thinking of him so much as their own repatriation, and the accounts the men under their command might take home. No one liked to see comrades in arms shot by their own officers.

When Jack was finally repatriated to an army detention centre, his mother wrote and advised him to just endure until he could come home: he was alive, thank God. He'd seen the worst of it. He wasn't so sure, though. The treatment he received there had been calculated to embarrass and demean. Being offered the chance to retrieve his honour in Ireland had been embraced thankfully. He was probably right in supposing that this *opportunity* was the government's way of solving a problem. His infractions during the war did not make him a criminal in the traditional sense of the word, nor even a traitor, so he might as well be working for his supper in Ireland rather than sitting around England in disgrace.

But he was becoming increasingly worried by the attitudes of his fellow Temporary Constables. It was sound logic to send men to assist the undermanned and beleaguered police force in Ireland, to maintain social order, but the men in Whitehall had not met the men they were sending over. His travelling companions, after their all-too-brief training, were behaving like soldiers heading back into the fray. They smoked hard, making light-hearted banter out of horrific war activities. It was worrying that the auxiliaries who led them were deliberately dehumanising the Irish patriots, referring to them as *the enemy*, rather than a civilian population that required policing.

Had war not intervened, these men might well have been grounded as bricklayers, carpenters or miners to support growing families. Instead, they were war-hardened and lacking in empathy. Permission to step beyond the moral boundaries of civilised behaviour obviously wasn't something that could just be revoked.

No good would come of it, Jack thought.

9

HANNAH

I've only gone a few yards down the slope when the Englishman himself steps onto the drive from the new hotel. He waves, and I pull Old Grey to a halt.

Smiling, he says, 'You're like a picture postcard from the past.'

'What, one of those faded brown ones?'

'Maybe,' he jokes, 'but those sepia pictures are filled with old-world charm, like you.'

The way he looks at me sends warmth to my cheeks. I roll my eyes, then say, 'Flattery is usually followed by a request. What are you after?'

'Well, I wondered, ah, can I ride with you for a little way?'

I can't take offence when this is said with such innocent eagerness. 'What, to experience the joys of rural Ireland?'

'Why not? It's a nice day for a jaunt in a donkey cart.'

Jaunt? I think and laugh. 'Go on, then. Climb up.'

He does so, awkwardly, and the seat that I used to share with my mother suddenly seems to shrink as his shoulder presses against mine. But his face breaks into a wide grin.

We trot down to the main road and turn west. 'Don't forget you'll have to walk back,' I remind him.

'I can manage a mile or so.' His sidelong smile catches me, and I realise our meeting had not been accidental. He had no doubt seen my cart outside Noel's house last night and had been watching for me to drive back down.

'Did you speak to Turlough?'

'No, he was nowhere to be seen. I had to wait in your barn until that downpour went through. I hope you don't mind.'

'Of course not. I hoped you'd do that.'

'Then, when I got back to the hotel, someone told me of a place down by the quay that Turlough stays in sometimes, but I haven't managed to get there yet.'

'I can take you there now?'

His eyes light up. 'Would you? Really?'

'I will, but don't hold your breath. If he's been told you're looking for him, he'll be long gone, and to be honest I don't think you'll ever find the truth of what happened to your granddad.' I give a quirky smile. 'Even those who were there at the time now believe the tales that grew legs over the years.'

'I'm beginning to realise that. But really, I wish I could convince people that I'm not trying to lay blame. I'd just like to know where Granddad Jack is buried, that's all.'

'Does it matter?'

'I made Great-Grandma a promise. I'd like to see it through. And if I don't, it won't be for want of trying.'

I click my tongue, and Old Grey turns obediently down the road towards Colla Pier. It's a beautiful day, the sea sparkling in anticipation of the approaching spring. If Turlough is there, maybe he will talk to me, if not to Justin, who seems fairly determined in his quest.

'It's beautiful here,' Justin says, echoing my thoughts.

'It is, so.'

'I heard you're to be married, now your father has passed.'

So much for keeping our news secret. 'I am. Have you been asking about me?'

I turn to peruse his expression but see no undercurrent of meaning. 'In the bar, I overheard, ah, stories,' he says hesitantly.

I glance at him, brows raised. 'Stories?'

'About Cathal wanting to inherit the farm. I'm sorry, it's not my business, but...'

'No, it's not,' I snap but feel the need to explain. 'I know he doesn't love me. I know he wants the farm. But I'm not able to work the farm myself.'

'I heard he's no farmer, that he does odd jobs and a bit of welding at the forge.'

There's something in his tone that I have to correct. 'Sure, he's a blacksmith, but he's keen enough to learn about farming. And you can't blame a body who grew up with nothing for wanting his own biteen of land.'

He presses his lips together as though he wants to say more but doesn't feel it's right. Well, it isn't. But what he said niggles.

'Cathal's a good man,' I add defensively. 'And there's no one else in Roone Bay who's offered.'

Even as I'm saying it, I realise it doesn't come out well.

'Do you love him?'

I stop the cart and turn to face him, amazed. 'You have a cheek!'

He flushes faintly. 'I know, but maybe you should be asking yourself whether you're selling yourself short.'

'I didn't think I was. There aren't so many options open to someone like me,' I say a little sourly, clicking the donkey on again. 'So, yes, it's an arrangement that suits us. We'll make it work.'

'You could leave the farm, get a job.'

'I didn't go to school. I have no school certificates. Who's going to employ me?'

'You didn't go to school?'

'It took a long time to get over the polio. Then Mam got ill and Dad was working the farm all the hours God sent. He didn't have time to be taking me down the hill every day.'

We arrive at Colla Pier. I snap the reins briefly. Old Grey plants his hooves solidly, and I slide to the ground. 'Wait here.'

He looks at the donkey warily. 'Is it safe? He won't run away with me?'

I'm amused despite my irritation. 'You're not used to animals, are you?'

'No. I always wanted a cat, but my mother sneezes when there's one anywhere near.'

I look up at him sitting on my cart with his worried expression. He's brave enough – or daft enough – to come to Ireland asking about things best left buried, yet he's afraid of an old donkey, too long in the tooth to run anywhere. 'If he runs, I'll pray for you both,' I say on a laugh.

I see the echo of a smile on his lips as I turn, feeling his eyes on me. I don't like people watching me walk, because my legs, from the knees down, are useless, which means I swing my legs from the hips and kind of lurch from one twisted foot to the other. As a teenager, I was so jealous of Aine's lithe body and slinky roll of the hips, but she was always protective of me. Even if I hadn't contracted the polio, I still wouldn't have her shape, though. She grew tall, like my brothers and my father, whereas I grew kind of stocky in comparison. I used to wonder if the polio had stunted my growth. But now I wonder if it's a legacy from unknown parents.

It's hard work walking on uneven ground, but I don't try to hide my clumsiness from Justin. He's a doctor and will have seen people in worse shape than me, and he'll leave Roone Bay soon enough, probably without learning anything about his granddad. I feel a little sorry for him, in truth, because even if his motives are innocent, the community has undoubtedly shut him out.

On the small track leading to the fisherman's hut, I stop to catch my breath and gaze at the majestic beauty of the sea stretching to the curved horizon. The truth is, polio or not, I'm glad to be alive. I call out, 'Turlough. It's me, Hannah.'

There's no reply. I knock at the door and push it open. It emits a heady smell of salt and fish that some would find unpleasant, but living so close to the sea has tuned my senses. That pungent odour will always be the scent of home. There's no indication, though, that Turlough has been here in a while.

Old Eoghan is sitting by the harbour wall, working away at fixing some small thing I can't make out. He looks up as I approach and smiles. 'Hannah! What brings you here? I'm sorry for your loss.'

'Sure, Dad was a troubled man,' I respond. 'He's in a better place now.' I'm careful not to speak ill of him, because he was one of a small community that created strong ties through troubled times. The past might be buried, but it's not forgotten.

'Sure, he is,' he agrees. 'With yer mam, right enough.'

'I'm looking for Turlough. Have you seen him?'

'Not for a while.'

'He must be around Roone Bay. I saw him up at the farm, just yesterday.'

He looks surprised. 'Did ye, so? Well, if I see him, I'll tell him you were asking after him.'

'Thank you.' I take a breath. 'Eoghan, were you, ah, were you with the army, with my granddad and Turlough, back in the day?'

He knows what I mean. He glances over at Justin who is sitting stiffly on my cart, staring towards us keenly. 'I heard there was an Englishman asking. He's stirring a pot best left alone.'

'He just wants to know what happened to his granddad.'

'Exactly what I mean, girrul. I heard the stories, of course, but I wasn't part of it at all. Too young.'

'He just wants to lay a wreath where his granddad is buried. He's not wanting to make trouble.'

'Does he, so? And what's the name of this granddad?'

'Jack Sanders. And he said there was another man went missing at the same time. Billy something or other.'

'Never heard the names, so.'

But he had paused just fractionally before speaking, and I know he's lying. What strange can of worms have I just cracked open?

I take my leave of Eoghan, walk back and heave myself up on the cart. Justin's gaze is intent. 'What did he tell you, the old fisherman? That wasn't Turlough, was it?'

'No, that wasn't himself. I learned nothing. He hasn't seen Turlough in a while.' I click my tongue and pull us full circle. Old Grey plods obediently back towards Roone Bay.

Justin sighs. 'These people will never tell me the truth, will they?'

'No, I don't think they will.'

'So why are you being helpful?'

I think for a moment and wonder if I feel some kind of empathy with his thirst for knowledge in light of my own uncertain background. But I say, 'Curiosity, plain and simple. Time enough has gone by, so I'm wondering quite what they're covering up.'

'There's no statute of limitations for murder,' he muses. 'I understand their reticence, in all honesty.'

'Would it be called murder when it's war?'

'Killing another human is always murder. But then, I took the Hippocratic oath, so my take on the sanctity of life might seem naïve to people who were fighting for the right to rule their own country.'

'True.' I smile to take the sting from the words. 'How long are you intending to stay?'

'I've taken a leave of absence, so I'm in no hurry. Which is just as well, as it turns out.'

Justin has a way with him that makes me feel comfortable in his presence, but I pull up at the end of the road, conscious of the fact that our little 'jaunt' is probably already food for gossip.

'This is your stop, I believe.'

He jumps down and looks up at me. 'Thank you for the ride. I don't think I've enjoyed anything so much in a long while. I'm staying at the hotel. I wonder if I could tempt you to have dinner with me one evening?'

I'm taken aback. 'Why?'

'Because you're kind, and I'd like to see you again.'

'I'm not sure it's a good idea,' I say doubtfully. I can just imagine the tongues wagging.

'Okay, but think about it. And if you find anything out, will you let me know?'

'Of course.' I nod, snap the reins and walk on, feigning a nonchalance that I don't feel. Inside, my heart is pounding.

10

HANNAH

With my four older siblings gone, even with Aine's help, Mam had worked harder than ever before. She never complained, and I was too young to notice the way weight fell off her and her skin turned to a grey pallor. I'd just turned twelve when she collapsed at the sink one day, and Aine drove her to the doctor in the cart. I learned later that when her monthly bleeding stopped and her belly started to swell, she thought she was pregnant again and had sighed with stoic acceptance. But no child was forming, and the pains that racked her body were something far worse. The doctor's diagnosis was a shock to us all. Mam told us with deep belief that God was calling her home, that we mustn't grieve; it was just her time.

It took two more years for her to die.

I only realised how hard my mother had worked when she became truly sick and the burdens of her labour shifted inexorably to Aine and me. Dad became sullen and silent, but one time I saw him bowed over a gate clutching it with his strong fists as if he'd like to break it. I slipped away because he wouldn't want to be seen crying. It was vaguely gratifying to realise that he loved her, in his own way.

Mam refused the medicine that was supposed to prolong her life, because she'd heard it made people feel more ill than the cancer. Ever practical, she said if it wasn't going to cure the cancer, what was the point? Dad couldn't really handle the workload on the farm after Mark left, but he had refused to give in. When it was clear that Mam was terminally ill, however, he lost the plot overnight.

It was hard to remain positive during that dreadful time, though I needed to for Mam. I wrote to all my siblings, telling them of Mam's illness, hinting that she'd like to see them, but none came back to visit. They professed a lack of funds, but reading between the lines, I realised they were avoiding the issue of nursing her. They had all fled Ireland, riding on the tide of change, while our farm was trapped in the past. I never blamed my siblings for leaving Ireland, but I was furious that they turned their backs on their own mam.

When she was ill, Mam told me: *You're my beautiful angel, sent by God in my hour of need.* At the time I was quite moved, but later I thought the words strange. As though I'd been given the polio to make me stay and nurse her instead of going out and getting my own life. I decided, after all, it was God that sent me the polio sickness and took away my running forever. He sent me callipers so that my useless legs could hold me up. For that, I hated Him. It wasn't fair. Why me? I wanted to be pretty and have the boys admire me, as they did Aine when she was dancing in the hall. Aine persuaded me to go with her to the local dance, just once. The eyes that followed me were filled with pity as I clumped to one side in the community hall and sat watching, a forever wallflower.

I never went again.

But now I'm wondering anew about Mam's words and what underlying meaning they might have held. She never said the same about Aine. So, did some other woman in desperate circumstances ask Mam and Dad to take me on? But if I was not their child, why do I have a birth certificate stating that I am?

I wonder if I'm the child of one of my older siblings. Mam might have taken me on rather than see me go to the nuns. That could explain Dad's strange antipathy towards me. I imagine the fury that would have made Dad accept the ruse and put his name to the deception rather than bear the stigma of a bastard grandchild in his home.

11

HANNAH

Cathal has been keeping his distance, and part of me wonders if he's doing the decent thing and observing the usual bereavement protocol. But the longer Mark is here, the more likely it is that Cathal has heard news of the inheritance. A few days later, I recognise the distinctive sound of his car grinding up the boreen. I hear the door slam hard, and I'm not surprised when he strides into the house wearing an expression of ire mixed with disappointment. Gone is any hint of his previous gentle manner.

'When were you going to tell me?' he asks, thrusting his head forward and slamming belligerent fists on his hips. He looks for all the world like an indignant rooster.

'Tell you what?' I ask innocently.

'About Mark inheriting the farm. Is it true?'

'Mark thinks so, but it's not so simple,' I say.

'I don't know what's not simple about your dad leaving everything to him. Did you know that all along? You've kept me hanging on a line, and now I find you're not inheriting!'

The petulant curl of his lip isn't one I've seen before. I'm taken aback by the terse rudeness of the accusations. He paces back and forth, and I realise that I'm finally seeing the man behind the deceptively beautiful mask. Pregnant or not, I'm glad to have my mistake so clearly exposed before my flagging self-respect took a nosedive. Though it pains me to realise the truth, the priest was right, Aine was right and even my dad was right. Behind Cathal's superficial mask is a young man who thinks the world owes him a free ride and believes his looks will win it for him. How close I came to making the biggest mistake of my life! How could I have been so stupid?

'I didn't know about the will,' I say calmly. 'It was a bolt out of the blue for me, too. Mam said I'd inherit, and Dad never told me different.'

He swivels. 'But is the will genuine?'

'I believe so.'

'Have you engaged a solicitor?'

'No,' I say honestly.

He's still pacing indignantly. 'There must be a way we can challenge it. I mean, you've looked after your mother and your father all these years.' He grins, and the Cathal I thought I knew suddenly pops into focus. It's a light-bulb moment that betrays the selfishness that drives him. 'Right, so. That's what we'll do. We'll challenge the will. We might still make something of this mess.'

'It would be great if you'd engage a solicitor on our behalf,' I suggest, trying hard to keep a straight face.

He's taken aback. He stops pacing to place his hands on my shoulders. His soulful expression betrays intense concern for my well-being as he says sincerely, 'But, Hannah, you know I can't act for you in this matter. You have to do it for both of us, for our future together. It's your farm and your dad's will. Don't you have any cash, any savings?'

'I don't have anything saved; nor did Dad.'

'What about the rent money for the fields?'

'I'll have to talk to Mickey Hoolihan about the rent,' I

agree, then my sense of the ridiculous gets the better of me. 'Of course, you could act on my behalf if we were married.' I smile inwardly, enjoying toying with him. I have no intention of telling him I'm pregnant, nor marrying him for the child's sake.

He winces visibly at the thought of marrying me without the benefit of an inheritance, and I fully realise the depth of his repugnance for me as a woman. He had probably steeled himself to make love to me, thinking it was what I wanted, and had viewed it as a necessary sacrifice in order to seal the bargain. Amusingly, I had been thinking the same thing. And he, after all, was marrying the farm, not me. His protestations of loyalty were probably as shallow as his pretty face. Of course, he hadn't intended to work the farm at all. Once we were married, he would have sold it and taken everything.

He's like Mark, only worse.

There's an internal debate raging across his features. He'd like to get angry with me for letting him down but doesn't want to entirely spike his guns in case by some strange chance I do manage to claw back the inheritance from Mark.

'Well,' he says, his tone having lost the belligerent edge, 'after you've talked to a solicitor, let me know how we stand.'

I know exactly where we stand, but I don't say that out loud. He makes excuses about needing to be at the forge for work, and I watch his car bounce down the boreen wafting little puffs of angry smoke. Cathal came here with fury in his grasping heart, and if he thinks he's leaving with the door cracked ajar, he's deceiving no one but himself.

I hadn't expected Mark to come tearing back from America to claw an inheritance out of the land, but in a way perhaps I should have. And maybe I should even be grateful that his actions have exposed Cathal's true nature. I'll write to Aine and tell her things didn't work out with Cathal quite the way I'd planned. I'm sure she'll be pleased.

If only I could find a new will!

I scour every nook and cranny of the house for hiding places, looking for loose boards and tweaking the old stones. I climb awkwardly onto a chair and search behind the best plates on the dresser, which haven't been used in decades, even though I suspect Mark has already done this. The cracked salt pot is now empty of everything except my own birth certificate, which I take out and peruse.

There is beauty in the curling handwriting in fading blue ink that states the facts: my parents' names, the date and location of birth, which was right here, in this house. So, a child was definitely born here. A child they called Hannah Barry.

I wonder again if I might be the child of one of my siblings – one of my sisters, perhaps. It's possible, but how do I find out? Can I outright ask? Even if it's true, with Mam and Dad both gone, I'm sure they will lie. But then I recall Lorcan Byrne's words. My father said I was not his biological child, nor Mam's. He said I was adopted. Would he have said that if I was his grandchild? A baby girl called Hannah Barry really was born in this house, but if I'm *not* Hannah Barry and was adopted from outside of our family, what happened to the baby who was born here? It's a mystery probably as unresolvable as discovering what happened to Justin's granddad. I sigh and get back to the task in hand.

I look at the meagre supplies in the kitchen cupboard. I have very little cash left to replenish the stock. I'm going to have to speak to Mickey about the rent for the fields. The only cash I have is that which I found in Dad's pockets the morning he died, and the weekly income from the eggs I sell at the market. Mickey might even offer to buy the farm, which would save Mark and me a lot of bother, if only Mark would be reasonable.

But Mark's not going to be reasonable.

The barn reveals no secrets, either, and if it hadn't been for Lorcan Byrne saying he'd actually seen the deeds, I would believe there were none. Dad, who was unable to read, had no interest in certificates and papers. Mark was supposed to simply step into his father's shoes as Dad had into his father's, so what was the need? Dad had lived in the past, dealing with neighbours and tradesmen as necessary, never worrying about the legality of something he knew he owned.

The fifteen fields he inherited had always been his first love, my mother the second. His children had arrived regularly over the first few years like strangers at his door. I don't actually blame them for leaving. I don't think he cared deeply for any other than his firstborn, as if bringing a son and heir into the world had been his greatest achievement. He hadn't expected Mark to also be his greatest disappointment. As for me, not only was I the last of his children, I was a girl, and disabled, too. I'd seen him glance at me with a curled lip, as though wondering quite what he'd done to deserve me. Now I wonder if his disdain was for a different reason entirely.

So, it seems my future no longer lies with Cathal. He will move on regardless. I kind of resent him for it. Once he told me he might take over John Drew's blacksmithing business, and it only now occurs to me that running a small farm is hardly the better option. I guess he just wanted to own the land for its value.

Thinking on John Drew brings my mind back to our old Irish Draught that John used to shoe. One day the gentle beast disappeared, and I never liked to ask what happened to her, fearing I already knew the answer. Ironically, John, who made his living from shoeing donkeys and horses, had been one of the first in Roone Bay to buy a motorised vehicle. In it he installed a travelling forge and began to take his work out to people who kept horses for pleasure, the huge Irish Draught horses having been replaced by tractors, the donkeys and carts by trucks.

When I mentioned to Dad that Cathal had asked for my hand, Dad said, *John Drew would throw his forge into the sea rather than leave it to a langer like Cathal.* I didn't believe it at the time, but I do now. Dad could be cruelly perceptive. It's a shame I didn't pay more attention to that while he was alive.

My somewhat introverted life has become an immense personal disaster. I think I would sit down and cry my heart out if it weren't for Noel. Maybe I should go to England after all. But will Aine's landlady want to take in an unwed woman who is with child?

I stand stock-still in the middle of the ancient kitchen and take a deep breath.

No! It's not the polio that has made a victim of me; it's me that has enabled it. I'm not going to be pressurised into running away. I will fight Mark, not just for myself but for my unborn child. Anything I salvage from this mess will be a bonus. Past conventions are being whittled away slowly but surely. I will keep my child and will need a home if nothing else. I'm used to being an outcast, so I'll weather the storm of disapproval. I have a right to a little happiness, but it will be up to me to fight for it.

12

HANNAH

Later in the day, Justin turns up unexpectedly, having walked up from the road below. He knocks at the open half-door. 'Good afternoon, Hannah,' he says. 'I hope you're well today? I'm not intruding, am I?'

Unlike Cathal, he waits to be invited.

'Of course not. Come on in. Will you have tea?'

'I'd love a cup. Thank you.'

'Sit yourself down, then.' I bustle about, fetching biscuits, putting tea in the pot, and settling cups and saucers on the table. 'So, did you have any luck yet?'

He shakes his head. 'Did you?'

'I haven't had a chance to speak to anyone.'

'And no news on Turlough?'

'If he doesn't want to be found, we won't find him.'

'Seek him here, seek him there...'

'Just like the Scarlet Pimpernel! Oh, what fun that story was. I read it over and over when I was younger. The dashing hero, the intrigue. We women are so desperate for a bit of fictional romance.' I chuckle, then mutter, 'After all, it's not something we get in real life.'

He sees the open book on the table. 'You read a lot, I think? Mostly novels?'

'Rarely novels. I mostly enjoy history. But some of the things people do to each other almost defies understanding. And you?'

'I like non-fiction of all genres. I'm not so good with novels.' He taps the open book. 'I read that one at school. Hardy is supposed to be a great writer, but that one is so miserable!'

I laugh. 'I agree, but the world isn't a kind place.' I change the subject. 'So, have you any idea what you will do now?'

He scratches his head. 'I have to say, I'm at my wits' end. People are being kind – well, they're not unkind, anyway – but I only have to mention Jack Sanders and they clam right up.'

'I'm sorry. I should have been more help, but I've had issues of my own.'

'Mark and the inheritance?'

'Is nothing secret in this town?' I grumble.

'Nothing except what happened to my granddad!'

After a moment, I realise he's made a joke and smile dutifully. 'Sorry, I'm miles away. The inheritance is a problem, all right.'

'Can I help in any way?'

'I doubt it. Noel O'Donovan is helping, if he even can.'

'That's kind.'

'It is. But as for your granddad, the thing you need to remember is that even if people do tell you any stories about what happened back then, you should take them with a pinch of salt. Everyone in Roone Bay was a hero and no one here ever killed any Black and Tans. Not your granddad Jack or anyone. If you listen to the stories, it was always the other way around.'

'It would be. But it's on record that Jack Sanders and Billy Devon disappeared from right here in Roone Bay.'

'Well, maybe they ran away to sea.'

He smiles. 'It's like the stories seeping out of the continent about the German occupation. Everyone's grandparents belonged to the resistance. None of them were collaborators, or kept their children alive by trading information that destroyed another family.'

'People were afraid of retribution. They still are.'

'I know. The truth is, unless one has actually been in those circumstances, we're not in a position to make judgement calls on who did what.'

'True, but if there are people alive today who executed – or murdered – your granddad and Billy, or even knew who did, they're not going to admit it, are they? You said yourself that there's no statute of limitations on murder.'

'But if someone local'– his eyes twinkle with amusement as they catch mine – 'was prepared to mention the fact that I promised Jack's Irish Catholic mother that I'd lay a wreath on his grave, people wouldn't have to do more than anonymously let me know where it is, would they?'

'Would you be digging for skeletons with identification tags?'

He looks taken aback. 'I wouldn't want to do that.'

'So, anyone could take you to any place on these hills to lay your wreath and send you home happy.'

He sighs. 'I know. I'm just hoping for a little decency, and I thought you might somehow be a conduit through which people could tell me what happened. I don't need names.'

'I'll put the word around, but I can't make any promises.'

I pour the tea and push the biscuit tin towards him. He takes one and dunks it in his tea, then cradles the cup between his hands. 'So, can I treat you to dinner at the hotel tonight?'

After a brief hesitation, I admit, 'I don't really have the kind of clothes...'

'You look lovely in what you're wearing.'

I laugh at the blatant lie. 'You have more blarney than an Irishman.'

'No, I mean it. You look, ah, comfortable in yourself. I have a strong dislike of daft fashions and painted faces. So, will you? Have dinner with me?'

I blanch, and his gaze softens. 'I believe you've had a hard life, Hannah. I think you've been put down so many times you don't know how to accept that I'd like to take you out for a meal because I think it would be nice for us to get to know each other.'

My astonishment must be written on my features. I'm at a loss for words.

He gives a satisfied little smile. 'Well, how about the day after tomorrow? That will give you time to get used to the idea. I warn you; I can be persistent. If you give me your number, I'll give you a call to remind you.'

'There's no telephone here,' I state, taking the wind from his confident sails. I don't mention that Noel will be having one installed; it's just taking a little longer to organise than he hoped.

He looks taken aback. 'But what would you do in an emergency?'

'Bring the donkey down to Roone Bay.'

'Good Lord,' he mutters, then takes a deep breath. 'I'll pick you up in my car at five, the day after tomorrow, then.'

'You'd bring your car up the boreen?'

'Others do. I promise I'll be brave about it.'

I laugh despite myself. I think he takes that as acceptance, as he adds, 'We can have a drink in the bar first.'

'No alcohol,' I say quickly. I've never had any, and seeing how it turned Dad, I'm not going to start.

'Okay, no alcohol,' he says without hesitation.

After he's gone, the butterflies in my stomach intensify. I don't know Justin, for all he seems nice. But he's at the opposite side of the spectrum from Cathal, and I'm starved of intelligent company. A small part of me hopes that Cathal hears about it. He won't just be jealous; he'll be furious.

I almost laugh out loud at the unkind thought, but it dies on my lips when I remember that tomorrow is the anniversary of Mam's death. It brings everything flooding back in a wave of sad nostalgia.

13

HANNAH, 1968

When Mam could no longer rise from her bed, Dad sometimes sat beside her, unable to voice his thoughts, clutching her hand the way he had once clutched the gate, fighting his demons. If he hurt her, she didn't complain but gazed up at him with sad resignation, probably knowing that he would be lost without her.

But when she was actually dying, he couldn't bear to be present. It had just been me and the priest.

The priest was beside me. I was sitting at her bedside, her limp hand draped in mine. Her body was still, her cheeks sunken; only the occasional quivering of her closed eyelids let me know that life hadn't quite departed. I didn't know whether she was cognisant, whether her life was flashing on replay, or whether she was already half in the realm of the angels. The room was cold and gloomy, the sky outside overcast, echoing my grief. Little light ever penetrated the tiny window, but that day a ray of sunshine would have been welcome.

Father Daniel's formal robe was impregnated with incense, the ever-present bible in his hands unopened as he murmured passages from memory, interspersed with prayer. 'Hail Mary, full of grace, the Lord is with thee. Blessed art thou among women, and blessed is the fruit of thy womb, Jesus.'

Her eyes had opened moments before she died. 'Look after Adrian, sweet Hannah,' she had whispered, her voice so faint I had to bend my ear to her lips. 'Promise me.'

I don't think I'd ever heard my father's name on her lips. I suspect she was recalling the handsome young man who had courted her. I tried to keep my face expressionless but couldn't stop the grief from shuddering up.

'Yes, Mam,' I said, thinking Dad was the one who should have been looking after me. But I would have promised her anything at that moment.

She lifted a hand and stroked away tears that overspilled onto my cheeks despite myself. 'It's been hard for you, Hannah, love, but be strong,' she said, like a final instruction. 'Trust in God. He has a reason.'

I saw the priest nodding his approval.

'I will, Mam,' I said.

But I didn't want to be strong. I wanted her back, as she had been before, but she was slipping away with quiet resignation, knowing God was gathering her into His arms. As I sat holding Mam's hand, watching the minuscule rise and fall of her chest, each hard-won, ragged breath promised to be the last.

'May Christ deliver you from torments, for He was crucified for you. May He deliver you from eternal death, for He deigned to die for you. May Jesus Christ, the Son of the living God, place you in the landscape of his Paradise. May He, the true Shepherd, acknowledge you for one of his flock…'

The words might have been coming from a recording, because the elderly priest wasn't looking at my mother, but staring out of the window as if wishing she would hurry up and die so that he could leave our miserable home and get on with his own life.

Perhaps I was being harsh, but I was thinking of myself, too.

With my mother gone, it would only be myself and my sister left to care for a father for whom I felt no love. Filial duty bound me, and now a promise, because promises were sacred as the bible. But it was for her, not him. My father gave me life, but in everything else he took all and gave nothing.

Mam had been a fire that was not so much extinguished as starved slowly of oxygen. For Mam it was a release. She had tried not to let the pain and increasing weakness stop her from her duties, but I remember the way she would freeze in the middle of some action and suck in her breath sharply to stop herself from crying out.

The priest's voice penetrated my maudlin self-pity. 'Though I should walk in the valley of the shadow of death, no evil would I fear, for you are with me...'

We're promised a different kind of existence after we've died, apparently better than this one. I will be renewed in Heaven, with legs that work as they should, but that seems bizarre. Will my mother be waiting for me there? And the grandmothers, and theirs before? All those generations drifting back – to when?

I was almost catatonic when the door crashed open. My father was standing there, wavering on the doorstep. 'Isn't she gone yet?' he slurred.

The priest was shocked. 'Have some compassion, man!' he said. 'Will ye say the prayers with us?'

'Devil take your prayers,' Dad said.

He lurched out, slamming the door behind him.

The priest met my eyes sympathetically.

I suddenly realised Mam's hand had gone slack in mine. I gasped, breathed out a whimper, then placed a hand on her chest, which was unnaturally still. The priest leaned over and made the cross on her forehead. 'Eternal rest grant unto her, O Lord, and let perpetual light shine upon her. May she rest in peace. Amen...'

I found myself sobbing uncontrollably.

He continues, 'May almighty God bless us with His peace and strength, the Father and the Son and the Holy Spirit... Will ye join me, Hannah? Our Father who art in Heaven...'

'... hallowed be thy name,' I hiccupped in unison.

When Father Daniel had performed his rites, he sighed. 'I'm sorry for your loss, Hannah. I'll be back into town now. Will I send up the undertaker?'

'Please, Father,' I said numbly.

'Be strong, girl. Always remember your mother with love, not as she is now. Her suffering is over, and she's with God now.'

He was right. I was relieved Mam was gone. She had suffered enough. But I didn't want to be strong. I wanted a *life*. Didn't I deserve a little happiness? Mam was Dad's strength, but she was mine, too. He was lost without her, but so was I. And now we would be bound together by a promise my drunken father would never know I made.

I suddenly remembered my sister, waiting silently in her room, for news. I should have shouted for her to come so that she could say goodbye.

I ran and burst into her room. 'Aine, Mam is—'

I stopped short. The old cardboard suitcase from my hospital days was open on the bed, and she was haphazardly piling her few clothes into it. 'What are you doing?' I asked, stunned.

'Leaving,' she said shortly. She stopped and swiped at her eyes. 'I'm sorry, Hannah. I couldn't be there to watch. I'm not strong like you. I stayed for Mam, but now she's gone, I have to get away. You know how it is...'

I was aghast. 'But, Aine, the funeral...'

'Mam's gone. Don't you understand? There's no heaven, no afterlife. Just gone. I don't need to watch a load of hypocrites crying over her, saying their stupid prayers. Them as didn't help her when she was alive, when they could have done some good.'

She folded the lid and leaned on it to do up the clasps.

'They were afraid of Dad.'

'I know. But they should have helped *her*.' Aine emphasised her words with a dull slap of her fist on the old case. 'They could have helped *us*.'

People don't interfere in family matters. They have their own problems to cope with. She knows that, but... I was stunned briefly into incoherence and finally blurted out, 'But what about me?'

She cast a guilty glance. I thought she'd stay and support me. I suddenly realised: of course she was going to leave. Like all the others. Self-pity washed through me.

'If you've got any sense, you'll leave, too.' She flicked her head towards the living room where Dad was snoring in the one upholstered chair. 'He'll drink himself to death without your help. You don't need to stay for him. He doesn't deserve it. Go and get yourself a life.'

'Like this?' I indicated my callipers.

'You're disabled, not stupid,' she said fiercely. 'Mam always knew you were clever. Prove it. Don't let them stop you from doing what you want.' She took my face in her hands, like Mam used to. 'You're pretty, Hannah. You're still young. Don't let him ruin your life. Leave now. Come with me, before he wakes up.'

'But I promised Mam—'

'Mam's dead,' she interrupted bluntly. 'I stayed until she was gone, now I'm going, too. The church will see her buried. She was always faithful. They'll do what's right. They know what Dad's about. I'm not staying to mind him, and neither should you. He never did any good for us. Come with me,' she repeated urgently.

'Where would we go?'

'London. Anywhere but here. I've saved a bit from my job in town. Hid it from himself, of course. Once we get there, we can find jobs.'

Things dropped into perspective. She'd already packed the one suitcase. She'd been working in Roone Bay, waiting on tables, and had given Mam a small sum each week; but while Mam and I had scrimped and made do, she'd been secretly saving to run away. She didn't need the burden of a disabled younger sister.

'I can't leave him,' I tell her. 'He can't care for himself.'

'You don't owe him anything.'

'Please don't leave.' My voice was a whisper of terror. I had never begged for anything before, but right then I was facing a loneliness too big to express. 'I can't manage the farm alone.'

'What farm? Some overgrown fields and some chickens?' She sighed. 'I'll send for you, Hannah. When I'm settled and have a job.'

'Promise?'

She reached out, hugged me and whispered, 'I promise.'

I didn't blame Aine for leaving. She was stifled here. I swallowed hard. I didn't want to be the one to dampen her dreams. It was just so sudden, I hadn't had time to come to terms with it, but maybe that was all for the good.

I pushed her away. 'Go on, then. Before Dad wakes up. You'll write to me, though?' It came out like a whine rather than a question.

'I will. I'll send letters to the post office. And money. Don't let Dad know.'

Holding on to the door for support, I watched her leave, as I'd once watched Mark leave. She walked swiftly down the rutted boreen, head held high. She was beautiful out of her drab working clothes. Just two years older than me, she looked so sophisticated, out of place in this rural community of ours. She was wearing neat black shoes that I'd never seen before and a small hat perched jauntily to one side. For want of money, she'd hand-made the coat and the dress beneath it, each neat, tiny stitch made by the light of a candle after the day was done. Now she was going.

Unlike Mark, at the corner she turned and waved.

I didn't doubt her eyes were filled with tears, as were mine.

She was going to get out of here and find a new life. I tried not to be jealous. She would do it; of that, I was sure. She was outgoing, amusing and exuberant – she would blossom in the city, with its noise, up-to-date fashions and dance venues. In that, alone, we were polar opposites. Because even if one day she did send for me, I wouldn't go. I loved the space I was born into: the rugged slopes with their ancient rocks, the steep foothills, the salt-laden air, the damp grass, the ivy that strangled everything... The thought of living in a city made me feel physically ill.

The future stretched out, terrifying in its solitude.

14

HANNAH

After Mam died, and Aine left home, I waited so long for word, I'd almost despaired, imagining her lost (in a variety of dreadful scenarios) before the first letter finally arrived, reeled off in a single breath of excitement. Now, as I'm getting ready for bed, I lay the ugly callipers on the floor and glare at them with loathing while rubbing cream onto the hard ridges they've created on my legs. I shouldn't hate them; they hold me up. But all the same, I wonder what it would be like to wear heeled shoes, like Aine, and a dress designed to flare as I twirled.

I reread some of Aine's letters before I sleep, touching the frail, blue, well-handled paper with deep reverence because it's all that connects us now. I remember sitting in the kitchen and crying when I read that first letter. I'd been so afraid for her, stepping out into the unknown with all the courage I could never, in a million years, have found. And I cried for myself, too, if I'm honest. With both Mam and Aine gone, I had never been so alone.

My dear, sweet Hannah,

I am sorry to be so long in writing, but I cannot tell you how hard it was in a foreign land with no money, no place to live, and there is such anti-Irish feeling here – for a while it scared me. You can be sure I had the kind of offers no girl should be subjected to! As you can see from the address, I am in London. I slept in waiting rooms and anywhere I could for a few weeks, even on a bench for two nights until a kind lady – Mrs Clancy – took pity on me. She's a war widow and has a spare room, and I suspect was grateful for company. She has a tiny house in the middle of a long row all joined together, which is strange, but there are lots like that in London. There's a space in the row opposite where a bomb took out five houses and all the women who were living there. The children had been sent out of town, so the poor weans lost their mams and their dads. We're on a slight rise, not enough to be called a hill, but I have a view over some rooftops through the gap, and on good days, when it's not foggy, I see a little curl of the Thames River. There are still lots of bomb sites here, broken buildings, piles of bricks, but there's plenty of building going on. We had a bomb scare the other day; all the houses were evacuated when builders found an unexploded bomb in the rubble. I've never seen anything like it. I knew about the Blitz, of course. It seemed like ancient history, but the devastation is all around us. Mrs Clancy lost her husband and two sons in the war, and now has nobody, so I feel truly adopted! Anyway, I got straight to and cleaned the kitchen! When she discovered I could sew, too, well, sure, she took payment in kind, I can tell you! It was a blessing, as it turns out. I've worked my fingers to a bloody mess making things for her and her friends who all clamour around bringing bits and pieces of fabric, since word got out. It brought in a few pennies, but guess what, a chara, it got me a job! I am learning to use a sewing machine in a factory! I got my first wages last week and it was like a blessing sent down from the good Lord himself! I gave half of it straight to Mrs Clancy, of course, and bought myself a decent pair of shoes and was finally able to start at dancing class. I will write again soon, a chara, but now you have an address you must write and tell me your news.

Your loving sister, Aine.

I remember experiencing a physical wave of relief, just to know that Aine was alive, followed by the gratification of knowing she'd found a safe home. More letters followed in the same vein, and in every one she asks will I go to London, but the more she tells me, the more I know a city is not for me. All the houses, the shops, the people crowded into one place. I love Roone Bay; it's my home despite everything. I see Mam's ghost in every room of our house, working away, bringing us all up, seeing her children leave one by one. Daft as it seems, I think leaving the house now would be a betrayal of all that she did for us.

Dearest Hannah,

I'm having a blast, love! There's so much dancing here, and music. And you know how I've always loved to dance, well, there was an advertisement for dancing lessons, and I signed up. It's not like any dancing we did in Roone Bay, by God it's not! Mam would turn in her grave, so! But me, I love this modern dancing. And you'll never guess what! I got a job dancing! There was some strange man came to the class watching us, and I didn't like it at all. I thought he was a perv, you know? And his eyes were on me. I was going to give him a piece of my mind, so, when the teacher came over and explained he was looking for girls to work for him, dancing in a club. He thought I had potential. Well, I decided to take the chance. At the factory, Mr Jenkins told me I was daft when I handed my notice in, to give up a good job to go dancing, but I get more for dancing than I'd ever get sewing collars. We do backing routines for bands. It's grand, so it is! You'd laugh at the costumes I have to wear. And wouldn't Mam say it's not proper! But us girls have a bodyguard to make sure men don't bother us. I don't think Mrs Clancy likes it very much, herself, but I creep in late and don't wake her, and I'm able to pay her more rent now and still keep the house clean for her, because the poor lady has the dreadful shivers. When I asked her, she said it was something left over from the bombing, but it got worse with age. She's a sweet lady, grateful, but I do find myself doing more and more for her, like she's my own mam.

Aine was always the bubbly one, the pretty one; with those long legs just made for dancing, I'm not surprised she's found her niche in London. She was dismissive of the things I love about Ireland: our cosy community and the bleak hills above the bay. She was always going to leave, and Mam's death had cut the final ties. She had told me she would go when Mam died, but her leaving before Mam's funeral, even, had shaken me to the core. We'd been together all our lives. Does she feel guilty about leaving me here to cope with Dad?? Is that why she begs me to go and live with her?

My siblings, other than Aine, have families, children I've never met. They must feel as distanced from me as I from them, but I'm disappointed that they betrayed no filial duty towards their own father. If they walked up the lane today, would I even recognise them? Aine was the only one who wrote back when I told them Dad had died. She's the only one kept in touch with me after Mam died, in fact. Her sporadic letters are like her, bright with life. She's happy out; full of herself, Mam would have said, somewhat unkindly.

Dearest Hannah,

I hope you are well, and that Dada isn't being the devil's own. I spoke to Mrs Clancy about you coming here, and she doesn't mind at all, bless her. I told her you wouldn't cost her a penny, that I would see you straight. She has another spare room. Just tell me you will come and I'll send you the fare. Last week I went to see the Beatles, live. You would never believe it. The crowds! And the screaming! I didn't know why the girls were screaming, but there I was, screaming, too!

I remember thinking I didn't know why she would be screaming about seeing beetles; sure, they never harmed a body. They must be bigger in England; poisonous, maybe. I realised later that they were a band of young men, changing the face of music. The memory of my naivety makes me embarrassed, even now. Later I heard the Beatles on a small transistor radio, but I did still wonder what all the bother was about.

When I wrote and told Aine about Cathal's proposal, her response had been immediate and vehement, heavily underlined. I read it again, now, with different eyes.

For goodness' sake, Hannah, don't throw your life away on a chancer. You don't love him, but the moment weans come along, you will be tied to the house, just as Mam was. Just wait a while longer. The right man will find you, just you wait and see.

I thought at the time: how long should I wait for some mythical Prince Charming to ride by, when Cathal was right there with the promise of a future.

But Cathal is no longer my future.

I realise now that he never was. Would I have seen my plan through, despite my rather big misgivings? I don't know. But I'm glad I saw sense before I was committed. Well, as if being pregnant isn't being committed. Our small community would think so, anyway.

Did I let him make love to me just to prove that I was a normal woman beneath the external trappings of polio? I don't know. It wasn't a memorable event, at any rate.

The mental image of Justin pops unbidden into my mind, and I briefly entertain myself with the fanciful notion that my Prince Charming has actually arrived but too late. Even if he had a fancy for me, and could see past my disability, how can I tell him I'm carrying Cathal's child? What would he think of me? But I'm going to love that baby despite Cathal and despite what people think of me. I will absolutely refuse to go to the nuns and let them send the child to America, or whatever they do with the unwanted babies. But I can't and won't foist my child onto an unsuspecting man.

15

HANNAH

A big vehicle arrives at the farm with a drill on a long arm, and several posts are erected, then the wire is looped up through the bare trees until it reaches the house. I'm not sure if Noel has paid for all that; though I have a feeling if I ask, he'll evade the question. The phone looks out of place, squatting quietly on the dresser. I don't know how to use it, and I don't know anyone to call. I've managed without one all this time, so I wonder if it was worth the expense if I'm going to be ousted soon from my home. As I go about my chores, it catches my peripheral vision like a huge alien frog.

Suddenly, the phone gives a loud, ear-bending double ring. I'm half asleep and leap up with a jolt, losing the book that was drooping in my hand. I warily approach the contraption, pick up the handset and hold it to my face, as I've seen others do. 'Yes?'

'Noel here. The phone company gave me the number. I'm just checking that it's working.'

'Oh,' I say, 'I suppose it must be.'

'Indeed, it must! So, have you a piece of paper handy? I want you to write my number down, and Grace's at the hotel reception desk. You can call either one of us at any time, day or night.'

'Just a minute,' I say and put the handset down. I find a pencil in a pot and an old receipt to write on, by which time the phone is ringing again. 'Yes?'

I hear him chuckle. 'If you put the handset back on the cradle, it cuts the connection.'

'Oh. Sorry. I'll get the hang of it. I've got a pencil.'

'Right...' Noel dictates the number and instructs, 'Put the phone back on the cradle, then lift it up and dial my number to try it out.'

I do and hear the phone ringing at the other end. It stops ringing, and Noel says, 'Hello.'

I giggle. 'It works!'

'Sure, it works. Now, Justin has asked for your number. Is it all right if I tell him?'

'He wants me to help with his search for information about his granddad.'

'He's been bothering everyone, but you know what it's like. No one wants to talk about that time.' There's a brief pause, and I hear voices in the distance. 'Caitlin just said she saw him drive out. He might well be on his way up to the farm. The number for your phone is written in the middle of the dial. Okay?'

'I see it. Thank you.'

'No bother. I'll be in touch. Oh, and Hannah? Don't let Mark upset you. You're not on your own any longer.'

'I won't. Bye.'

The contraption makes a buzzing noise in my ear before I put the handset down. *Not on my own any longer*, I think. Was I always on my own? Did everyone except me realise that?

I wait expectantly for a while, but Justin doesn't arrive. He obviously had some other destination in mind, and I wonder why I feel quite so disappointed.

· · ·

The next day I feel tired, as though I haven't slept at all. I finally force myself to take out the pad of writing paper and update Aine on what's happening. I write with a light-hearted humour about Mark and Cathal's inadvertent exposure of his true nature. I tell her about Justin and his search for his granddad. I give her the facts without giving any hint that I'm very possibly on the verge of breaking down, or that deep inside I think I'm falling in love with someone I can't have. I've been pretending to be strong all my life, but my resolve has drained overnight. The whole fabric of my existence is unravelling one stitch at a time, and now it's so thin I feel that a breath of wind might blow it away.

Why am I here at all? What is the point of me?

I fold the letter and slip it into an envelope, just as Mickey Hoolihan knocks briefly at the door as he passes under the low lintel. I'm pleased to see him. After Dad's funeral, I was a little surprised he hadn't contacted me before now about the rent for the fields. I hadn't liked to ask.

'How are you doing, Hannah?' he asks.

Maybe he sees blank confusion on my face because instead of waiting for an answer, he joins me at the kitchen table, resting thick forearms over the scuffed wood, compassion in his expression. Mickey is a good man, neighbourly, though he's never interfered with the pattern of my family's life. He dresses like the poorest of farmers, and his slow speech make people think he's stupid, but he's not; not at all.

I take a deep breath and force out a smile. 'I'm coping. Sorting things out,' I lie.

'I heard that Mark is back, staying at the new hotel.'

'He is,' I say dryly. 'He didn't come back to see me or pay his respects to Dad, though.'

'He wants his slice of the inheritance.'

He gets it immediately, and I'm too tired of covering for Dad's shortcomings to start covering for Mark's, too. 'Actually, he wants all of it. He was ranting and cursing, pulling the place apart looking for the deeds to the property. He accused me of hiding them, but I've never seen any deeds.'

'I thought maybe Mark had come to offer you a home over in America.'

'Quite the opposite.' I can't keep the snippiness out of my voice. 'He just wants me gone so he can sell the place.'

'Sure, Mark doesn't need the money, does he? I heard that him and that langer Cathal Carrol were in the bar last night, having a hooley with the lads. Mark was splashing money around, being the big *I am*. Seems your brother made himself a small fortune over the water.'

'It's the impression he wants to give,' I say with a curl of the lip.

'Ah. I thought maybe he'd grown up and discovered some decency in himself.'

'Not at all, he hasn't. He told me he built up a small business making rustic furniture.' I indicate the chairs and the table that Granddad had made. 'He wants the money to expand his business, get better premises, hire some help. He'll put me out of the house to sell the farm.'

'Would he now?' Mickey is still for a moment, musing, then he pulls a small brown envelope out of his shirt pocket and pushes it across the table. 'I was meaning to come down and give you the rent for the fields. Now your father is passed, we have some business to discuss, but it will wait a while longer. Let Mark play out his hand first.'

I don't quite know what he means by that, but the money is sorely needed. 'Thank you,' I say.

He leans back, arms folded across his chest. 'Put it away, girrul. Mark doesn't need to know. So, what will ye do?'

I flush faintly. He just called Cathal a langer, so probably he's aware of my near-miss. 'Aine has always said I can go to her in London.'

'And will you do that?'

'I don't know. She loves London: the nightlife, the dancing, the shops... But me...' I shake my head. 'I can't imagine being in a city. All that concrete, all those people. If I have to go there, it will be the end of me, I'm sure.'

'Sure, God will provide. Don't you worry now. Something will turn up.'

I give a grim laugh. 'Well, if there's going to be a miracle, it had better be soon.'

He pats my arm as he rises, grating the chair along the flagstones. 'You'll not be wanting for a home, girrul. The missus says you can come up and live with us if that's your wish. Now our Jennifer's gone to Dublin, we have a room to spare.'

I'm startled speechless, and he looks embarrassed as I tear up; not from gratitude but at the unexpected magnitude of the kindness of my neighbours.

'But if Mark sells, won't you get a share of the sale?' he queries from the door.

'Not if Mark has a say in the matter.' I grimace. 'It turns out that I'm excluded from the will entirely. Apparently, Dad told the solicitor that I'm not his child. I don't see how that can be possible. I mean, if I'm not Hannah Barry, where is she, and where did I come from?'

His jaw drops fleetingly, then he shakes his head. 'I remember your ma giving birth,' he says, frowning. 'You were definitely born in your house, here, and your mam wasn't one to, ah, play around.'

My humour gets the better of me. 'She wouldn't have had the time, anyway. But I'll get nothing if Mark has his way,' I add grimly.

'I hoped he'd turned out better than that.' Mickey is silent for a long while, churning this information over, then says, 'I'm after remembering something strange. I didn't mind it at the time. I thought the missus was out of sorts, but...'

I wait, curiously, while he finds the words.

'Well, your ma and my missus were always real friendly. Since school, you know.'

I didn't know that. I always thought Mam didn't like Sally Hoolihan; she called her an interfering busybody.

Mickey grins at some internal recollection. 'Your ma used to come up to the farm with you and Aine, and let rip about your da never there and the older kids being lazy. Then you got the polio and were sent off to Cork hospital. The missus helped your ma through that time, while you were gone, you know.' The grin slips. 'But when your ma brought you home, the missus went to visit, and your ma sent her away, angry, like. She caught a glimpse of you, poor wean, with those iron things on your legs. She said you looked different, thinner, and your mam said what did she expect, after all the trouble. We all thought it was the polio, but what if...'

He leaves the question hanging for a moment. He shakes his head, then looks me straight in the eye. 'What if you really were a different child?'

16

HANNAH

Later, Noel rings me on the new telephone and explains that he's been talking to Justin. Instead of going to the hotel for a meal, we're to go to Noel's house. I can't stop the little smile that curls my lips. Noel is incorrigibly nosy. But it suits me. I've seen the big hotel dining room through the window and find it daunting. Apparently, Noel will come and collect me to save Justin from having a nervous breakdown driving up the boreen in his little car.

'I don't want to be a nuisance,' I say anxiously. 'You've already done so much for me. I can come down in the cart.'

'Sure, I won't hear of it,' he says, 'and that's the matter ended!'

He comes up early to fetch me, so that I can settle, though quite what he means by that, I don't know.

I'm shown into his library where a turf fire smoulders. I breathe in deeply. If I do end up in London, I'll take the scent with me, in my memory, along with the sea and the hills. I peruse the well-stocked shelves. A large number of books are about breeding and racing horses. Of course, that's how he made his fortune. But there's also a selection of other material. I pull a book down and try to settle as instructed, but the luxury and warmth are unusual and somewhat disconcerting.

I'm lost in the past when the library door opens, and Mrs Weddows shows Justin in. He looks around appreciatively and whistles at the walls of books as she closes the door behind her. 'Wow, I wonder if he's read all these,' he jokes. 'The English lady who runs the hotel said I was to come up here for dinner. She said that Noel was picking you up and warned me that *invitation* means it's an order. She's amusing.'

'That would be Grace, Noel's granddaughter. She's beautiful, isn't she?'

'In a superior, English kind of way,' he says in a low whisper. 'I find that kind of blonde beauty a bit scary, actually. Give me a country lass with roses in her cheeks.'

I laugh. 'That sounds like the words of a poem. Anyway, she's not so scary when you get to know her.'

'So, why the change of plans?'

'I had nothing to do with it. It was Noel's suggestion. I think we're both in for a grilling. He seems to want to know about everything that's going on in Roone Bay. I'm wondering if Mickey Hoolihan has said something to him about when I had polio. You're not the only one with a mystery to solve,' I say, cracking a quick grin.

'Who's Mickey, and what mystery?'

I repeat what Mickey had told me about his wife being pushed away by Mam after I'd come home from hospital.

He listens, wide-eyed. 'Well,' he says, pulling his chair nearer to the fire. 'It sounds far-fetched, if you want me to be honest. Would it even have been possible for your mam to bring home a different child? But it does seem that we need to find out what really happened at the hospital, or you will never rest easy.'

'I have no idea how to even go about that.' Then it hits me:

he said *we*. 'Thanks for the offer, but you have your own agenda.'

'Yes, but I have an ulterior motive for wanting to help you.'

My brows rise in query.

His smile pops dimples into his cheeks. 'Well, if I help you, then you'll feel obliged to help me. Besides, I'm feeling lonely. You talk to me, and no one else will. I get the feeling they'd rather I just went home.'

I echo his smile. 'Isn't that the truth now?'

'It might be the sensible option, but I really do have a need to find out what happened. I mentioned I've taken a leave of absence from my practice, and I don't want to go back with the mystery still stealing my peace of mind.'

'Not just the flowers on the grave, then?'

'No, though that part is true.'

'Well, if it's any consolation, you've made me a little curious,' I admit. 'I'd like to know, too.'

'Great! Then I might finally make some progress!'

At that moment, Mrs Weddows knocks lightly and puts her head around the door. 'Dinner is on the table. Will ye please to follow me?'

Noel and Caitlin are there already, and stand up to welcome us, then we all shuffle in towards the table, and Mrs Weddows lifts a lid from what looks like a huge casserole. The rising scent makes my stomach growl, but Caitlin pushes the handle of a ladle towards me. 'Guests first, and don't be shy. There's plenty.'

Justin seems to take things in his stride, but I feel awkward, out of place, like a servant invited to dine with the lord of the manor. Caitlin soon puts me at my ease with a few well-timed observations about the locals. Then Noel asks Justin whether he found Turlough.

'No,' Justin admits. 'He's not wanting to be found, I guess.'

'So, have you discovered anything at all about your granddad who disappeared – Jack Sanders, I think you said?'

'Jack, that's right. I already know what's in the official records. He and Billy Devon disappeared the day the barracks was burned. I guess that's significant in itself. One other man was discovered shot dead and taken back to Cork for burial, but that's all. No one has even heard of the barracks, if you believe the locals. There's a conspiracy of silence about the event, anyway.'

'So,' Caitlin says, 'just enjoy the holiday. You'll end up leaving with what you came with, and maybe that's no more than you expected?'

'I suppose I'd better come clean. I didn't only come to find Jack's grave. There's a little mystery that I'd really like to have cleared up. If I'm not boring you,' he adds.

All the forks go still.

Noel's eyes light up. 'Fire away, then!'

'Great-Grandma kept everything Granddad Jack ever sent to her. He was her son, remember. He went off to war as a youth and was in the trenches in France. There was some sort of scandal, I don't know what, but he came back to England under a cloud. He spent some time in a veteran's hospital, then went to Ireland where he disappeared. My great-grandma never saw her son again. My father wasn't interested in the letters that she'd kept, so when she died, he gave them to me; mostly because they were still in their envelopes and I have an interest in postage stamps. I read the letters, of course. If she hadn't wanted them to be read, she would have destroyed them, after all. It was a strange experience, like a voice from the grave. I felt a bit closer to Granddad, though, knowing he'd written them. He sounded gentle and kind, but he was a very troubled man.'

'Not surprising he was troubled,' Noel says, 'if he'd been in the trenches. Go on.'

'Well, this was all like old history, interesting, sad, but done and dusted. Reading Jack's letters verified everything my great-gran had said, that Jack was a decent man. He had intended to be a policeman like his father, only he got caught up in the war, and maybe got damaged somehow, in his mind, you know? Trauma or something. They didn't call it that, back then. And, of course, there was that hint of a scandal – I never knew what – and it seems he was advised to volunteer as a temporary policeman in Ireland and not come back to England until things had cooled. He was with the Black and Tans, all right, but anyone reading those letters would know he wasn't a thug. I had no thought at all about looking further, only I found something strange. When I quizzed Dad about it, he didn't know what I was talking about.'

'So, what did you find that was so strange it sent you scurrying over the water?' Noel asks, leaning forward slightly.

Justin's grin is mischievous as he holds on to the moment a fraction longer. 'Well, I nearly missed it, actually. But once I'd found it, it preyed on my mind. There were several birthday cards amongst the letters. The script was always formal and unemotional, which was a sign of the times, I guess. *Happy Birthday, Mother. I'll see you soon, God willing*, or something similar. Anyway, I read each card, too, and put them back in their envelopes. There was one birthday card that I was just putting away, but when I glanced at the envelope, it didn't make sense.'

We're all poised for the next comment, tense with curiosity.

He grins, enjoying that he's spiked our interest. 'Well, it's my interest in stamps, you see. The first Irish Free State stamp was on the cover, but it was issued in 1922. Two years *after* my granddad was declared missing, presumed dead.'

'That's weird!' I exclaim.

'Weird as him rising from the grave, I tell you. I put it down and picked it up again, willing it to change, thinking it was maybe my mistake. But every time I looked, it remained the same.'

'Might a card have been put in the wrong envelope?'

'Possibly, but even so, the envelope was posted from Ireland, and the handwriting matched all the ones that came from Jack.'

'Might someone else have belatedly found the card and posted it on his behalf?'

'I considered that and started to quiz Grandma Rose. She was Jack's wife, you see, my father's mother. She was the only one left alive who actually knew him. I was curious to know what kind of man he'd been. She'd married again, of course, once Jack had been missing long enough for the marriage to be declared void. She was happy enough to talk about Jack. She said they didn't have much time together, what with the war, then him coming to Ireland, but she'd known him since school. She said he was a sensitive child and a caring young man. Just think how the Great War would have affected someone like that: men fighting each other in the trenches with bayonets and rifles. He survived the trenches and came back to England, and after his time in hospital he went straight over to Ireland as a Temporary Constable instead of going home. He was stationed here, in Roone Bay.'

'I wonder what happened that meant he ended up in Ireland, instead of going home?' I query.

Justin shrugs. 'I don't know the details, just that, according to the "missing, presumed dead" notice that was sent to Great-Grandma, it turns out that the barracks in Roone Bay was burned to the ground the day Jack disappeared. According to an archived newspaper report I found in the library, nothing was saved from the fire, and no bodies were found other than one Black and Tan who was shot dead in the fracas, but he had been left outside when they torched the building, maybe an act of respect for the man's family? So it was assumed that the missing officers were taken somewhere else, up in the hills, to be executed. It's what they did,' he says, glancing around apologetically. 'I'm not saying it was right or wrong.' He takes a deep breath. 'So, I want to know how that card was sent after he died, and who sent it? Although Great-Grandma asked me to find Jack's grave and have it, oh, blessed, or whatever Catholics do, I stumbled onto a bigger mystery.'

'I'm sure there's a simple explanation,' Noel states.

Justin pushes his hand through his hair in exasperation. 'I'm sure there must be, if only people would speak to me! The simplest answer would be, as you said, that someone found the card and posted it. But the other possibility – admittedly less likely – is that he posted it himself.'

I'm silent for a moment, taking this in. 'You're suggesting he might not have died when the barracks was burned?'

'I don't know... I've known all my life that my granddad died at the hands of the IRA, but what if he didn't die? What if something else happened?'

I frown. 'You think he jumped ship and joined the IRA?'

'I doubt it. From what I understand, his sense of honour and duty wouldn't have allowed him to do that. I did wonder if he simply couldn't handle the situation and ran away from his post. It would have been difficult for him to come back to England if he'd done that.'

'But he had a wife and child there!' Caitlin says, shocked.

'I'm trying to keep an open mind, but I'd rather not discover that he abandoned his wife and son – my father.'

'Harsh,' I comment.

'Absolutely.'

I say hesitantly, 'You say he was a good man, but the Black and Tans weren't exactly known for being good people. But maybe you're right, maybe he was changed by the war and struggled mentally afterwards. I've read that many men who came home were unable to cope with civilian life, after what they had seen.'

'All I know is what my great-grandma told me, and the letters he sent to his mother around the time he was sent back to England confirm what she said. He was troubled but not out of his mind.' Justin sighs. 'I don't believe he is still alive, though. He would have made contact years back if he was. He had a loving relationship with his mother, and I can't see that he would just have left her not knowing... It's more likely, as Noel says, that there's a simple explanation. But it bothers me that I don't know.'

17

JACK, 1920

In Dublin, Jack was kitted out with a rifle, a handgun and a uniform of sorts, which had been cobbled together from what was available: dark green RIC trousers that looked black from a distance, a dark beret, and a sand-coloured jacket that he guessed was redundant stock from some eastern-based regiment. Once attired, his sense of unease escalated; he felt more like a soldier than a peacekeeper.

The volunteers had been told they would get training, and they did, but it was far from the civilian policing he was expecting to learn about, concerning the rights of citizens and upholding the law. Instead, the training was suspiciously like that he'd received as a soldier, which revolved around controlling violence with force and taking prisoners rather than de-escalating situations with calming dialogue.

After a couple of unsettling weeks, the men were provided with their destinations. Some would stay in Dublin, and some would go south to what was referred to as 'Bandit Country'. Jack was sent south. As he was transported through Ireland, he tried to see the scraggy countryside though his mother's eyes, to find beauty in the grey rocks that thrust up through an impossibly green scrub. It was a hard call. This land was nothing like West Somerset, where he'd spent his childhood, with its cosy farmlands drifting over steep rolling hills, and its deep, secret valleys crowded with deciduous trees. This was a bleak landscape, its thin layer of barren soil tilled by desperately poor people.

At home, his family weren't rich, but neither were they struggling to survive. Life was hard for labouring folk – it was the world over – but he'd never seen poverty such as his mother had described when she talked of her childhood, and it seemed it wasn't much better now. She recalled running to school in winter with no shoes and being so hungry her belly looked caved-in; just days ago, he had witnessed barefoot children begging on the streets of Dublin. She remembered her childhood with nostalgia, the warmth of a large family and close community, but she had left Ireland through necessity, and he could see why.

It took two days to get to his destination, which was the second-to-last on the agenda. They made an overnight stay in Cork city, and he was disturbed to find that armed men were on watch for enemy action outside their lodgings.

With the back canvas of the lorry rolled up to provide the men with air, he watched the scenery roll by. At first it was a little like southern England, but it got ever bleaker the further south they travelled, more like the rugged northern English counties, though the long ridges of rock were rounded against the skyline rather than the sharp escarpments he'd seen in Yorkshire and Derbyshire.

Half a dozen men were dropped off at another RIC barracks along the way, and they took to the road again for another hour or so. Jack's destination was a barracks on the outskirts of a small town called Roone Bay; a den of iniquity, by all accounts, which blatantly supported the rebels who were secreted in the surrounding countryside.

Jack was to become a policeman of sorts, assisting to bring the rebellious, ignorant Irish to heel, and traitors to justice, which had the ring of righteousness about it. He was intelligent enough to suspect that the truth of the matter was wrapped in propaganda, though.

The self-styled Irish Republican Army's slogan 'England's difficulty is Ireland's opportunity' still rankled through the millions of bereaved families in England. They resented the Irish nationals who hadn't supported the war; that their menfolk were strutting arrogantly alive, on two good legs, rubbed salt in those wounds.

Jack recalled the uniformed officer, only three days ago, marching self-importantly up and down before the volunteers who were lined up in the recruitment yard awaiting transport.

These people are TRAITORS, he had roared. *This insurgency is an act of WAR! The Irish must learn to OBEY the LAW, like every MAN, woman and CHILD in ENGLAND. You men have been trained by the British ARMY. Your JOB is to bring LAW and ORDER. You will assist the RIC, that's the ROYAL IRISH Con-STABULARY, for those who don't remember. They are in service to His MAJESTY, the KING, as you will be...*

He had shouted certain words to emphasise them, as if the men before him were imbeciles. Jack had served under men like this – officers through parentage rather than ability. But it was true that the Irish police officers, despite being largely Irish by birth, were being ousted from their jobs, boycotted and cold-shouldered by the populace, because the Irish Government had declared Ireland a free state. The RIC, being part of the English establishment, was being treated by the Irish as an illegal force.

The brutal execution of the leaders of the Easter Rising in 1916 had not quelled the insurrection so much as given it fresh impetus. He was sure the British Government thought they were acting in the interests of peace, taking a hard line to suppress a small, treasonable uprising when the country was beleaguered enough already, but in fact it had the opposite effect. It created a wave of anger that swept through Ireland, inciting rebellion in those who previously hadn't wanted to be involved in an uprising at all. Also, the news wafted over to America, reaching the wider diaspora of Irish emigrants, provoking fresh resentment against the centuries of suppression the Irish had suffered as a people under English domination.

And the world was looking on in judgement.

But Jack was in Ireland to assist the RIC officers to do what they had sworn to do: uphold the law; nothing more. Presently, he understood, they had to go about in groups for fear of the renegade forces who were conducting guerrilla warfare from the vast, scrubby hills of West Cork. It wasn't so much open warfare as skirmishes, as the ragged, self-styled Irish Republican Army mainly sought to steal RIC weapons and scare the men into abandoning their posts. Those who refused to be intimidated were sometimes obliged to force shopkeepers to sell to them at gunpoint, because the citizens were as afraid of the rebels and retribution as they were of the Black and Tans. Some of the more isolated barracks had even been torched, their beleaguered occupants relocated. And there had been a few incidents that had ended in deaths on both sides.

Were these untrained, self-styled soldiers daft, Jack thought, to pit themselves against the might of England's war machine? According to politicians, Ireland had been a carbuncle on England's backside for centuries. His mother, brought up in the wilds of Kerry, had flashed her dark Irish eyes with fury when the men from the Easter Rising had been hanged for treason, and slammed the newspaper on the table, vowing to never read another word that was printed. *They were Irish*, she argued vehemently, *not English, so how could they be traitors? We should be allowed to rule our own country.* His mother's Irish temper was legendary, and like any person who had emigrated through necessity, she was torn between her new country and the old; loyalties die hard.

Jack's father had been a policeman, English through and through, and arguments could sometimes explode through the house like a storm, his father shouting, *Well why don't you go back to your precious Ireland, then?* and his mother screaming, *I will, so! Just you see!* But the squall would soon pass, leaving a settling calm in its wake.

Jack didn't know the right of it, in all honesty.

18

HANNAH

Last night, Caitlin insisted that I stayed here, in the Big House, and it would have been rude to refuse, but despite being warm and well fed, I feel out of place. Perhaps that isn't enough to sustain life after all. I miss the familiarity of my own home, basic though it is. This morning, despite pressure to stay, I tell Noel and Caitlin I have to feed the chickens and check on Old Grey, which isn't exactly a lie. Caitlin provides me with a waterproof coat she says she doesn't need. Another little untruth to make me feel less bad about accepting their charity. Any hint of trouble with Mark and I'm to phone them, or even just turn up at their door.

The hills are stunningly atmospheric this morning, peeping through layers of thick white mist that sit in the hollows. As Noel drives me up to the farm, I can see clear across to Steel Hill, which is briefly lit by a sombre orange tint as a break in the slow-moving clouds sends shadows marching across its rugged surface. Driving the cart provides plenty of time for reflection, but the car gets me home in an instant. I wonder whether the people scooting around in their cars ever truly experience Ireland any longer.

I'm an anachronism in this new age; certainly, I haven't seen another donkey cart in Roone Bay for a while. Visitors gawp at me as I drive by, as if I'm doing it to provide entertainment, but I love the slow pace of the cart.

Mark's hire car is parked at the foot of the boreen, where it meets the track to our farm, and when we arrive, Cathal's old Ford is parked in the yard.

'Do you want me to come in?' Noel asks, concerned.

'Not at all,' I say. 'I'll be fine.'

Despite what's going on, I have no fear that Cathal or Mark will cause me physical harm. If Cathal is getting chummy with Mark, I suspect that he's given up entirely on his plans to marry me for the farm.

I find the two men seated companionably, their legs stretched towards a roaring fire that is gaily devouring the wood I'd been rationing through the long winter. I look around at the kitchen, which I seem to have lived in forever. A stone flagged floor. The nails banged into the open beams on which scythes and tools are still racked. The big kettle hanging on a chain over the fire. The chairs my granddad made. I feel a burgeoning sense of nostalgia. When I leave this house, I'll be leaving a bit of me behind in the damp walls.

'Ah, here she is,' Cathal exclaims. 'We were wondering where you got to.'

'I stayed at the Big House last night,' I say and enjoy the surprise on the faces of both men.

'How come?' Mark demands, barely hiding his jealousy.

'Noel's going to help me sort out the inheritance.'

He casts me a sarcastic glance. He has no idea that I know of the codicil that he hasn't shared with anyone else, that he only inherits if he lives here and works the farm for ten years – I suspect he's doing mental gymnastics trying to find a way around that one – but he's annoyed to hear that I really intend to look into the will further. I suspect that Mark got here as quickly as he could after discovering Dad had passed. Maybe he'd expected me to just step back and allow the will to be served in his favour. Whatever his reason, the longer people remain in ignorance of the issue, the better. I don't want neighbours staring after me with pity for my further misfortune.

'So, you two know each other from before?' I ask.

'Not really. We met in the bar and had some good craic,' Cathal says. 'Mark's been telling me he came back to pay his respects to your mam and dad's grave. I was just up to see you and we got chatting. He's done well for himself in America, from the sound of it.'

I don't doubt Mark was bragging about his furniture business, making it sound far more than it really is. I expect Cathal's hoping that if Mark is so successful, he won't need to be clutching at the inheritance from a tiny run-down Irish farm. Mark will be wary of sharing his plans with Cathal, though. As Noel said, his plans to oust me into the street penniless won't win him any friends.

'So, how long are ye staying in the old country?' Cathal asks Mark.

Mark shrugs. 'I don't know. It might be my last visit. I don't have family over here any longer, so I'm going to take a stroll around, remind myself of the place before I leave.'

Cathal misses the implication that I'm not considered family. 'Sure, check out the old stomping grounds, eh? Shall I tell the lads you're up for a jar tonight?'

'Sure, why not? It should be a blast.'

'So.' Cathal stands. 'I'll be leaving youse to catch up, then.'

He nods to Mark, gives me a sly smile and a wink, and leaves. He's being as guarded with the truth as Mark is, and he's holding on to the hope that if I win the farm in a legal battle, he can come running back to claim my hand.

But Mark isn't so slow. 'What was all that about?' he asks. 'He's not sweet on you, is he?'

My slight flush gives me away instantly.

'Well, well,' Mark says with a smirk, tipping the chair back on two legs. 'A romance in the air? He must be desperate to be interested in you. So how long has that been going on?'

'Nothing's going on,' I snap. 'He's being kind and helpful, and that's more than I can say for you.'

'Helpful my arse. That one's a langer. He'll be wanting to marry you for the farm. You're a fool. The minute he got that ring on your finger and his name on the deeds, it would be up for sale. How will that go when he realises you aren't inheriting it at all?'

'He already knows,' I say, knocking the sneer from Mark's lips.

'What does he know?'

'The Dad left you the farm and that I'm going to fight you for it,' I say innocently. 'What else is there?'

Mark scowls at me for a moment. 'Well, he's no good. Don't say I didn't warn you.'

'I thought you liked him?'

'Just because I'm being sociable doesn't mean I don't see him for what he is.'

'And I wonder if he sees you for what you are, too,' I snip.

He gets up and throws another log on the fire.

'I thought you were going to take a look around?'

'I don't need to look around to remember why I left. All those people in America who emigrated? Their kids and grand-kids, you know, have this wonderful romantic vision of an Ireland full of fairy mounds and leprechauns and rainbows. Really, it's just a scruffy little island where people live in hovels and scratch a living on thin air and myths.'

'While in America the streets are paved with gold? Everyone lives on hope and faith, Mark, and myths provide food for starved minds.'

'Since when did you get so hoity-toity?'

'I'm just sorry you feel that way. Dad loved this farm, before Mam died and you left. He imagined you taking over the farm after him. You broke his heart.'

'Don't go getting maudlin on me,' Mark said. 'Dad was soured the moment he realised Mam was going to die, and that was before I left. And don't get any ideas. This place isn't yours, and going down the old Irish-blarney road isn't going to make me change my mind. If Dad had wanted you to inherit, he'd have made a new will.'

'Who's to say he didn't?'

Mark's mouth drops open, then he recovers himself. 'If he had, you'd have mentioned it.'

'Probably,' I agree. 'Unlike you, I wouldn't have kept something that big from the rest of my family. But maybe it's time to take yourself back down to the hotel? Clouds are gathering, and the heavens are going to come down with a passion.'

I'm lying, of course, but it serves its purpose. Mark heaves himself to his feet, glances out of the window and mutters something obscene under his breath as he slams through the door without bidding me goodbye.

After he's gone, the winter sun fights through the rising mist, and I sit by the fire and read. I might as well enjoy the unaccustomed blaze while I can, while I can still call this place my home.

19

HANNAH

It's mid-morning the next day when I hear Justin's car arrive. I smile, thinking he's taken the bull by the horns and driven up the pitted boreen. Justin hasn't Cathal's size or looks at all, but there's something wholesome about him that makes my heart give a little skip and jump. I didn't ever want to feel sorry for myself, but right now, I do. If it weren't for Cathal's baby growing inside me, and the ironwork on my legs, maybe I'd stand a chance.

He knocks politely at the open door. 'May I come in?'

'Of course,' I say.

'I brought scones.'

'Did Mrs Weddows send them?'

'No, I got them in the café. Don't tell her I said so, but they smell just as good.'

'Noel put a telephone in for me,' I say, proudly pointing. 'He said to get the number from the middle, there.'

'Ah, yes, he told me. I was going to offer, but, well, I thought you might be a bit too proud to accept. I should have phoned before turning up today, but I was afraid you'd tell me you didn't want to see me, then I would have been stumped.'

'Noel's a very generous man.'

'He is, but the people in Roone Bay care about you, you know.'

'No, they don't. In all the years I was living here, minding Dad, no one asked if I was happy. Until a few days ago, I was thinking that I couldn't imagine living anywhere else. I was going to marry Cathal just so that I could stay here, but now... Well, let's just say I realised my mistake in time.'

'I'm so pleased to hear you say that. Noel said Cathal wouldn't make a farmer, not in a hundred years.'

'And he wouldn't want to live here, either. I was fooling myself.' The kitchen is both familiar and awful. Suddenly I don't want to stay here at all. 'Mark called this a hovel. It's been my home, so I never really thought I'd have anything better, but after staying at the Big House, I'm thinking he might be right. The truth is, I didn't ever want to marry Cathal. I just want children, and no one else asked.'

I end on a hiccup, and before I know it, Justin's arms are wrapped tightly around me, and I nestle my head into his shoulder.

'Let it out,' he says softly, and I do.

I find myself sobbing uncontrollably: for a lost life, for the lack of love, for Dad's coldness, for Mam dying and for my confused parentage...

As my sobs abate, I find Justin is rocking me gently, his head resting on top of mine. I'm too shy to put my arms around him, though that's where they want to go. But I'm afraid to give too much of myself because I know this moment will pass. I don't know anything about him, and the last thing he needs is for a disillusioned and uneducated culchie to throw herself at him.

'I'm guessing that was quite a few years' worth of tears,' he says softly as I take a deep breath and push myself away.

'Sorry about that. Did you come for something specific?' I ask finally.

'A cup of tea?' he suggests. 'To go with the scones?'

I give a damp laugh, and busy myself with plates and knifes and cups. When we're both seated, he asks me what it was like growing up on a farm.

I tell him about our Irish Draught, and how upset I was when he disappeared one day. 'It was my own fault for getting too fond of him,' I say wryly. 'Because on a farm, animals are business, not pets.'

'That's sad.'

'I used to be scared of the cows,' I admitted. 'They were just so big. Dad told me to get over it, so I tried. Then one day there was this big black cow in the yard. I walked up bravely and petted it. Dad looked out of the milking parlour and started jumping up and down and screaming. As the cow wandered over to him to see what the fuss was all about, Dad screamed at me to get in the house. I realised he wasn't joking when he threw himself over the ditch to get away and fell into two feet of muddy water. It turned out I'd been petting Mickey Hoolihan's bull.'

Justin is laughing so much he's nearly crying. 'What happened then?'

'Well, Mickey came running down the hill with one of his cows on a lead. The bull dutifully followed them all the way back to the field.'

'My childhood was a lot less scary,' he said. 'The worst thing I can recall is taking myself off for a walk up the hill when I was about six and getting lost. I wasn't too worried until it started to get dark. When I saw some lights, I headed for them, and a nice lady took me home in her car. By then the whole village was out searching. Some people were out for hours before news got around that I'd been brought home.'

'Were your parents angry with you?'

'No, they were so scared... Just relieved I'd been found, I

guess. I had some scary moments, too, as a young doctor. A child once had an epileptic fit in my surgery and I just froze. It was the child's mother who did all the right things.'

'Did she call you out on it?'

'Quite the opposite. She was very nice and told me I'd be able to handle things like that when I grew up.'

'Oh. That was a bit of a put-down.'

He grins. 'She was right. I learned a lot from studying, but it was experience that turned me into a doctor.'

I relate other memories that have him clutching his sides with laughter. He tells me more about his childhood and keeps apologising because it was so boringly safe. But I'm fascinated to hear about his modern school that taught boys and girls in the same class, with teachers who didn't whack the backs of their students' hands with a ruler. After hearing of my brothers' and sisters' experiences, I was quite happy to have been excused school. It was only as I got older that I realised it wasn't missing school that was the problem; it was not having gained any certification. There are few career openings for anyone – particularly a woman – who has no school certificates.

When there's a lull in the conversation and our mugs have been pushed aside, he asks, 'So, has Mark been bothering you?'

'Not really. He doesn't want to work the farm, but he can't sell it without the deeds, and no one knows what Dad did with them.' I tell him about the proviso to the will, that Mark should be sharing the proceeds with his siblings if he doesn't intend to stay and work the farm, and add, 'I feel that I should tell them despite what Lorcan said.'

'Be careful,' Justin says quietly. 'Don't say anything to Mark that might make him lose control. I get the feeling he has a temper on him.'

'I think you're right. I won't say anything to anyone, not yet, but I don't like the subterfuge. I'm not him.'

'I wouldn't have offered to cuddle you if you were.'

I dutifully smile. After a small silence, I admit, 'I'm wondering if I'm even related to him.'

Justin compresses his lips. 'Mickey suggested that your mam brought a different child home from the hospital, but it sounds a bit far-fetched to me.'

'Stranger things have happened.'

'Well, we're as likely to get to the truth of that as we are to finding out the truth about my granddad. I haven't lost hope, though. But it's a shame people are so secretive about things that happened so long ago.'

'It's not so far distant that people aren't afraid of repercussions. In Ireland, family bonds still have a strong hold on the community.'

'More so than in England, I think. My father was a distant figure in my home life. Parents in general didn't tend to show much emotion to their children, but times are changing. I'm trying to be the kind of father my son can talk to.'

I try to hide my dismay. 'You have a son?'

He nods. 'Paul is three, nearly four in fact. I've never been gone from home for more than a couple of days before, so I guess he'll be missing me.'

Of course he's married, I think. For a daft moment I'd been wondering what it would be like to be married to a man who was interested in the things I read about, who would discuss history instead of asking was dinner ready. But any faint stirrings of hope die a death in that moment. I don't know why I deceived myself into thinking anything different. He's out of my league entirely. I should have known that. He's here to find out about his granddad and will disappear back to England soon enough, whether his curiosity is satisfied or not.

I hide my disappointment behind a bright voice. 'So, you'll be leaving soon?'

'Not instantly. Even with the sabbatical, I can't be away for too long. Paul will think I've abandoned him.'

I pull myself together. I will have a child to love, too. That will have to be enough.

20

JACK, 1920

Driving south from Cork city had been a jolting, bumpy ride. From the occasional dialogue Jack tuned into, his colleagues found the journey nerve-racking, expecting every moment to be attacked by rebels. But Jack remained slightly distanced – unaware, or uncaring, he wasn't sure. For most of the journey to his posting in Roone Bay, he turned inward to his past, pondering at the vagaries of fate that had brought him to this place at this time. He'd been resigned to dying in the war, but his very survival had been criticised and challenged, then finally put down to something vaguely called war neurosis.

He had intended to join the police force when he finished university, and if that had happened, he would have been exempt from the draft, but he'd had last minute doubts about his vocation. He'd married his school sweetheart, so as a married man he was exempt from conscription for a short while. But men on the front lines were being gunned down like ducks at the fairground, and each year the war continued, the rules changed.

When his conscription papers arrived, he was almost glad. The stress of waiting had worn him down, added to which, able-bodied men who went about their normal business in England were continually vilified by the women whose husbands and sons had already been drafted, making life almost intolerable.

His pregnant wife, Rose, living with his mother by this time, was filled with her own terror: pregnancy, the fear of dying in childbirth, of not coping with a baby and no husband's shoulder to lean on. His mother's stoic nature finally broke on the day he donned his uniform. She sobbed that at least her husband had been spared seeing his own son sent to war. His father's sudden death from a stroke when Jack was in his mid-teens had left her stunned. She put her face in her apron, keening as if Jack had died in the trenches already.

Against all the odds he had survived, only to find himself a pariah in his own country. Those who hadn't been there didn't understand that cowardice wasn't something he'd deliberately chosen. He didn't think he was a coward, really. But what happened couldn't be undone, and emotions were volatile. It was almost a relief to be sent to Ireland. He'd been only vaguely curious about Ireland up to now; it was just a troublesome island on the fringes of his awareness.

His mother had spoken about the country passionately as he was growing up, bewailing the poverty that had forced her to leave yet in the next breath extolling the virtues of being brought up poor. There were things she brought with her to England and never lost: her religion, which her husband had tolerated, her sweet songs, which her husband loved, and her tempestuous nature, which was what had attracted his father to her in the first place.

Despite the connection and the nostalgic stories, Jack had had no yearning to visit Ireland. Like Scotland, with its turbulent history, there was an undercurrent of anti-English animosity that he didn't want to experience. Yet here he was, with his oh-so-very-English accent that had been pummelled into him through school. He wondered if he would be tempted to explain to the indigenous population that he was half Irish by birth but doubted it would make any difference.

He had a feeling in his bones that this enforced atonement for inadvertent betrayal on the battlefield wasn't going to turn out well. But in truth, what gave him that sense of foreboding at this moment wasn't the problematic Irish; it was the men he was forced to associate with. Sure, they'd been soldiers in the Great War, but he'd seen little evidence amongst them of what his father would have called *basic decency*.

To Jack, being a soldier or a policeman was about upholding ideals like the law or democracy or the freedom to choose one's religion. In Ireland, he had rationalised, he wouldn't be fighting for his country but keeping the peace; he could do that. His father would no doubt have approved; except that in England the police didn't carry guns. One of the reasons these unemployed ex-military men had been recruited was that they were all familiar with weaponry. That, in itself, was worrying.

Whatever the right of it, Jack just wanted to be good and fair. He'd accepted the commission and that was just that. He would make the best of a bad job and then go home. He hadn't bargained for the insidious niggle penetrating his conscience that he shouldn't be here; none of them should. He wouldn't express this to his senior officer, but he had a sneaking belief that the Irish should be allowed to govern their own country as his mother had maintained.

He was startled out of his reverie by the driver shouting over his shoulder, 'Nearly there!'

Unlike the impressive four-storey red-brick building they had stopped in overnight in Cork, the Roone Bay barracks comprised a basic single-storey building created from local stone. It was sturdy, the walls being three feet thick at the foot, with external shutters on the sash windows, more to protect the occupants from the Atlantic squalls than to guard against attack. He'd been warned that these squalls sometimes charged across the landscape in such fury a man could barely keep on his feet, but he'd lived near the sea in West Somerset most of his life. He'd experienced the fierce winter storms that from time to time galloped across the landscape and turned the adjacent sea into a raging maelstrom, so suspected there was a little blarney going on.

The hills were misted by a light rain when they arrived. Jack jumped down and stretched his legs, grateful to be on his feet, but within moments droplets had gathered on his hair and nose, driving in on the back of a chill breeze. He shivered and hurried into the barracks where a fire was smouldering in the hearth. It was the bleakest time of winter, but at least the landscape wasn't a sea of churned mud, dead men and dead horses.

He thought longingly of his tiny cottage in West Somerset. He had marched to war leaving his mother with his pregnant wife, and come back briefly once, on leave, to find Walter, his son and heir, in her arms. He recalled Rose carrying their baby on her hip as she walked around the garden, pointing out drooping snowdrops and the green thrusting tips of crocuses waking up from their winter slumber. That was nearly two years ago. His son would be toddling now, on his own feet. The trees would be bare and skeletal once again, the grass struggling through brown, rotting mulch, dreaming of spring. Thoughts of home had sustained him while he was in the trenches, and he'd built on them until he'd become unsure of what memories were real and what weren't.

The leave had been traumatic, the time with his family all too short, the dread of his returning to France hanging over them like a dark shroud. It had been nowhere near long enough for him to recover his sanity. But pride had forced him to march resolutely to the train station when the time came. The expression on his mother's face had echoed his uncertainty: would this be the last time they'd meet in this life?

He had later received a letter from Rose, who told him that

his mother had fallen to her knees in the kitchen and sobbed unconsolably after he'd left, under an overwhelming flood of prescience that she would never see him again. That letter, worn indistinct by handling, rested in his breast pocket, as close as he had come to his wife in over a year. He was sure she must have written, as he had to her, and supposed that their letters had simply been lost, trampled underfoot in the muddied hardship of the war. Like the men he served with, he never wrote to tell his family that war was hell on earth, the stench of death in every breath. He'd never detailed the terror of that living nightmare, though they must have had an inkling.

In the early days of the war, women back in England were buoyed up with news of small victories, and the work they voluntarily took over from the men who left. The men – in some manly conspiracy – had withheld the true horror from their wives and loved ones, but newspapers, though regulated by the war machine, had finally leaked the truth. Photographs of tanks driving over the piled bodies of the dead overwrote the idealised notion of the war as something romantic and virtuous.

The mental images of home had sustained Jack through the horrors of the war, and he decided they would sustain him now, in Ireland. He would live for the moment he could finally go home, having surely paid for the unwitting crime of falling to pieces under the appalling conditions. It was hard to recall home, though. It was a lifetime distant, becoming less real as time went on. He would do as his mother advised in her letter and make it through one long day at a time, as he had in the trenches in France.

Little Walter would be turning three, soon. He would be toddling around the garden, his chubby fingers reaching out to grasp at the earthy treasures as Jack's had once done; turning stones to seek out spiders, woodlice and snails, which the temperate Somerset climate propagated in abundance. Jack's heart ached at this precious time he was missing out on with his son, but he knew in truth that staying away was the best thing he could do for Walter.

He'd been given an unspoken choice: West Cork or the hell of social censure in a village that wouldn't provide employment for cowards. His family would have equally suffered had he chosen the latter, so it had been no choice, really. But his mother had the right of it. Unlike so many, he'd survived the war, and he would survive this. Times would change. People would grow less vindictive as time passed. He would serve his time and count the days. Once home, he would pick up the threads of his lost life and blot out the past. The 'war to end wars' was ended. Thank God there would never be another. Thank God his son would never have to experience what he had experienced, which had left him not so much broken as distant from peacetime reality. He felt a lot older than his twenty-four years.

21

HANNAH

I walk in through the open door to my home to find Turlough sitting in Dad's chair by the cold fireplace. I recognise him first by the sour smell of unwashed clothes and the faint reek of fish from the shack. He's fast asleep, his mouth open, issuing a gentle snore. I did wonder, with Justin's arrival, if I would ever see him again. For someone who spends his life in the uncaring hills, he certainly seems to know everything about everyone. I don't doubt he's heard about the man who has come seeking his dead granddad. And maybe, after all, Turlough does know something of it, if he'd been running messages for the IRA, as the rumours suggest.

I quietly light the fire and fill the kettle, setting it to boil over the flames. I turn my head to find him watching my movements. Like the wild creatures, he has the ability to be uncannily motionless.

'You're a good girl, Hannah. You did well by your parents.'

'Thank you.'

I'm pleased that he's in one of his more lucid states. Sometimes the words that come out of his mouth make no sense at all.

I cough, trying not to blanch at the stench of him. 'There

are clean clothes upstairs. Dad won't be needing them. And you can wash at the tap.'

His eyes close as if tiredness has overtaken him again, but there's a faint hint of a smile on his lips. 'Sure, I probably need it. There aren't many of us left now, are there?'

'Left?' I query.

'From back in the day.'

Ah. 'No, I guess not.'

'I heard that an Englishman has come asking questions. I thought it would happen one day.'

'I wondered if that was why you came. People told you he was here, asking me to help?'

'They did.'

'And will you speak to him?'

He's silent, so I nod. 'It's okay, no one is going to bother you about the past, if you don't want to talk.'

I go upstairs, gather a pile of Dad's clean working clothes and put them on the chair along with Dad's razor. 'I have chores in the barn; I'll be back in half an hour.'

'You're a good girl, Hannah,' he says again as I leave, knowing that he might be gone when I come back.

He'll either choose to talk or not. There will be no pressuring him. But he didn't come here for the wash and the clothes, however much he needs them.

I heave open the barn door, which is drooping on its hinges. Inside, subtle light filters through the moss-edged corrugated plastic sheets Dad set into the roof many years ago. At one end of the barn where the slates have slipped, the afternoon sun bites through the holes in brilliant dust-filled shafts. That end of the barn is slowly rotting for want of care.

The chickens, who were gathered at the barn gate zigzagging with excitement at my approach, welcome me with soft cooing noises. I fill the water trough and scatter feed.

There are none sitting today, so I scour the barn for pockets of eggs, then sit on a straw bale and watch my hens peck eagerly at the meal I've scattered. A hen might lay an egg every other day, and where one has laid, others follow. When there are seven or more in a batch, the last might choose to sit them all. Chickens have no loyalty towards their own eggs, and when the chicks hatch, several hens will share the duty of care, taking turns to tuck the brood under the warmth of their downy feathers. I contemplate the strangeness of nature. As always there's no answer to be found, just an acceptance of what is.

When I go back into the house Turlough is less hairy and a trifle less smelly. He's a tall man, raw-boned and lean from his outdoor life – Dad's clothes are too tight on him, the trousers rising at half-mast, but he isn't minding. I gingerly take the discarded clothes outside. I'll throw them in the midden later. In a year or so, the rough-spun cotton and wool will have gone back to nature. When the newly made compost is scattered in the fields, only the buttons will remain, to be harvested by magpies as treasures for their nests.

'Will you take a breakfast?' I ask, though it's clearly midday.

'I will.'

Luckily, the provisions I bought yesterday include bacon and black pudding. I throw more wood over the smouldering peat to bring it back to flame and put a skillet on the hotplate. I throw spuds into the boiling kettle, and soon the bacon is sizzling.

'Will you speak to the Englishman?' I ask hesitantly.

'I don't remember anything.' He shakes his head in panic.

'Memories aren't shed so easily,' I say softly. 'He means no harm, but I think he won't leave until he has answers. He's just looking to find out what happened to his granddad back in the day. He disappeared, and another man with him.'

'Gone, all gone,' Turlough mutters, his eyes sidling away from me.

'He made a promise to his great-grandma to find his granddad's grave. Jack's mother was an Irishwoman, from Kerry, you see. She was Catholic. Justin promised to lay a wreath and have a priest say a prayer. That's all he wants to do.'

I thought that mentioning an Irish connection and the sanctity of a promise might prompt information, but it was the name that did it. 'Jack?' he echoes, swivelling his head sharply.

'Jack Sanders.'

'Jack Sanders?' he mutters. 'There was a man shot. I didn't know his name. There was Johnny Crowley from Roone Bay, who was let leave. And there were some others let go on the day, sent back on the road to Cork, they were, like dogs with their tails between their legs.'

I'm turning the eggs, trying not to startle Turlough into clamming up. I'd heard that John, the local RIC officer, had fled Roone Bay on the day the barracks had been burned. Some tales were too stretched to be anything but distant echoes of reality, but that was fact. His wife and children had quietly departed Roone Bay just days later, with all their belongings. Gone to a new place where his previous occupation hadn't been known, it was presumed.

After a while, Turlough's voice came again, low and hesitant. 'We were watching them,' he said. 'Me and Conor. We weren't supposed to. We would have been given the fear of God by our mams if the men saw, but we saw Aisling with the Englishman. Jack, he was called. He shouldn't have touched her. That was wrong. That's why they took him. He shouldn't have touched her.'

Oh my. Did Justin's granddad rape some woman called Aisling? There were stories of the Black and Tans pillaging and destroying homes, and raping the women while their men were out working the fields or traipsing the hills as soldiers. If he'd done something like that, he would have been hounded and shot out of hand. It would explain why the barracks was burned the same day Jack and Billy went missing.

I put the plate in front of Turlough, and he eats quickly, shovelling the food in with little care to tasting it.

'Turlough, who was Aisling? What did Jack do?'

I don't know if he's heard me. He lifts eyes that were seeing something far beyond the walls, far into the past, and his voice is suddenly distinct. 'That's why they torched the barracks, don't you see? Some were let go, but Jack and Billy were taken.'

'Where were they taken?'

'To the hills.'

'What did they do? What happened to them?'

My voice is soft but urgent, because I'm sure I know what they did but need to have it confirmed.

And as though I've pressed a switch, Turlough begins to sob openly as he tells me, 'The captain said he raped a woman. I was a boy. I didn't know what the word meant. I didn't know that men would even do something like that. He swore blind that she'd invited him in, but the captain said no, she didn't. She was a good woman whose husband wasn't there to protect her.'

Tears are running freely down his face.

'What happened then?' I ask quietly.

'They took him up to the execution stone on the hill. The captain sentenced him to hang for his crimes against the people of Ireland. *Five years ago*, he quoted, *the English sentenced our brave leaders to death, and so will we punish the criminals they send to rule us*. They hanged him. Me and Conor, we watched them hang him.'

When Turlough winds to a halt, I have tears in my eyes, too. Five years previous to the burning of the Roone Bay barracks would mean the Easter Rising, during which Patrick Pearse declared Ireland a free state. But all the leaders captured at the time were tried for treason against the English crown and shot by firing squad, not hanged.

Justin's suspicion that Jack had been summarily executed was no longer in doubt, only he hadn't been shot but hanged. A jury-rigged hanging was, by anyone's reckoning, a slow way for a man to die. A chill creeps up my spine at the thought of children watching a man being hanged, though it's long in the past. I wonder if witnessing that horrific scene was what turned Turlough's mind.

I thought the name given to the tall standing stone up on the hill above the bay was historic, but maybe it earned its name a lot more recently. I imagined two young boys, hiding behind rocks, watching as Jack was slowly strangled at the end of a rope. No wonder Turlough said he could never sleep again. It seems that Granddad Conor had also witnessed the event. Given that Dad's hard and pragmatic nature had been handed down from him, I wouldn't be surprised to find that the event had not damaged Conor as it appears to have damaged Turlough.

'What did they do then, Turlough? Did you see where they buried the bodies?'

Turlough pauses so long I think he's run out of words, but he adds in a small, confused voice, 'I was just a child. I shouldn't have even been there, but me and Conor thought it was brave and clever to be following the men, and them not knowing we were watching. I see it in my dreams still.'

'And those men who hanged him, are any still alive?'

'I don't know. I don't know.'

But he looks away from me, and I sense the lie. So, there's someone alive in Roone Bay who was there when Justin's granddad was executed.

'Can you get them to tell the Englishman, so he can lay a wreath and go on home? He isn't here to make trouble, I promise. No one else has to know what happened.'

'I have to go,' Turlough mutters. 'Too much. Too long. The breath is gone. Too long. I can't sleep.' He pushes himself to his feet muttering the words over and over under his breath.

I rise and put my hand on his arm. 'I'm sorry. I won't ask

again. You don't have to go. It will be cold tonight, and Dad's bed is empty.'

'Too long, too long,' Turlough repeats. He backs through the door, turns and scuttles up the hill in ungainly haste, and within minutes, like a deer, he's melted into the landscape.

So, the mystery is solved.

Do I tell Justin, or leave him believing his granddad was a good man?

22

JACK, 1920

The barracks was cold and totally lacking in home comforts. There was a fireplace in the living area, and on it one boiled the water for tea and cooked a meal, if you could call it that. Jack found it peculiarly antiquated. The thin mattresses in the bunkroom were inadequate, as were the ex-army blankets. Mist hung almost permanently over the hilltops and settled on the grass overnight. It was never quite freezing, but there seemed to be an all-pervading damp that seeped into his bones, making him ache. He held his hands towards the fire, which never warmed the room he was in, and longed for home, but he was beginning to forget what home looked like.

Hearing news of atrocities in Dublin, the officers went out in groups of three, always leaving three behind in the barracks to guard the building, and weapons were always at the ready. The people in Roone Bay tolerated them at best, casting worried glances and sidling away quickly rather than engaging, but they saw no sign of the dreaded IRA.

Jack found the regime restricting and one morning simply stepped outside, started to walk and didn't stop. He breathed in deeply of the cold, fresh air and wondered whether this infraction would be reported. He doubted it. The rest of the men would just think him daft to put himself in harm's way.

The Atlantic stretched out into the distance, a bank of dark clouds hanging on the horizon. Away to the east, a cold, golden sun was rising in clear air, burning away the morning mist like tufts of angel wings, sending shafts of light across the landscape. It was so beautiful it caught his breath. Suddenly he got it. This was the landscape his mother loved. It was just waiting for him to see it. He stood silently, entranced, soaking in this new experience and feeling the tension of the barracks slide away into the bright dawn.

He took another few steps up the rocky slope and saw and heard the dog at the same time. A small collie was planted aggressively in front of him, hackles up, teeth bared, growling. Jack knew dogs well and stopped short. He hunkered down and presented his knuckles. The dog sneaked forward, breathed in deeply then braved a snatched lick.

Jack's tension unwound. 'Come on, boy,' he said in hushed tones. 'Come on. I'm not going to hurt you.'

He kept a low dialogue going and gradually eased his hand towards the dog's muzzle, until he was able to smooth it under the chin. He turned and sat on a boulder, and the dog sidled between his feet and leaned back, seeking the warmth of his body. Jack's sigh echoed that of the dog as he gentled it with both hands. Over the past three years, he'd had little physical contact with man nor beast, save that of aggression. He missed the old dog back in England that he'd had as a puppy, and all the grief he'd been storing up came tumbling out in the cold and lonely morning on the rocky slopes of an Irish mountain. He bent and snuffled his tears into the dog's fur.

A small sound to his right made him leap to his feet and reach for his rifle. It was not where he'd left it. From several feet away, the dark circle of the muzzle was aimed directly at his chest, as if the young woman holding it was familiar with the weapon. Her feet were braced, the stock hitched to one shoulder, the sights level with her eye. Jack grimaced and held his hands away from his sides in a gesture of compliance. The flap over the handgun on his belt was fastened; no way could he reach it before she fired. Not that he would shoot her in any event. He wouldn't shoot a woman, even in war. He shrugged, realising that he had done everything he'd been told not to do and put himself in exactly the situation he'd been warned about.

He sighed. He'd survived the war, and now this.

Nothing left to lose, he dropped his hands and turned slowly to face the Atlantic. The sun had risen a little further, and the brilliance on the water twinkled like a million stars. He held that vision in his mind as he waited for the inevitable smack between the shoulders that would bring death swiftly on its heels. Not even the call of a bird broke the unearthly silence.

After a moment, she asked softly, 'Why would ye turn your back on me?'

'I've always loved the ocean. If I have to die, the last thing I see will be something beautiful.'

She gave a faint chuckle. 'That's not very complimentary.'

'Are you going to shoot me?'

'I should.'

He took that to mean no and turned back to face her – slowly, so as not to spook her into firing. She was petite, fine-boned, with white skin and a shock of unruly black hair. Her clothes were ragged, damp, and the stout boots on her feet were several sizes too big. He thought he'd never seen anything so lovely. He smiled. 'You're right. That sight is much more beautiful than the ocean.'

The rifle was lowered slightly, and a cocky grin broke out. 'Sure, don't ye have the blarney?'

'Are you with the Irish Military?' he asked.

'Not exactly. But I expect I'd get a medal if I took you in.'

'They'd shoot me, for sure.'

'They would.'

'I won't hurt you,' Jack said.

'I know.'

'You do?'

'I saw you with Ben. My dog. And I watched you cry.'

'You weren't supposed to see that,' he admitted. 'No one was.'

'So, why the big grief?'

'May I sit?'

'Sure.'

He sat back down on the damp rock. She perched on another rock several feet away, facing him, and planted the rifle on its butt between her feet. He could have taken it from her at that moment.

'It all got to me. Missing home. Missing my mother, my wife, my dog. And my little boy. He won't even know me when I go home. Life wasn't supposed to be like this.'

'You were in the war?'

He nodded. 'Too long.'

'So why are ye here? Youse English shouldn't be here, in my country.'

'I know. I'm sorry.'

And it came tumbling out – his grief for the life he was supposed to have had. His dreams of being a copper like his dad. His young love cut short as war engulfed the nation. And the reason he was now in Ireland.

'And you love her, this Rose of yours?'

'I don't know. We were childhood sweethearts and married in haste because of the war. Well, because' – he sighed, finally admitting a dark secret – 'I guess I didn't want to die without knowing a woman's touch. Maybe when I go home, I'll find I do love her after all. But I'm not sure of anything any longer.'

But he missed the warmth of a woman's body, the feel of her

breath on his neck, the soft touch of her skin against his. He wanted to cry again.

'What's your name called?'

He smiled at the strangeness of the sentence. 'Jack Sanders. And you?'

'Aisling.'

'Just Aisling?'

'That's enough.'

She rose and walked towards him without fear, leaving his rifle leaning against the rock. She leaned down, put her hands on his shoulders and pressed her lips against his forehead. Then she stepped back. 'Go home, Jack. Go home before it's too late.'

23

HANNAH

As I drift towards sleep my thoughts churn endlessly around my own situation. What if little Hannah had died of the polio, and Mam had brought a different child home? Not so much a charitable act as prompted by grief, a child to hold in her arms to fill the empty place where her own child should have been. Had I heard that this had happened to someone else, it would seem like karma. A child lost and another who needed a home; how could it have worked out better?

I had heard that during the epidemic some parents abandoned their damaged children, not able to cope with them, too poor and struggling with their own survival. But this isn't any child. This is me, and I need to know. Had I been abandoned? Did Mam take a stranger's child – me – home in the place of her own dead daughter? And if so, did my brothers and sisters know I wasn't their real sister? Surely they would have realised. It would explain Dad's coldness towards me. Does Mark know that's why I was cut out of Dad's will?

And what of the woman who abandoned me? Had she told everyone her child had died? Did she assume I'd been sent to an orphanage? Did she want to know if I'd been adopted? Had she been informed that Mam had taken her child? Did she even care? Did she have a death certificate stored away somewhere, all the while knowing her child was still alive? Did she ever wonder if that child was safe or happy?

And supposing I did find her? What then? What's the point of knowing? Do I want to confront her, or hug her? What good would that do after all this time?

These thoughts spin around in endless circles.

So improbable but so possible. With Mam and Dad both gone, I'm left with no one to ask if it's true, why Mam did what she did or why Dad accepted it.

The long night of inner turmoil is exhausting, but morning brings new resolution. I need to find out, or at least try to. Knowing won't change what happened, but like Justin's search for his lost granddad, it's the unknown that rankles and sits in the brain like a canker. Whether it settles my mind or not, whether it achieves anything or opens new threads of confusion, quite simply, I need to know.

I feel strangely comforted by the decision.

It's early when I harness Old Grey and trot him down into town. The sun is low, bringing an orange glow to the clouds. Leaf buds hang expectantly on blackened branches, dripping dew onto limp grass. Winter is a time when nature holds its breath; even trees need time to rest. In a month, the buds will explode into emerald-green jewels, then thicken into rich foliage. Nature is balance. Dark and light, winter and summer. The one without the other would be endlessly the same.

Maybe Justin has had a sleepless night, too. He's walking sturdily up the rise from the quay, a newspaper under his arm. I pull up alongside. He turns, and his smile is like summer peeping through the winter clouds. 'I heard you coming,' he says.

'I'm going to see Noel. Will you come with me?'

Maybe he guesses that I have news to impart, but he nods, instantly, and climbs up onto the cart, putting his arm along the seat back to give me space.

At the top of the drive, we jump down. I drop the lead, and Old Grey stands like a statue, and will wait patiently until I return.

'I hope Noel is up and about,' I say.

'If he's not, we'll wait.' Justin pats Old Grey's neck. 'I can be patient, too.'

'Old Grey would win, hands down.'

We laugh companionably.

Caitlin comes to the door at my hesitant knock. Betraying no surprise, she ushers us into the living room. Noel is already in his usual chair by the fire, today's newspaper rumpled on the table beside him. He smiles a welcome.

'Come in, girrul; sate yourself down. And yourself, Justin. It's early to be visiting I'm thinking. So, what's the bother? Has that brother of yours done the dirty and kicked you out?'

I laugh. 'Not at all, though he's no doubt been thinking about it. What Mickey Hoolihan told me got me thinking...'

I recount what Mickey had told me. 'But, you see, there's no telling whether there's truth in it or not.'

'But what if there is?' Justin adds for me, and I remember his offer to help me look into it.

'I mean, what kind of mother would abandon her child?' I ask of no one in particular.

'It's sad enough, sure,' Noel agrees, 'but it wasn't unusual for children to be abandoned during the epidemic. It happened where I was, too, in America. Poor people with big families were already struggling to survive. Parents couldn't afford the long drive into the city to visit their sick children even if they wanted to, and some simply didn't have the resources to cope with a child who ended up disabled. But maybe when your mother visited and was told her child had died, she saw the abandoned child – you – and brought her home. Perhaps you should think of the beauty in that action rather than the sadness of abandonment.'

I wonder if that could even be true, but, somehow, I know it is. A lifetime of feeling *different* suddenly falls into place. Dad hadn't wanted Mam to bring a stranger's child home in place of his that had died. Mam had treated me as her own, but to Dad, I had always been someone else's child in his home.

They're all staring at me as I muse, then say out loud, 'But if it is true, I don't have legal adoption papers, and I've always been called Hannah. So, was what Mam did even legal? Did the nurses agree for Mam to take the child? I don't see how that could have happened at all.'

'I doubt it was legal,' Justin suggests, 'but think about it. The nurses had seen so much sadness, they probably saw it as a small miracle for the abandoned child.'

Noel adds, 'There must be a nugget of truth in there somewhere. I mean, why else would your father have cut you out of the inheritance?'

'Dad needed me to look after Mam, then himself after she died. And then he was prepared to abandon me after his death,' I say, feeling my lip curl.

'He doesn't sound like a very nice person,' Justin agrees.

And nor was your granddad, I almost snap but manage to hold my tongue. It's not Justin's fault. It would be kinder leaving him to believe his own fairy tale.

'If you were in hospital for a long-enough length of time,' Noel muses, 'and you came back vastly different, well, the polio would have been blamed. If it wasn't a legal adoption, once it was done, maybe your dad felt he had no choice but to go along with it. If he'd spread the word, there would have been a police investigation into the legalities of your mother "stealing" a child. Kidnapping is a serious offence, no matter what prompted it.'

Caitlin says, 'But surely your brothers and sisters would have known, or guessed, at least, that you weren't the same child?'

'Maybe they were afraid of the repercussions, too, like Dad. Maybe it was easier for everyone to simply believe Mam when she said I was Hannah. Anything else would have brought trouble to the door.'

Since Mark arrived, I've been wondering about my future, but that has paled into insignificance beside the empty page of my past. Who am I? Who is my real mother? I feel no desire to create new bonds with a mother who abandoned me, but if I don't find out who she is, the mystery will haunt me.

For the first time since meeting Justin, I understand the compulsion that drove him all the way here from England simply to know the answer to a mystery that had plagued him since his great-grandmother died. Knowing won't change the past, but it might well change the future for the person who's no longer in thrall to endless speculation.

'Right,' I say. 'I want to know where I come from. I want to know why Mam brought me home from the hospital. I want to know if the nurses were complicit, or whether she stole me. Maybe there's a body still alive who can tell me these things.'

Noel nods. 'The best place to start would be Cork hospital, see if we can't find out the names of the nurses on the polio wards, and go from there. I suspect that at least one of the nurses, or even a doctor, must have been in on the deception. I don't see how she could have done it otherwise.'

'They must,' I agree. 'But will anyone remember after so many years? Would I even be able to track anyone down?'

'Or will they be afraid to speak,' Noel adds, obviously thinking about Justin's own quest. 'But we won't know if we don't ask.'

'We?'

'Well, you won't be driving all the way to Cork in the cart now, will you? I'm going to help.'

'Don't bother arguing,' Caitlin warns. 'I haven't seen Noel so animated since the hotel opened its doors. He was getting bored, so he was. And I'm going to help, too.'

Now it's Noel's turn to grin. 'And if Caitlin wants to help, I'm not the man to try to stop her. A dragon she is, when her will is crossed.'

They smile comfortably at each other.

'Oh, this is fun,' Noel says, his eyes twinkling.

'I hate to burst your bubble,' Justin remarks, 'but shouldn't I be the one to take Hannah into Cork? I'm a doctor. I know my way around the system. People might be more prepared to talk to me.'

At that moment, Justin's stomach gives an angry growl.

'Should we carry on this discussion over breakfast?' Caitlin suggests, and we all laugh and follow her downstairs.

'So,' she asks Justin when we're seated around the big kitchen table, 'Grace says you have a little boy back at home in – where did you say?'

'Near Porlock, on the west coast of Somerset. I have a practice there.'

'Ah, yes, you said you were a doctor. So, your wife will be looking after the children, then?'

'I'm not married. Paul is my sister's son. Sadly, Amanda became ill in the last trimester and died soon after the birth. Her treatment was too little, too late. If I'd been there... Well, the baby survived, but she didn't. Her husband felt unable to take care of the child on his own. He works abroad a lot, so in the end I adopted him. He doesn't get to see much of his father, in truth.'

Do I detect a note of censure in his tone?

'Oh, so sad,' Caitlin says. 'I'm sorry for your loss.'

'It was a huge shock,' Justin admits. 'Anyway, between my

mother and Denise, the nanny I hired, Paul isn't wanting for much. I'm hoping that one day, when I marry, my wife and I will be able to provide a more stable home for him.'

'You're engaged?' Caitlin asks.

He shakes his head. 'No. Maybe soon?'

He casts a quirky smile at me, which I doubt is missed by Caitlin or Noel. I mustn't read too much into it, though. The only one I'd hurt by doing so would be myself. It's only through my interactions with these lovely people that I realise how foolish it was to believe that I could be content with Cathal. In hindsight, it's easy to see that loneliness had overwritten common sense.

I flush, but he carries on. 'My mother, of course, would love for me to start a family, and I'd like to provide Paul with a brother or sister. But that's not a good reason for marrying the wrong woman.'

'Absolutely,' Caitlin agrees vehemently.

'It's early, still. I have no commitments here, so we could go to Cork straight away,' Justin suggests, moving the conversation away from dangerous territory.

'Old Grey is still outside, with the cart. I need to take him home,' I remind everyone. 'And the chickens need to be fed.'

'Don't you be worrying about that now,' Noel says. 'I'll pop on up to the farm to check on the chickens, and I'll put Old Grey in the meadow with mine. One more won't make a difference.'

Caitlin frowns. 'He says that every time. We've become the unofficial home for unwanted donkeys.'

'That one isn't unwanted,' I correct her. But if I move to England to live with Áine, I can't think of anywhere better for my faithful old donkey to go.

'You really don't want me to come and help?' Noel says, hope in his eyes.

'You can if you wish,' Justin says. 'I just thought—'

'He needs to go up and do the chickens,' Caitlin interrupts, glaring at Noel. 'Let the young ones be after doing the running.'

'But—'

Caitlin puts her hands on her hips. 'If you want to be useful, Noel O'Donovan, you get yourself into Roone Bay and find out something about Justin's granddad.'

Judging by his ludicrously hangdog expression, Noel knows when he's beaten.

24

JACK, 1920

A few days after Jack's strange meeting with the IRA girl, an auxiliary officer came down from Cork and blustered through a rehearsed pep talk. The officer had been snuggled warmly into a thick felt coat and stout boots, and flanked on the journey by his own bodyguard detail. Marching importantly up and down in the freezing living area, smacking his gloved hands together to get the blood supply going, he said that there had been action just a few miles away to the east. They had to remain VIGILANT. This was better than the trenches, eh WHAT?

Jack assumed that this officer, the plum in his voice betraying an advantageous background, had been drafted at sixteen years of age in the last few months of the war and had never served in the trenches. Arrogance sat visibly on his lack of experience. Perhaps he'd been eagerly awaiting his chance to go war, only for it to end. Jack snickered under his breath – accepting a post in Ireland as an auxiliary was the next best thing; doing his bit for the country, eh what?

Next to him, Billy Devon made an obscene gesture just out of the officer's line of sight. Jack had instinctively disliked Billy the moment he had met him. Billy was a diminutive middle-aged soldier with a pronounced cockney accent. He'd volunteered early in the war and somehow miraculously survived. His small, wiry frame was misleading. Jack imagined that enemy soldiers would have mistaken him for a child and learned, too late, that small didn't mean innocent or nice. He had anti-social habits, and Jack was more than half convinced that Billy enjoyed being disgusting, exaggerating things he discovered his comrades didn't like, as if it gave him some kind of superiority over those who were bigger than him.

Jack wasn't alone in his aversion, but he learned to keep his features neutral in the face of blatant provocation, because the sly smile that followed a wince of distaste betrayed hidden triumph. The thing Jack most hated about him, though, were the brazen lies about his exploits during the war, which were told with gleeful attention to foul detail. If he had done half the things he boasted of, Jack would be surprised. But it wasn't what he recalled that turned Jack's stomach so much as the man's unbridled enjoyment of airing memories that a decent man would spend the rest of his life trying – and failing – to forget.

The officer led them to understand they were lucky being out in the sticks. It was far more dangerous in Cork, with the sniper bullets, the bombing and burning of buildings. Jack thought he was lucky to be away from the city, too, if that spoiled child in a uniform was an example of the officers in charge. Johnny Crowley, the resident guard, soured by the way his fellow countrymen had turned on him, heard him out without comment but quietly muttered, after he'd finished, 'The daft bollix.'

Jack couldn't help but agree.

Jack wrote to his wife and mother, letting them know where he was, and was conscious of the fact that his letter was somehow superficial. He'd been away from home for so long, he could find little emotion in himself for the wife he barely knew and the son who was a stranger to him. He had known her as a child – they'd gone to school together – and he recalled, with some nostalgia, the exquisite excitement of her flesh against his in the night, but he couldn't quite recall her features; the fresh young face of Aisling now overlapped his memories.

During the day, the men took to the Crossley Tender, with its anti-grenade mesh, and trawled the area, seeking out possible IRA safe houses or signs of military training in progress, but for the most part these missions were more like outings, any sign of the disruptive IRA fading like mist into the hills before them. They sometimes stopped men to search for hidden letters and arms, or bid good morning to women, tipping fingers to their brows in greeting. Always, they were greeted by emotionless expressions and silent suspicion.

Jack took to sloping away in the mornings, taking the air, he would have said. Johnny told him he was treading dangerous ground and would no doubt wake up one day to find himself dead. He had no idea that Jack was hoping to meet Aisling again. She rose again and again in his mind like a secret, precious gift. Here and now, she was more real than his own family, who were a lifetime of experience distant and held the veiled nostalgia of a faded photograph of people long dead. Here, Aisling was flesh and blood, with the danger of an Irish lilt in her voice, the hint of mischief in her smile.

It was almost a week after his first encounter with her that Aisling appeared before him again. He saw her shape gradually materialise through the mist like a wraith and knew at the first hint of a shadow who it was, just as he was sure she recognised him.

'Ye'd wake the dead with your grunting and gasping,' she said.

'It's all uphill from the barracks,' he said. 'But certainly, I'm not as fit as I should be. Too much sitting around over the last year or so.'

She perched on a flat rock and patted the space beside her, and he dutifully sat, resting his rifle at his feet. 'You're not afraid someone will see us?'

He smiled gently, staring out towards the sea, though the view was scarred by lowered clouds. 'Are you?'

'Not at all.' She looked around and pointed to a large boulder. 'If I give warning, though, crouch behind there and be absolutely quiet.'

He raised one brow in amusement. 'And if my lot come up from below?'

'They'll sound like a marauding army, which they are, of course. I'll be gone before you can say Jack Sanders. But if my lot see us, I'll be forced to shoot you.'

He turned to assess her. 'Would you be able to? If you were told to shoot someone, could you?'

'I really don't know,' she answered seriously. 'You were in the war, weren't you? What was it like?'

'Bad,' he said mildly.

'Were you afraid?'

'All the time.'

'And did you kill anyone?'

He pursed his lips. 'Yes. Possibly several. I don't really know.'

'How could you not know?' she asked curiously.

His lip curled. 'We were in trenches or shell holes filled with water. We were cold and hungry and numb all in the same breath. Smoke from the guns and big artillery filled the air. It was enough to choke a man. Bullets and shells would be screaming overhead. We'd bury our heads under our arms as earth and rocks and bits of men fell like hail. Wounded men and horses would be screaming and screaming, and we'd be shooting at shadows…' He paused and shook his head as if to clear it.

Suddenly, she jumped up, her head tilted. 'Hide! Quickly!'

He looked her calmly in the eye and didn't move. He heard the clatter of a rock tumbling in the distance from further up the mountain path.

She glanced at him fearfully. 'Jack, run,' she hissed.

Shadows moved out of the mist, and he waited for the men to come and take him away. As the shapes materialised, he didn't know who was more surprised by the encounter: Aisling, himself, or the two mountain goats.

He caught her eye, and they began to laugh.

25

HANNAH

As I climb into Justin's car, he reaches for my hand and gives it a comforting squeeze. 'Are you all right?' he asks. 'You're not worried, are you?'

'I am, of course.' I pause, then explain. 'I mean, is it sensible to try to trace a mother who couldn't be bothered to take her child home from hospital?'

'You don't know what the circumstances were. She might have regretted that action all her life. Maybe she was ill. Maybe she tried to find you and couldn't. She might not even still be alive, but maybe you have brothers and sisters who would like to know you? The thing is, you'll spend the rest of your life wondering if we don't try to find out.'

'That's the crux of it,' I agree, sighing.

He pulls out onto the Bantry road. He's a confident driver but careful. Even so, I'm not used to being in a car and feel as though we're rushing along the road too fast. After a while, though, I relax and watch the countryside passing by. It's mild and clear today, though temporary waterfalls cascade down the mountainside.

For a while, we wind up a small road that weaves through

dark forestry plantation, tall pines marching in regiments up the steep hillside. The day seems to brighten when we emerge from the plantation and turn onto the Dunmanway road. We head east, wind-scoured rocks clawing the sky on one side, the Atlantic briefly visible on our right, a strip of black against the white winter sky.

'That's some scenery,' Justin says, slowing to take it in. 'Do you ever get used to it?'

'I haven't, in all the years I've been here.'

'Would you move away?'

'From choice? I don't know. I might have to move away, start a new life somewhere else.'

'Because of Mark and the inheritance?'

'That and Cathal. When people know—' I stop abruptly. 'I doubt Cathal will tell the truth of the matter.'

Justin picks a different thread out of the weave. 'People will understand that you were lonely, that it would have been a potentially disastrous relationship. I don't think anyone in Roone Bay has a lot of respect for Cathal, in truth.'

'I didn't know that.'

'I'm surprised, in a small community, that no one had the decency to tell you.'

'That's the Irish mentality. They never like to say bad things about anyone. Except the English, of course,' I add with a laugh.

He casts me a sidelong glance but flicks his eyes quickly back to the road. There's little traffic, but the rain has sprung potholes up through the tarmac. 'Would you think about moving to England?'

'Aine has been asking me to go and live with her in London. I might do that, but...'

'But?'

'I don't know if I could cope with all those people.'

'It doesn't have to be London. Where I live, in Somerset, is a small town on the edge of rolling hills and not so far from the sea. I love it there. The scent of salt, the storms, the seagulls, the fishing vessels and holidaymakers. Not so dissimilar from Roone Bay. It's also got the same bad weather,' he adds, smiling. 'From my house I have a good view over the water – towards Ireland, in fact, although it's too far away to see, and Ireland is further north, of course. The sea isn't clear, like here. We're on the outer edge of the Bristol channel and when the tide is on its way out, it pulls a huge fan of brown muddy water from the estuary out into the sea. As a child I used to wonder when all the mud would be washed out, and the sea would be blue like in the picture books, but it hasn't happened yet.'

I smile. 'I've never travelled far from Roone Bay. This is all I know, really. I was in Cork hospital when I was ill, but I've never visited the city since. I have siblings in America and Australia and England, and I've never left Cork. I'm a pretty sad case.'

'I think you're the opposite of that, actually. You seem to possess a quiet inner strength, and I sense you've got a kind heart,' he says quietly.

We're both silent for a moment. Then he asks, 'Do you recall much about your childhood, before polio? Do you mind me asking?'

'I don't mind at all, but I don't recall much before hospital. I have a few mental snapshots, and I don't even know if they're true. I remember playing with a small dog in a kitchen that had a big black range at one end. I told Mam that, and she said I must have just wanted a dog so much I invented it, but now I wonder if it was true. I remember someone singing a song about a bird in a gilded cage. I couldn't have made that up because I didn't even know what the word gilded meant. But Mam couldn't sing a note, so it was all confused.'

I think for a moment. 'My memories seem to start in hospital. Strangely, I recall being ill, but almost happy to be there, because for a long time the nurses and doctors became my family. I'm told I was three when I contracted the disease. Or Hannah was. It's hard to think of it that way. No one ever discovered how I – she – contracted it. Mam said it might have been while we were at the market. No one else in my family got it, which was lucky for them.'

'They might not have even been aware they had it,' Justin says. 'The virus is highly contagious, but some people who get the virus just feel ill for a while, like having a cold. They can pass it on, though, and the next person might get it badly, especially a child. That's why it was originally called infantile paralysis. It's only when the virus goes into the spine that it becomes dangerous.'

'I read that. But because I was so young, hospital became my life. I thought I'd forgot about home, my sisters, my brothers, my dad – but maybe I'd never met them,' I add bitterly. 'I even forgot how to speak Irish – if I'd ever known, that is. Mam said my first words were in Irish, but if I wasn't Hannah, maybe I didn't know it at all. This is so confusing. Anyway, when Mam came to pick me up, I could only speak English because that's what everyone in the hospital spoke. I was four years old by then. Because it took such a long time to recover, the hospital had set up schooling for residential polio children. They taught me how to read, thank goodness, because I don't know if that would have happened at home. Dad only spoke Irish, though, and when I got home, I didn't understand him at all.'

'But you learned Irish, or relearned it?'

'Maybe it was already there – who knows? But I learned it quickly enough, anyway.' I pause in recollection and blink hard as I pull to the surface memories that still have the power to hurt. 'The worst moment was when Mam came to pick me up.'

'Really? That's weird.'

I shake my head. 'Not really. The nurses told me my mam was coming, that I was going home. I was really excited but didn't really know what going home meant by then. Then this lady came into the room. She held her arms out to me, and I realised she was going to take me away. I screamed and clung to the nurse because I didn't recognise Mam. The nurses were my family, the children in the ward were like brothers and sisters, but this woman was a stranger. I remember Mam had tears running down her face because I didn't recognise her. I was pushing her away yelling for my real mam. I came to terms with that, and rationalised that I just didn't recognise her because I was young and ill, because of the length of time I was away from home.' I close my eyes briefly. 'But now everything is turned on its head. Maybe I really didn't recognise her, because, you know, perhaps she really wasn't my mam.'

Justin shakes his head and says softly. 'But she took you home, and loved you and made you part of the family.'

'I guess she tried.' I sigh. 'I don't remember anything before the polio. I have a good memory for almost everything, except those early years. I suppose it was the trauma of being taken away from home so young and then being told memories that were never real. I always felt strangely disconnected from the family, except for Aine. And, of course, I was disabled. That was never over. Mam tried to help me to adjust, but as I became a teenager, she became focused on her own declining health. She was always religious, but she became immersed in it, praying all the time. Dad said she was making sure she was going to Heaven, not the other place. I thought he was joking, but now I'm not so sure. If she took me home illegally, perhaps she thought that her big sin would override all the good she'd done in her life.'

'But your family. They were supportive?'

'Aine was. She was the only one who kept in touch with me, after. We were always close. My other brothers and sisters were so much older. I never really knew any of them well, and they didn't really try to know me or Aine. They just left as soon as they could.'

'Well, luckily, you came through just fine. You don't seem bitter and peeved at the world, like your brother, though you surely had more reason to.'

'It's hard to be positive sometimes, like when I drive the donkey cart into town and people stare.'

Justin smiles. 'I stared, too, but it was because you were enchanting. When I saw you driving that donkey cart, I thought you'd driven straight out of a fairy mound into the modern world.'

I laugh. He's dispersed my self-pity in a sentence. 'Well, my life was no fairy tale, nor was Mam's. She said, when I was a baby...' I falter, thinking that baby might not have been me. I take a breath and carry on. 'She said she would carry her baby on her back, in her shawl, as she went about her chores. It was what women did. They couldn't afford prams or pushchairs. She used a drawer from the chest upstairs as a cot until the baby was too big for it. I used to feel sorry for her hard life, but what I feel towards her at this moment is anger.'

'Not surprisingly.'

'She tried to be a good mother. She worked hard. She made clothes by the light of an oil lamp, because the farm, back then, had no electricity.' I think back. 'Sometimes the scent of a turf fire brings strange memories, like someone singing the old lullabies and rocking me to sleep in a cradle. Mam told me I imagined it, but now I'm thinking it's a memory from my real mam, or maybe one of the nurses.'

'You sing, though,' Justin says. 'I've heard you humming to yourself a few times now.'

'Do I? I didn't realise. Aine said I have a good voice, but Dad used to tell me to shut up that racket if I started singing by accident. I used to listen to a man singing the old songs, when I went to the market with Mam. I was fascinated by his sweet voice and the beautiful stories. He was disabled, too. I felt some kind of empathy, I guess. He had wooden crutches by his side.

He would be begging, a hat by his feet. Back then I thought he was really old, but now I wonder whether he was old at all. No matter we were poor, Mam always put a coin for him, and some eggs. I don't know what had happened to him. Damaged by war or sickness or just born like it. I enjoyed going to market with Mam. I loved riding in the cart with her, because I had her to myself on those days. I was able to listen to the singing and the gossip, too. That was the only time I got to understand what it was like outside of our farm.'

'So, you were fairly isolated?'

'That's how it was. Work from morning to night, and then some. It wasn't all bad, of course. In the summer, one of my older sisters would bring Aine and me to the barn or the field while they worked. I remember coming home sitting astride Old Grey's back with my callipers sticking out sideways. I remember once watching the sun sink as we were coming off the hill, me perched on top of a mountain of hay in the wagon. I wasn't unhappy, exactly. Just a bit sad sometimes because I was different.'

'It must have been tough, all right,' he agrees.

I laugh. 'You'll have me feeling sorry for myself all over again. Okay, here's a happy memory. When I was able to walk by myself with just one stick, it became my job to collect the eggs in the barn. I was so proud to have my own job. I remember carefully carrying the eggs, one at a time, to a little wicker basket, because eggs were too precious to waste. Then Aine would bring the basket in to Mam, in case I dropped it. I'm sorry, that's not a very exciting story! I'm boring you.'

'Not at all. I'm fascinated. My childhood was so different. I was protected. We had a warm house and warm clothes. I thought I was hard done by if Father Christmas didn't bring me the right toys.'

'It was a hard living on the farm, but the worst thing was knowing that Dad hated me. I used to think it was because instead of working, I had to be cared for. Now I wonder if he was irritated because I wasn't even his child.'

'Harsh to blame the child.'

'It's in the Bible, though, isn't it? God will visit the sins of the father on his children and his children's children...'

'Not a nice sentiment. Are you religious yourself?' he asks.

I glance at Justin. 'Do you mind if I am?'

'Mind? No. I just think people should move away from assuming the Bible is a definitive text. They're somewhat confused stories from an ancient civilisation. The people who told those stories lived in a brutal world. We don't live like that any longer.'

'Are you an atheist?'

'Not at all. I believe in God. I just think I should be free to do that in my own way. I try to help people, which is why I became a doctor. But also, I try not to harm anyone in thought or deed. That's my creed, really. I don't think women getting pregnant out of wedlock is a sin, for instance.'

I jolt. I wonder why he's chosen that particular example and respond somewhat sourly, 'I've never understood why the man in the matter is never deemed culpable.'

He grins. 'Sure, it takes two. Always did, always will! I used to love going to church as a child, though. The space, the singing, the stained-glass windows, the whole community atmosphere. I only stopped going when I realised a lot of it didn't make sense in the modern world.'

'Mam used to take me to mass. Same thing, really. I remember the priest telling us that hard work made poor people good people, and the poor would inherit the earth. But he lived in a big house with a housekeeper and was never hungry. I wondered, later, how he could say things like that when he was so comfortable.'

'There are double standards everywhere,' Justin says.

'Always,' I agree. 'But I didn't have anything to compare our lives to. Apart from the priest, everyone was poor, like us.'

'What about Noel O'Donovan?'

'Oh, he didn't come back to Ireland until I was a teenager, around the time Mam died, I guess. The Big House was just an ivy-covered ruin back then. But when he did it up, he was so far out of our league, he was like a king out of a fairy tale.'

'Not a prince?'

'Don't be daft. No, he was far too old to be a handsome prince!'

Justin laughs loudly.

As we pass through Dunmanway, I decide I've said enough about me. 'This is Sam Maguire's birthplace, you know.'

'Who's Sam Maguire?' Justin asks.

'He was a famous footballer. There's a trophy named after him. Michael Collins went to school here, too.' I glance at him with a half-smile.

'Okay, don't get cocky. I know who Michael Collins is.'

I laugh openly. 'The annual Ballabuidhe horse fair is held here, too. Travellers from all over Ireland gather here, for the horses, you understand. There will be races and shows, and the shops will be closed as the horses are chased through the town.'

'Really? Isn't that dangerous?'

'I guess. Shopkeepers cover their windows with wood because the crowds push back into them to get away from the hooves. But I don't think anyone has ever been hurt.'

A bit further on we cross the Bandon River and drive through Ballineen and Enniskeane, the towns grown so close they are spoken of in the same breath. 'There was a big battle here, in 1922 I think.'

'What was that all about?'

'The treaty between England and Ireland that allowed Ireland to become a free state omitted the six northern counties that wished to remain allied to England. The IRA want all of

Ireland to be free of English rule. *Ireland for the Irish*. That's essentially what all the Troubles are about.'

'I feel chastened by my ignorance,' Justin says. 'I've seen the fighting on the news but never really understood why Irish were fighting Irish. I thought it was Protestants against Catholics.'

'It is, sort of, but it's more complicated than that. Historically, the north was largely populated by settlers from Scotland and England, so is mainly Protestant, whereas those in the south historically migrated from paganism to Catholicism a long time ago, through an influx of monks and missionaries. The northern counties have close trading ties with England, but I think they're also a little afraid of coming under the dominion of the Catholic church.'

'The church is losing its dominion, though.'

'Is it? If you lived here, you wouldn't believe that.'

Justin is silent for a moment, then asks, 'You say you've had no education, and have been cut off from society for most of your life, but you seem very well informed and balanced in your views.'

'I read a lot,' I say simply.

As we drive into Bandon, he asks, 'So what is Bandon famous for?'

It's like this all the way to Cork. I point out the tower houses that were destroyed by Cromwell's cannonballs, and I point out the wrecks of homes abandoned during the famine, and the shells of mansions abandoned when their tenants could no longer pay rent. I point out the tall round tower that the early Christian monks created for their own safety. 'They made the door over fifteen feet above ground level, accessed by a ladder that would have been hauled up in the case of an attack.'

'It makes you realise how harsh life must have been in those days,' Justin remarks.

'Ireland was tribal, dominated by clan warfare, and if you count the generations, it's not really so long ago.'

Justin gives a laugh. 'And we now think we're so civilised. I wonder what people will think of us a thousand years from now?'

The grey, towering mountains are behind us now, and as we drive up a green river valley towards Cork city, I find myself musing on Justin's granddad rather than my own problems. We're driving the reverse journey that Jack must have taken going south, through a scrubby landscape from which the rebels had once enacted their guerrilla warfare. It must have seemed like heaven to Jack after the endless sea of mud and slaughter in the trenches of France.

26

JACK, 1920

When Aisling appeared again, Jack was sitting on a rock staring out over the ragged countryside. He hadn't heard her arrive but was instantly aware of not being alone. He jolted out of his reverie as she took two strides and sat beside him. The hard knot inside his chest eased just slightly.

He had wondered whether he'd imagined Aisling into something other than she was because he was starved of female company, but something deeper fired through his body at the slight contact. She was beautiful, but it wasn't that. She was like a wild animal, sleek and natural as the ground she walked on. She had no fancy clothes, no airs and graces, but was as wholesome and enticing as the scent of brown bread straight from the oven. His senses were fired, and when she looked into his eyes, he knew she felt the same way. How bizarre, he thought, to have found his soulmate under such circumstances. He wondered how much time they would have before fate intervened; before they were torn apart by circumstances beyond their control.

For a few moments, they sat in companionable silence. The rain had stopped a few days back, and there was a strange warmth on the breeze. The Atlantic was like melted glass. The sky was blue with drifting tufts of white clouds.

'Hard to believe there's so much hate in the world when you see this,' he commented.

'So, what were you thinking?' she prompted. 'You were away with the fairies.'

He was tempted to lie, as he'd lied so often, but felt compelled to tell her. 'I killed a young lad during the war and he haunts my sleep.'

'Why did you kill him?'

'If I hadn't, he would have killed me.'

She gently touched his arm. 'I'm sorry. I shouldn't have asked.'

But it was too late – the mental door had cracked open. The rugged scenery around him faded, replaced by the memory of blood and carnage.

'I did things in the war I'm not proud of, but we weren't human; we were animals. It was kill or be killed; survival at its most basic. When I stabbed that young man with a bayonet, it wasn't to kill him – it was so that I didn't die. I will never forget the blank terror in his eyes. I've often thought about that young man's mother, back in Germany, or wherever he had come from, wondering where her precious son had died, and how, and I can't tell her. I don't know who he was. Just the enemy. She probably hoped he'd died cleanly, quickly, but it wasn't likely, not from a bayonet wound in the stomach. There was no time for mercy killing in the height of battle... You don't forget things like that. Not ever.'

'But you survived,' she said. 'You should have gone home, back to your family.'

'I couldn't,' he admitted. 'Home was a lifetime away. A cosy little cottage in a cosy small town on the edge of the sea. My family wanted their son, husband, father back. Someone who would walk to the bakery to buy a loaf of bread and chat to the neighbours on the way. But I was no longer that man. I was afraid I'd hurt them; my family, I mean.'

'It will fade with time,' she said sympathetically.

He shook his head. 'I don't sleep. I don't forget. I have the same dream, night after night. I'm searching for the boy's mother, but she's running away from me and I can't catch up. She thinks I want to harm her, but I just want to tell her how sorry I am.'

Aisling had tears in her eyes, and he realised they weren't for the young soldier but for him, for his never-ending nightmares. He bowed his head into his hands, but the tears were long dried.

She was silent for a moment, then said, 'Then you should remember him. It's only right.'

He turned his head towards her, a questioning frown lowering his brow.

'He didn't want to kill you, either. Remembering makes you a decent man,' she added in explanation.

He didn't feel decent at all. He wanted nothing less than to take her in his arms and cry on her shoulder. Maybe it showed in his eyes, because her mouth screwed into a grimace.

'Let me show you something,' she said.

She stood and took his hand. He allowed her to lead him along a small track. She might have been leading him into an ambush for all he knew. After a while, she let go of his hands to bunch up her skirts to aid her upward scramble. Jack had no idea how high they were, but the boulders they navigated were huge, and it took all his concentration to keep up. She was nimble as a mountain goat.

'Where are we going?' he grunted.

She flashed a smile over her shoulder. 'You'll see.'

He wondered if he was being led, a lamb to the slaughter, to the IRA hideout in the hills. If so, he didn't fight it. If he was shot and buried up here, at least his unwholesome memories would die with him. He scrambled over yet another boulder and suddenly Aisling was gone.

He heard a giggle behind him and turned. She'd slipped into a small cavern in the rocks. He slipped down beside her, ducked under an overhang, and exited in a small hollow where bedrock formed a natural wall over which a small stream tumbled and rushed, not quite vertical enough to be called a waterfall. The small pool below it was filled with dark, peaty water, the surrounding boulders speckled with moss and lichen. He was enchanted. To one side there was a bush – blackthorn, maybe – covered with tattered strips of cloth spiked onto the thorns, which he already knew meant people had been here, praying, their current religious affiliation sitting uneasily on the remnants of druidic practices.

'Is the pool deep? Where does the water go?' he asked.

'It's not deep, but it's not for bathing. You'll get lynched if you're found naked in there.'

He gave a half-smile. 'I'd get lynched in or out of the water, probably. So, where does the water go?'

She grinned. 'Tír na nÓg, where the fairies dwell. This is a holy well. Give the lady a token with your prayer. Maybe she will take the bad memories from you.'

He smiled at the strange mix of legend, myth and religion. To him the tattered strips of cloth marking prayers seemed more pagan than anything. He wondered what had been prayed for up here. For a lovestruck woman to have her love returned, for a neighbour to get boils, for a child to be made well... He searched his pockets and found a cotton handkerchief, his initials embroidered into one corner. He bit the tiny hand-stitched hem and tore off a wide strip. He wasn't just humouring her. In this place, on this day, he felt as if he had truly stepped out of real life and into a fairy tale. He closed his eyes and made his wish for internal peace, before reaching up and piercing the strip of fabric onto a thorn.

'Can I tell you my wish?' he said. 'In England, when we blow the candles out on a birthday cake, our wish has to stay untold, or it will never come true.'

'It's not a wish; it's a prayer. There's a difference between magic and the mercy of God. You can tell me if you want.'

He nodded. 'I wished that there would never be another war. I wished this could all be over.'

She's still for a moment, then nods. 'Take off the jacket, so. Be just a man for a moment, and not the enemy.'

'I'm not your enemy.'

'That uniform says otherwise.'

He unbuckled the belt and cast off the sand-coloured jacket and shivered in the damp chill of this strange grotto, yet without it he felt lighter, cleaner.

'May I drink the water?'

'Sure, it's pure, from the mountain. It's the peat makes the pool that colour.'

He kneeled, dipped his hands, cupped them together and drank. The water tasted strangely bitter, but was chill and refreshing.

She sat on a rock and watched. 'So,' she said finally. 'If you don't want to be here, why don't you go home, leave the fighting behind you?'

It all spilled out, and she listened intently without interrupting until he wound to a halt.

'Your mother is Irish, so?'

He nodded.

'Well, that makes you only half English. We can work on that half together.'

He laughed. 'I must get back. My colleagues think me a fool for walking out on my own.'

'Sure, aren't they right? One of these days you'll be shot, wearing that uniform.'

'Maybe it would be a good thing.'

'So, you have a death wish.'

He shook his head. 'To tell you the truth, war has ruined me. I don't know what I want. I don't know who I am any longer.'

'But back in England, your wife is waiting for you.'

'I know, but—' He paused, trying to find the words, and they ripped from him with agonising honesty. 'I don't want her any longer. I have a son, too. But he won't know me. If I go back, I'll be a stranger to them.'

'If?' she queried softly.

He nodded guiltily. 'War does that to a man. Changes him. It changes everyone, I guess. The things we did... the things we saw... and we're supposed to slot ourselves back into our old lives as if it hadn't happened. I don't think I can do that.'

'You could stay in Ireland.'

He indicated his uniform.

She laughed. 'We'll burn it together.'

27

HANNAH

As we come into the outskirts of Cork, Justin says, 'Now all we have to do is find St Mary's Hospital.'

I'm staring, wide-eyed and overwhelmed by the miles of streets we pass through, the number of tall buildings, the cars, the people, the bustle and the noise. I shrink lower into the car. Cork is a small city. What would it be like in London, travelling miles and miles without seeing any countryside?

We get lost several times, and we stop twice to ask for directions, the responses of which I have to repeat to Justin, who can't understand the Cork accent, which he says is like a stream of vowels without consonants. We detour accidentally around the university campus and the abandoned and dilapidated city jail with its hanging gate, which had last housed republican prisoners during the 1920s, about the time Justin's granddad was serving in Ireland.

We eventually find the hospital, which is still a hospital, thank goodness. The receptionist is polite when we ask about records from back during the polio epidemic.

She looks down at my callipers and her tone softens. 'You were here as a child?'

I nod. 'I was three when I was brought in. I remember a Nurse Bergin and a Nurse Philips. There was a doctor called, ah, maybe MacNamara? Those are the only names I recall.'

'You must have a good memory,' she says, impressed.

'Well, they were like my family for a long time.'

'So, what information exactly are you looking for?'

Her eyebrows nearly disappear into her fringe as I explain what we discovered.

'Goodness, I don't think I've heard anything like that before,' she exclaims. 'Well, I don't think there's anyone still working in the hospital who was here twenty-five years ago, but there are records, of course. You'd need your birth certificate to prove who you are...' She hesitates. 'Well, a birth certificate, anyway. Did you bring it with you?'

'I should have thought of that,' Justin says, clapping the heel of his hand to his forehead in annoyance. 'But in any event, we'd need to know what other girls of similar age were in the hospital at the same time.'

'Well, I don't know if that contravenes the privacy laws, but you couldn't see any records today, anyway. You need to put in a request to the registrar, who would then search out the right records.' She pauses in thought, then says, 'I have an idea. Hold on.'

The receptionist slides the small window closed, turns her back on us and makes a call. There's a brief muttered dialogue before she comes back to the window. 'Might you recall a nurse called McGuire?'

I shake my head. 'That name doesn't ring any bells, I'm afraid.'

'Well, Geraldine was a ward sister here during the epidemic. She retired a few years ago. She doesn't remember your name; so many children passed through her care. Anyway, she helped with a project some years later that studied how the epidemic affected Ireland, so she's interested to meet you. She might be able to answer some of your questions.' She scribbles as she talks, then pushes a piece of paper towards us. 'That's her address, and her phone number if you get lost.'

'Thank you,' Justin and I say in unison.

Geraldine McGuire lives in a small modern bungalow on the north side of the city. She's a large woman with steel-grey hair screwed back into a loose bun with a clip. She comes to the door using a walking aid, her hands swollen with arthritis.

'I hope we're not intruding?' Justin says.

'Sure, I wasn't busy at all. I'm fascinated by your story, actually. I don't know if we'll find out anything that will help, but... Well, come on in and seat yourselves down. It's nice to talk about the old days, back when I had legs men liked to look at!' She gives a belly laugh and shows us into a room cluttered with glass ornaments.

'What a lovely room,' Justin says. 'So much light. And that glass seahorse is stunning.'

Geraldine preens, and I smile inwardly as Justin delivers his best bedside manner.

'It was a present from my daughter. She's working in Australia now. She's too far away, really, but nurses in Ireland simply don't get paid as much as they should.'

'Nor in England,' Justin comments.

'Are you a nurse?'

'I'm a doctor,' he says somewhat apologetically, adding, 'but I've never treated anyone with polio. I suspect you could teach me a thing or two.'

'We were all learning as we went along,' she says softly. 'It was the worst time, really. All those poor children...' She glances at my callipers. 'But you got off lightly, Hannah.'

'Compared to some, I did,' I agree. 'But I do wonder what

my life would have been like if I hadn't got polio at all. Did the hospital receptionist tell you that I'm almost sure that Esther Barry, who took me home, wasn't my birth mother?'

'She told me that, sure, but it's a strange tale, far-fetched, maybe.'

'It was a bit of a shock to me, to say the least. I'd always thought my parents were, well, my parents. Only when Dad died, I was told that might not be the case. It's all a bit third-hand, and there's no proof, but I can't see why anyone would invent something like that.'

'But who would have told you such a thing?'

I explain about the will and about Dad's unwritten words.

Her eyes widen. 'But even if it's true, it was a bit harsh to cut you out of the will, wasn't it?'

'Yes,' I say bluntly, 'but it does explain Dad's attitude towards me all these years. We were told that you had helped with some kind of project about those days.'

'I did. It was a few years back now, though.'

'Oh, so, you can't help?' I ask, disappointed.

'Well, I'm not sure I should let you see it, but seeing as it's personal and it was so long ago... I do have some of the information I collated for the national survey. I don't think I was supposed to keep it, but no one ever asked for it back.' She hesitates and adds, 'Really, I shouldn't, but in your case...'

'We won't divulge anything to anyone,' Justin assures her.

She struggles to her feet, opens a cupboard door and rifles through piles of papers. 'It would be at the bottom of the pile, of course. This is the basic list of children, with dates of admission; then there's this lot, in alphabetical order. I did have a list of the parents' names and addresses, but it's not here. So, what year were you brought in?'

'Nineteen fifty-seven. I was three.'

'Ah, how unlucky. That was the year the vaccination was

introduced in Ireland. A year later and you wouldn't have got the polio at all. Now.'

She hands Justin two stacks of lined sheets covered in faded handwriting, bound by green ribbon, and sits down heavily, gasping for breath. Justin and I, seated close on a coach, lean forward, our shoulders brushing.

'Hundreds of children,' I whisper.

Geraldine nods. 'Yes, and quite a few didn't get to go home at all. The poor mothers, too. Many couldn't get into the hospital; it was too far. They were too poor, and Cork is such a big county, see.'

'Mam said she only managed to get in once before picking me up. It took all day to get here and back, and she was only allowed to stand outside the door and wave at me through the window.'

Geraldine nods. 'That would be right. We couldn't let any parents in. It's quite contagious. And, well, times were different, then. There were so many changes in the system while I was there, especially when we were dealing with children. But the polio epidemic.' She compresses her lips, remembering. 'We'd never dealt with anything like it.'

'I guess we should start from the date of your discharge and work backward,' Justin says.

'It would have been late in 1957. I was there around seven months. Mam said I'd recently turned four – that would be in October – but I don't know the exact date I was brought home.'

'So,' he says, setting aside the later pages, 'let's start in December and work backward...'

The list is handwritten on sheets of lined paper, with basic details: the child's name, the area the child came from and the final prognosis prior to hospital discharge. Several were simply marked deceased.

Justin reads more quickly than me. His finger glides down

the list, then he waits for me to catch up each time before flipping the page. Then he stabs it in triumph. 'Here you are!'

It seems weird to read my name on an old sheet of paper, in a stranger's house. *Hannah Barry, discharged with lower limb paralysis.* We go back and forward a month each way, analysing the data. Of the children mentioned around the time of my discharge, only one girl child of four years old had died.

'Mary O'Brien,' I whisper with hushed reverence. 'Might that be me?'

Geraldine gathers the papers and flips back and forth, pursing her lips before coming to the same conclusion. 'Maybe.' She looks me straight in the eye. 'This is an incredible story, though. Even if you find Mary's mother, she might not believe you or want to know at all. Or you might be wrong altogether.'

'I know,' I say dryly. 'It seems incredible to me, too, which is why I want to verify it. If it's even possible. I'm not looking for anything except an answer.'

'So, how might we find out who her parents were?' Justin muses.

Geraldine rifles through the other pile of papers. 'Ah, here we are. The child was taken back to Masseytown, in Macroom, to be buried,' she says. 'You could look in church records for her birth, which would maybe establish the identity of Mary O'Brien's parents, but after that, well, who knows? If her parents tell you their child died, there's nothing will prove otherwise.'

'You've been an enormous help,' Justin says. 'If we need to come back one day and take another look at the records, would you mind?'

'Not at all. But maybe you'd let me know the outcome? There were several nurses working with me back then. I'm curious to know who would have agreed to such a thing.'

'She won't get into trouble?' I ask anxiously.

'Not at all. There's nothing written that will convict anyone. And if Mary O'Brien was abandoned, it was an act of compassion as far as I can see. It's just an incredible story, and me working there at the time with no clue. Like you, I'm just curious to know.'

28

HANNAH

The road to Macroom is fairly level, cutting through fields that presently lie dank, the yellowing grass waiting for spring. Cows huddle despondently under straggly hedges and the skeletal branches of stunted trees clawing blackly towards the sky. It could be seen as miserable, but it's all part of the greater joy of nature. Without the dark of night, I would never see the stars. Without winter, I wouldn't see the beauty in spring.

The mountains I'm so familiar with are nowhere in sight. It feels peculiar to be so far from home, and yet Aine didn't think twice about going to London, nor my other sisters and brothers to the other side of the planet. So why is it so hard for me to leave Roone Bay?

It's bizarre, being ferried across Cork by a man I barely know, trying to trace my birth mother, when all my life I'd had no inkling that it was anyone other than Mam. What possessed her to do such a thing? Maybe she intended to tell me one day, when I was old enough, but I was barely fourteen when she died, when she begged me to care for her husband. Maybe she thought I wouldn't have stayed had I known the truth.

Maybe she was right.

Macroom is a busy market town built around the River Sullane. There's a many-arched bridge over the river, but as we drive across, I see old cobblestones through the clear water that must have once been a ford. We pass the impressive remains of a mediaeval castle. There's big history all around us: clan fights from the early mediaeval period, King Brian Boru's famous battle, the famine, the mills, the brickworks and Mount Massey, the mansion that was burned out by the IRA. The facts are popping up into my head like released corks.

We navigate our way to the church and make our way inside. The young priest who greets us looks bemused at our strange quest. 'I find it hard to believe the story, in all honesty. Surely Mary's mother should be left in peace, after all this time?'

'But what if it's true?' I ask. 'Wouldn't my mother want to meet me?'

'I don't know.' He purses his lips and finally says, 'Well, maybe it's part of God's larger plan. Follow me.'

He takes us into a small room where the records are locked behind ancient carved oak doors. 'You're lucky,' he says. 'Church records are being centralised now, but I still have the books going back to the dates you're referring to.'

He pulls a vast tome from a cabinet, places it on a table and turns the yellowing pages reverently, quickly scanning the beautiful script detailing births. Eventually he comes to an entry relating to Mary O'Brien, who was two months younger than me – or I am two months younger than I thought I was! The child's mother is listed as Kate O'Brien, seamstress; the father, Thomas O'Brien, handyman.

'Handyman?' I ask. 'What does that actually mean?'

'Well,' the priest muses, 'it has all the hallmarks of someone with various skills – carpentry and the like – who would likely have been employed in local businesses or by one of the more affluent households. More than that, I can't tell you.'

'A seamstress might have been employed in a local shop?' I suggest.

'I would suggest,' the priest says, folding the book and placing it carefully back on the shelf, 'that you begin by enquiring in the older, more established businesses, such as a hardware shop, where a handyman might have purchased tools, or an establishment where a wealthy lady might have bought fabrics.'

'I can't walk so far,' I remind Justin.

'You can take my arm, lean on me. And if you need to rest, say so, and we'll find a place to have a coffee. Okay?'

'Okay.'

'You have a good husband, so,' the priest says, smiling.

I flush, but neither of us disabuse him. We thank him for his help, and Justin drives down into the town.

Although there is a new supermarket, around the wide market area old-fashioned shops cluster, their frontages bordered with carved wood, the faded lettering above them proudly pronouncing local names and occupations. Dan McCarthy, victualler; Mickey Sweeny, butcher; Buckley's hardware; Sheehan's; Leary's...

Justin walks around the car to help me out. 'Right,' he says, parking my hand inside his elbow and patting it. 'That stays right there. No argument.'

Over the next few hours, we ask countless people for information about a Kate and Thomas O'Brien, seamstress and handyman, who were working around the Macroom area in the fifties. As I tell the almost truthful story of trying to find my birth mother after I'd been adopted as a child, I'm amazed at how helpful people are, or want to be, anyway. Even if they don't know the answer, they keep us talking, as if knowledge is going to fly down from the sky, if only they wish hard enough. Sometimes it takes a long, convoluted dialogue before they admit they can't help at all. I'm getting tired, and despite leaning on Justin's arm, I grit my teeth and cope. It's what I've always done.

Justin must feel the weight of me settle heavily on his arm. My legs are aching. The whole of me is aching. Walking isn't easy; I walk from my hips, lifting each dead leg in turn, swinging it out and dropping it. I remember the nurses in hospital teaching me how to do this, me clutching two parallel hand bars, even then realising that this wasn't a normal part of growing up. Here, I see people striding about their business and envy them their ignorance that the simple act of walking is such a precious gift.

'I'm a bit tired,' I say finally, unable to disguise my exhaustion any longer. 'Maybe we should just go on home?'

Justin halts immediately and turns to face me, his face the picture of guilt. 'Oh, Lord. I'm so thoughtless. I didn't realise it was so late.'

I take a breath. 'I'm fine. Sure, we can drive on home.'

'How about I find us a hotel, and we'll have another try in the morning? If we go home without the truth, would you have the courage to come back again? You'd spend the rest of your life wondering.'

I know he's right, but I wonder now if this is all worth it. 'It's a fool's errand, really,' I say despondently, 'and a hotel will be too expensive.'

'Don't worry about the cost. It's my treat.' He puts an arm around me. 'And don't give up yet. We might be close to the truth.'

'I just think we've wasted enough time. We should be back in Roone Bay finding out what happened to your granddad Jack.' I feel a little guilty for withholding what Turlough told me, but ignorance is kinder than the brutal truth.

'That can wait a few days. Besides, with me out of the way, Noel might actually have got someone to talk to him.'

'Really, I think we should drive back.'

'It's late, and it'd be dangerous driving all that way in the dark when I don't know the roads. Hannah, please stop arguing and just let me look after you?'

His concern reaches into parts of me that have lain dormant for a long time. A flood of longing almost brings tears to my eyes. How I wish for someone to look at me like that every day when I wake up. It doesn't even have to be love; just the concern of one caring person would be enough. But I learned long ago that self-pity is for the weak.

Justin stops a woman walking past. 'Excuse me, can you tell me where we can best stay for the night?'

'Sure,' she answers and points behind us. 'There's the big hotel, right there, see? But' – she leans forward slightly and drops her voice – 'look, if ye don't be wanting the bells and trimmings, half a mile down the road towards Millstreet, there's a small hotel, Tim Pat's. Likely that would suit better.'

'Thank you kindly,' Justin says, and to me, 'Right. Back to the car.'

'But—' I begin.

'No,' he says. 'My mind is made up.'

He's laughing as he says it, so I think if I did insist, he would drive on home, but selfishly I don't want to. I really am exhausted, and I'd like this adventure to last a little longer before reality cuts back in. I don't yet want to face the fear of a future that now seems to rely entirely on the charity of Aine, or neighbours I barely know.

29

HANNAH

I think that the hotel, from the elaborate portico, might once have been the home of a merchant or a wealthy mill owner. On my own, I would have felt the need to find a tradesman's entrance, but Justin walks me through the front door as if he owns the place. A diminutive, neat older woman at the front desk introduces herself as Deirdre, and asks do we want a double room? Her smile is infectious, but I flush slightly as Justin calmly replies that we need two singles. She leads us up a carpeted stairway to a corridor that is slightly uneven and has two more angled steps along its length.

'Mind the stairs,' she says to me. 'This part of the house was built on later. The owner wanted taller ceilings in the new rooms below so that he could hang a Waterford glass chandelier.' She laughs at this human folly, but it's beyond me to imagine the kind of wealth that could afford such a thing.

Upstairs, Deirdre points to a door at the end of the corridor. 'The bathroom is there. Some hotels are putting bathrooms into each room, but I'm afraid we're a little too settled in the past to provide that kind of luxury.'

This is luxury, if the truth be known. My ancient and basic

farmhouse still doesn't have a bathroom at all. But times are changing. Even my own brother won't stay at the old home for want of his own comfort. My mother would have said I'm getting ideas above my station, that staying overnight in Noel's renovated mansion, and now a hotel, will be the ruin of me. It's only now that it occurs to me that my mother had truly accepted the church's teachings, that we were poor by the grace of God. Actually, I think, looking around at this evidence of a once-privileged family's home, it was the rich who promoted that concept, not God. After all, if everyone had aspirations of grandeur, how would they remain superior, and who would do all the work?

'These are yours.' Deirdre stops at two adjacent doors and opens the first. 'The keys are in the locks inside, so bring them with you when you come downstairs.'

I find the sage-green decor in my room a little tired, but the hotel emits an aura of calm that seems to settle comfortably around my shoulders.

'Why don't you rest a while?' Justin advises.

I limp to the bed and sit, gratefully. I reach to unbuckle my callipers, but Justin kneels. 'Let me,' he says.

I almost freeze, then nod slightly. No one has done this for me since I was a child. I feel embarrassed as he gently removes the ironware. He smiles as he lifts both of my legs and swivels them up onto the covers. 'Lie back, close your eyes and relax.'

To my shock, he sits at the foot of the bed and begins to massage my swollen ankles. I lie with my eyes closed as he performs this strangely intimate act. I can't use my own legs because the nerve endings in the muscles were destroyed by the polio, but I can still experience sensation. Being a doctor, Justin must know this. I find I'm drifting into a peculiar state, neither totally awake but not asleep.

'There,' he says softly. The bed creaks as he stands. 'Now, may I kiss you?'

I feel his weight shift. My eyes pop open. His face is so close, the warmth of his breath is tickling my lips. He wants to kiss me? I reach up and gently pull him towards me.

His kiss isn't the brush of goodnight. It's a full-on, committed kiss, and I'm responding with all the released passion of my stifled life.

Finally, he disengages himself from me, his eyes crinkled with amusement. 'I'm going to remind you of this later, sweet Hannah.'

I lie still and hear the door close quietly behind him. It's only then that I realise tears are seeping from under my closed eyelids. I've rarely been the recipient of kindness, let alone love, and I tell myself Justin's actions are those of simple compassion. He's a doctor, after all. He knows about these things.

I feel well rested when he knocks to take me down to dinner. The dining room is tall, with windows that look out over a once-manicured garden, now comfortably overgrown, with possibly a river at the foot beyond a line of mature trees. I suspect this will be magnificent in the summer, but presently the bare branches are interspersed with the dark green of spruce and holly that still hosts a scatter of blood-red berries.

The ornate ceiling rose sports a magnificent glass chandelier. I point it out to Justin. 'Look, the chandelier!'

He laughs and shakes his head. 'The waiter told me that the original one was sold a long time ago for a rather astronomical sum. That's just a copy.'

'Well, I wouldn't know the difference.'

'If you put the two side by side, you probably would. The old glass had a high lead content that made it really glitter; modern glass looks kind of dull in comparison.'

'You know about this stuff?'

'I learned a bit about lead poisoning, of course, when I was training.' He sees me glance at the cut-glass wine glasses that wait on the table. 'You don't have to worry about the odd drink from a crystal glass. It's more dangerous for the people working in the factories than it is for people who buy or use the products.'

'When I get home, I'll get a book on glass from the library,' I state. I don't like half-knowing things. But even as I say it, my situation returns in full force. It's not my home; it's Mark's, and he's going to sell it. I might be leaving Roone Bay for good. I take a deep breath. Wherever I go, there's sure to be a library.

Justin picks up the menu. 'What would you like to order? Don't worry about the cost. It's my treat.'

'Everything is so expensive! I could feed Dad and me for a week on the cost of just one of these meals. I've never been to a restaurant before.'

'What, never?'

I shake my head.

He grins. 'Well, girrul, just enjoy the experience.'

I laugh at his attempt at a West Cork accent, but the look on his face is that of Santa giving a child a coveted toy. 'Very well. The chicken would be grand.'

'Would you like a glass of wine?'

I shake my head. 'Just water, thank you.'

The food is divine, served on bone china plates, eaten with silver cutlery. I lean over and whisper, 'I don't know which knife to use. I'm as out of place here as the donkey that strayed accidentally into a meadow of thoroughbred horses.'

He laughs. 'Hannah, I think you're absolutely charming just as you are. When there's an abundance of cutlery, start at the outside and work in.' After a moment, he says, 'So, we could stay for another night if we don't have any joy tomorrow. I'm sure we could trace the family if we persevere.'

'I don't want you to waste your time on me. We've visited so many shops, talked to so many people. It's probably pointless carrying on.'

'It's not pointless, and we haven't visited them all. I'm really happy to keep going. Let's see what tomorrow brings.'

'I've taken up too much of your time already.'

What I really mean is that I'm already indebted, and can't find it in me to be more of a burden on his time and finances. I think he knows this, so says, 'Okay, we'll discuss it in the morning. It's too early to sleep, though. I have a fancy for a nightcap. Will you join me in the lounge?'

I nod agreement, and Justin rises to give me his arm and leads me through to the lounge bar. He's a real gentleman, and if I never have another such experience, I will hold this one in my mind as long as I live.

I ask Justin if he always wanted to be a doctor.

He shakes his head. 'I grew up intending to be a policeman. It's sort of a family tradition. But, oh, I don't know, something pulled me towards medicine. I'd still be doing something good for society, but in a different way.'

'Did your parents mind? That you changed your mind, I mean?'

'Not at all. They were happy that I wanted to go on to university and do something good with my life. Did you ever have any thoughts about what you wanted to do when you were younger?'

I shake my head. 'My future seems to have been pre-ordained. The polio kind of set me in a pattern of acceptance that I wasn't like other people, and Dad solidified that belief. I'd never be able to get a job. I should be grateful to be alive. Then with Mam being ill, and all the rest, well, I guess I never had time to consider the alternatives.'

'But all the reading, the self-education! Did you never think of rebelling against this, ah, conditioning?'

'I did, of course, but couldn't see how. I had no money. And after Aine left, I didn't have anyone to talk to. Leaving just seemed so scary, such a big move.'

'That must have been so lonely.'

'I was telling you how it was, not looking for sympathy.'

'Well, you have it anyway. No wonder you were contemplating a liaison with Cathal. You were grasping at life, not realising other options would come along.'

'What options?' I grumble. But he's so kind, so thoughtful. I want to ask him why he never got snapped up by any of the clever women he must have associated with, but I can't think of a way to say it that doesn't look as though I'm fishing for the position. He tells me anyway.

'My mother's only regret is that I haven't married and produced more grandchildren. But becoming a doctor took a lot of time and energy. I had nothing left to give to a family. I would have been one of those absent fathers, or else given myself a nervous breakdown trying to do both.'

'So, you never had a sweetheart?'

He smiles in soft recollection. 'I had a long-term girlfriend. I thought we were in love, but she got tired of waiting. She wanted a family. So eventually she decided to leave.'

'That's sad.'

He shakes his head. 'No, it isn't. She wanted the family more than she wanted to be with me. I was pleased to have discovered that before we ended up being a couple who stayed together for the family but didn't love each other. Then, of course, becoming a GP in my home town, I found I was a very eligible bachelor. A standing in the community, a good wage... there were several local women – good women – who would have married me in a heartbeat, but I'd rather stay single than marry someone who didn't ignite a spark inside me.'

'What's it like, your home?'

'I still live with my mother.' He flashes a twisted smile. 'Sad, I know! But the house has been in my family for generations, and basically, I'm to inherit it. Granddad Jack grew up there. I guess I wouldn't be able to afford to buy it today. It's got four bedrooms and is quite prestigious in the village. It's two hundred years old and made out of local stone. People say it's quaint, but I would rather say it's traditional. It's set back from the road behind a low drystone wall. We have a garage and a lovely garden behind, with apple trees and shrubs. My family grew vegetables there during WW2, through necessity, you understand, but when times got easier, we turned it back to lawn and flowers. It takes a lot of time and energy to grow vegetables, and we're all busy people.'

'What does your mam do?'

He laughs. 'What doesn't she do! If there's a committee, she belongs to it; if there's a charity, she's busy fundraising. She's one of the mainstays of our little community. And on top of that, she's helping the nanny and me to raise Paul.'

'She sounds lovely.'

'She is. I have never regretted my decision to go back home. I don't want to live anywhere else, really. After my training, I bought into the local practice and will probably be there until I die. The height of my ambition is not so very exciting, you see.'

The waiter approaches and says deferentially, 'There are two ladies in reception, asking after you.'

Justin and I snatch a shared glance. 'Are you sure it's us they want?' he asks.

The waiter nods. 'The couple who were asking after Kate O'Brien, they said.' His eyes flick to my callipers, so I'm pretty sure I know what description was given, and how we were so easily identified.

'Can you show them in here, please?' Justin says.

'Certainly, sir.'

'Thank you.'

Two ladies, one about my age, one maybe a generation older, approach us. We stand to greet them. As their eyes adjust to the subdued light, they stare openly. Then the older lady gives a gasp and puts her hand to her mouth. I can see why. The younger woman at her side is so similar to me, I might be looking at my own reflection in a slightly distorted mirror. There's a moment of stunned silence while we take each other in. From the depths of my childhood, a word rises.

'Mammy?' I whisper.

'Oh God, oh God,' the woman whispers. 'Mary?'

30

HANNAH

'Mrs O'Brien?' Justin asks, taking charge of the situation.

The older woman nods, not taking her eyes from me.

'Please come and join us. I'm so sorry, this is a bit of a shock, but, well, it's a shock for us, too. Would you like tea?'

'I don't understand,' the woman says, moving automatically to the proffered seat to sit bolt upright, her bag on her lap. 'It can't be. It's impossible.'

'Please bring a pot of tea,' Justin says to the waiter, who is hovering, agog with interest.

A few minutes later, I'm seated opposite women who are surely my mother and sister, separated by nearly thirty years of lies, and the waiter has placed a large tray between us.

'Strange how tea helps,' Justin says, pouring, filling the awkward silence. 'So, presumably you're Kate O'Brien, and...?'

'My youngest daughter, Ann,' she says, then repeats, 'But I don't understand...'

'I'm Justin, and this is Hannah. We have reason to believe she might be your daughter.'

At this moment, none of us doubt I am, though I have a knot in my chest as I wonder how this woman is going to react towards the daughter she'd abandoned all those years ago. I'm shocked by her next words.

'My Mary died. They phoned me at the shop where I was working. That's how I found out,' Kate says, her eyes never leaving my face. 'I couldn't get into the hospital for such a long time. They told me our little Mary had given up the struggle and just stopped breathing one night.' She takes a shuddering inward breath as if breathing for her child. 'The hospital arranged the burial. We had a funeral service for our baby, but... I don't understand. I mean, how could this even be? Why now?' She takes a shuddering breath. 'Did you always know? Why didn't you come before?'

There's anger in her voice now, but I dispel it with a few words. I shake my head. 'I didn't have the slightest reason to believe I wasn't Mam's child. Not until Dad died.'

'But—'

'Let me explain.'

As I tell them about the will and what the solicitor told me, the accusation on her face gradually slips away.

'So, you see, I had to try to find out, but' – I shake my head in bemusement – 'I never expected this.'

'And, ah' – she indicates Justin – 'your husband...'

I flush, mortified, but Justin takes up the story without faltering. 'No, we're not married. We met only recently, when I came over to Roone Bay to try to trace an ancestor.' He reaches for my hand. 'We both had quests and decided to help each other out. But in all honesty,' he adds, 'we're as surprised as you to find out that Hannah's speculation has turned out to be true. We expected to find nothing at all. I mean, it was so long ago, people must have moved on, died. But why the nurses would have swapped the little girls over is a mystery that almost defies belief. Except that...'

'Except that here we are,' I say numbly and turn my gaze to the girl sitting opposite me, whose expression is sliding slowly from suspicion towards acceptance. 'And it seems as well as discovering a mother, I have a sister, too.'

Kate gives a smile of pride. 'Five children who lived. Three boys, two girls, including Ann, here.' She pauses and adds, 'Maybe three girls, after all.'

'Oh, goodness,' I say under my breath. 'I have more sisters and brothers? But will they want to know me?'

The girl opposite me smiles suddenly and nods, as if she's made her mind up. 'Sure, they will. We all will.'

Justin carries on, 'We thought that Esther's child had died and Mary's mother had abandoned her. That was why Esther took the girl home and brought her up as her own. It seemed like an act of charity, of goodwill. Happenstance, if you like.'

'I didn't abandon my child,' Kate says indignantly. 'I would never have done that.'

'I, ah...' Whatever Justin was going to say dies in his throat. We all stare at him as embarrassment creases his features.

'What?' I ask.

'Well...' He takes a deep breath. 'The only other possibility is that your mother found her child dead and swapped the children. Maybe it wasn't the nurses at all.'

'My mam *stole* a child – I mean, stole me?' I say, aghast.

Kate shakes her head, as if to clear it, and says in a low, agonised voice, 'I *grieved* for my Mary. How could a woman do that to another mother?'

'We don't know that she did,' Justin says. 'I was just proposing an alternative possibility. It might have been a nurse...'

'No,' I say with certainty. 'It makes sense that it was Mam. The nurses would have known that Mary's mother hadn't abandoned her.' I pause, then add, 'But to deprive a mother of her child, and deprive the child of her real mother...' I echo Kate's confusion. 'Could Mam really have done that?'

However, the truth is sitting before me; a fact in everything except proof. My long years of feeling not quite *belonging* are justified, after all. It wasn't just the polio and my disability; it was because I truly didn't belong. Mam had taken another woman's child, maybe in a moment of irrational grief, but she'd always known I wasn't her child, and Dad had known, too. But if he'd informed anyone, Mam would have been in serious trouble. And he would have been running the farm without a wife at home.

'So selfish,' I whisper but still don't want to believe it. 'If we could find who was nursing the children at the time...'

'We've been lucky getting this far,' Justin says. 'Maybe trying to apportion blame at this time is counter-productive.'

'But what if it wasn't a mistake? Shouldn't someone have to account for it?'

'Who? Your mother passed years back, and your father is gone, too,' Justin says reasonably. 'People who have suffered the loss of a child don't always think rationally. It was over twenty-five years ago, and maybe it's unfair to instigate an enquiry now? It might destroy the lives of people who are blameless, which is equally as hard to prove. Whatever happened, there's no undoing it. The question isn't who did it, but where do we go from here?'

I can't take my eyes from Justin's face as he speaks. Empathy, kindness and compassion, added to sheer common sense. He's undoubtedly a good doctor and will surely make some woman a good husband one day. I try to dampen the increasing wish that it could be me.

I reach over the table and clasp one of Kate's hands. She flinches, then accepts the contact. 'Justin's right. You're my mother,' I say firmly. 'I know that as surely as I've ever known anything. Not that I recall much from before hospital. It was as though my life started at that point.'

'And I thought my life stopped at that point,' Kate says. 'When the polio epidemic started, we were all terrified for our children. God help us, but we were all hoping it would be someone else's child, not our own. When you first fell ill, I didn't realise what it was. You were crying, and had a sore throat and a bad headache. I remember giving you cough medicine and feeling annoyed because I had work to do. I didn't think it was anything bad. Just the flu.

'After a couple of days, I remember you screaming for me in the night. I was so tired. I thought you were just being naughty. I tried to make you get up, stand up, and you couldn't. You fell on your face on the carpet and didn't move except for the screaming. That was when I knew it was polio.'

She shudders with the memory.

I jolt. 'I told Mam I remember falling on a carpet,' I say, 'but she said I must have misremembered, because I never had a carpet in my room. There were no carpets in the whole house, just bare floorboards and Mam's rag rugs. I remember the carpet, though, because I couldn't move anything, and all I could see was this long stretch of red leading away towards the door.'

'It *was* red,' Kate agreed. 'I wrapped you in a blanket and took you to the doctor. He called an ambulance, and they took you away. I only saw you twice after that. I was allowed to go as far as the little window in the door to the ward. There were rows and rows of beds with little children, all with polio. I waved and waved, and finally you saw me, but you got really upset and screamed because I didn't go in and pick you up. The nurses told me it was best to stay away, then.'

Kate is crying as she speaks. 'I stayed away for a long time. I don't know how I lived through those weeks. I phoned several times and spoke to someone on the telephone. They told me you couldn't swallow at one stage. They were giving you wet rags to suck. They told me you were being given extra air to breathe, so I thought that was the end. When the polio stops a child from swallowing, or stops the muscles that do the breathing... I'd learned about it by then, you see. But still you survived.'

She takes a deep breath. 'Then one day they phoned me. I knew it was bad before the nurse said anything. They told me you had died. We were advised not to open the little coffin for fear of infection. It was the most awful time. I'd had two miscarriages before, but having a child of three years old die was the worst thing ever. It took me a long time to get through it. I had good neighbours, a good husband and other children to care for. But I thought about you every day. And now I find you were alive all that time, and that some other child had died. How could your mother do that to me? How could she?'

'We don't really know what happened,' Justin reminds everyone. 'It might have been a mix-up in the hospital.'

'A mother knows her own child,' Kate says harshly, wiping her eyes.

I swipe my eyes and realise Justin's eyes are bright, too.

'I'm sorry – I didn't mean to get upset. It was a long time ago.'

'Some things stay with you forever,' he says gently. 'And polio is such a cruel disease.'

There's a long silence, and I sense we're all thinking of all the children and families who suffered.

'The nurses must have known us all, too. Surely they would have known which girl survived and which one died? I guess we'll never know the truth of what happened.'

'This is all very miserable,' Kate says on a slight hiccup. 'When you were taken home, were you happy? Were they good to you, these people?'

As I tell her a little of my life, I try to underplay the desperate poverty, my lack of schooling, the years I spent nursing the people I believed were my parents. I dwell on the farm, the chickens, Old Grey and most especially my relationship with Aine. 'Certainly, Mam treated me as her daughter,' I say finally. 'She was kind and caring while I was little, though her illness gradually reversed our roles. But my father was always cold towards me. At least now I understand why.'

'Now it's too late,' Kate snips, swiping away tears for the poor unloved child I had been. 'What a horrible, selfish man. I'm glad he's dead. If he wasn't, you wouldn't have found out the truth.'

'It wasn't all bad,' I say softly.

But she's right; if the solicitor had died before Dad, I never would have learned any of this. I would never have known why Dad cut me out of the will. I think about Mark. He knows I'm not Dad's daughter, from the terms of the will, but he doesn't know the truth – that I wasn't Mam's, either.

'So, please, tell me about your family... my family,' I amend with a slight laugh. 'I'm curious to know what my life would have been like had I not been taken home by the wrong mother.'

After a faltering start, Kate talks, and gradually the tension eases. She's still a seamstress, mainly making wedding dresses these days. It's quite lucrative, she informs us, pride mixed with unpretentiousness. She reaches for Ann's hand and tells us that Ann designs the dresses and is gradually taking charge of the business along with her sister. All of her children – my sisters and brothers – are still in Ireland. Three are married, including Ann, who has a baby of her own, presently being looked after by her husband. The old ways are surely changing, I think. Dad never provided Mam with relief from the unending care of their children. It just wasn't how things worked.

'Do you remember anything about what happened? Kate asks. 'I know you were just three when you left home, but surely you recall something about me, about your home life? Before you were taken?'

'Did you used to sing to me?' I ask. 'I have a snatch of a song in my head, something about a bird in a cage...'

Kate smiles. 'You mean the music hall song?' She sings

under her breath, in a sweet voice, '*She's only a bird in a gilded cage, a beautiful sight to see. You may think she's happy and free from care, she's not, though she seems to be...*'

'Oh!' I say in wonder.

'Mam is always singing,' Ann says, smiling for the first time. 'She has a wonderful voice, so she has. And about a million songs!'

Kate laughs. 'Not quite so many.'

'I always wondered if I was misremembering,' I muse, bringing a new wave of sorrow to Kate's features. 'Mam never sang, yet I had that in the back of my head the whole time.'

'Well, I think this is just like a fairy tale,' Justin says, smiling. 'Your own family have pretty much disowned you...'

'Except for Aine.'

'All except your sister,' he amends. 'And now you've found an entirely new family who want to know you. How about that?'

31

HANNAH

I hide a yawn behind my hand.

'We're pretty tired,' Justin says. 'It's been a long day, physically and emotionally. Maybe we should all step back and get used to the idea?' he suggests, rising from his chair.

Justin's right. I'm exhausted. I rise, not taking my eyes from this woman, my mother, who looks as confounded as me. 'We can't go back and change things, but we can create new bonds, can't we?'

'We surely can.' Kate's tears are now sliding openly, for the grief she'd shed for her lost child, the grief that she should haven't have had to experience. I realise that we've all slid quietly towards the belief that it was the woman I'd called Mam who had swapped the babies.

Kate stands, too, clutching her bag like a lifeline. She takes a deep breath. 'Well, now,' she says resolutely. 'It's time for you to come home. You don't have to worry about the future any longer. We have a spare room...'

'No, I can't. Not yet.' I rest my hand on her shoulder. 'Gladly, I'll visit, meet the family. That will be a moment, I guess! But you need to talk this through with everyone first. I'd love to visit, when we're all a bit more used to the idea. This is so much to take in. I believe you're my birth mother, but your family have no idea...'

'But what will you do? Where will you go? You will come back?' She looks panicked. 'Promise me, if you have nowhere, you will come to me?'

'I will, of course. This is all so very strange.'

'Happy strange,' Justin amends.

'Happy strange,' I agree, echoing his smile. 'We'll get to know each other, of course, but right now, I have to go back and sort my own life out so that I can move on. We will write.'

'We will, surely! I want to know everything. I mustn't lose you all over again. Can't you stay a while?'

I hear pleading in her voice but shake my head. 'There are things that need sorting, not least the confusion in my mind. I don't care about inheriting the farm now. I've come to terms with that, but I have to make my own way. If we write long and often, next time we meet, we'll be a little bit closer.'

We've gathered in a huddle by the table, talking of leaving, yet no one wants to make the first move.

'It's best that I drive you home, too, Mam,' Ann says gently. 'Father will be wondering...'

'My father?' I ask in astonishment. 'I have a father, too?'

'Sure, you have,' Kate says firmly. 'You should come...'

Ann shakes her head. 'I don't think Dad will be so easily convinced. Hannah's right – we all need time.'

Kate nods, finally accepting this. 'But, Hannah... I can't call you Mary, can I?'

'I've been Hannah for too long to change now.'

'You won't forget, will you?'

I laugh in astonishment. 'Forget? How could I?'

Kate hesitantly holds her arms out, and hesitantly I walk into them. We cling tightly for a long moment, the invisible bonds of mother and child rising through the mists of trauma.

She writes her details on a scrap of paper, and I tell her to send letters to the post office at Roone Bay until I know what I'm going to do. We make promises, inviolable pledges, for the future. Then Justin and I stand at the front of the hotel and watch them walk away into the darkness of the car park; my birth mother and a sister I didn't know I had. My mother stops once and stares back at me for a long moment before turning away again, as stunned as I am by the day's unexpected revelations.

'Are you all right?' Justin asks, eyeing me keenly.

I laugh. 'I'm more than all right. You have—' I search for the words. 'You, this trip, everything. Thank you. I've been only half awake my whole life, and suddenly doors I didn't know existed have opened. I'm not bound to the farm. I'm not going to marry Cathal. I don't care about the inheritance; the man I thought was my brother will take everything, and suddenly I don't mind. Everything I thought I was, the life I had thrust upon me, it was all a lie. I feel lighter, freer, as if I've finally been given permission to leave. I want to leave. You did that, so thank you!'

'Glad to be of service,' he says lightly, but his features settle into an expression of satisfaction, and I think he understands that I've made a decision to find my own future. The internal inadequacy that had been fostered by the man I thought was my father has dissipated. He didn't love me, never did; and now I know why, I realise that the anger he felt towards Mam for her actions had been directed unfairly onto the child she stole, as if it were my fault. I should feel hurt, but what I feel is unburdened.

'Well, you have to admit, neither of us expected that,' I say to Justin as we turn to go in. I'm drooping with pain and exhaustion, and I don't think I'm hiding it too well as we make our way towards the stairs and I struggle with the first step.

'Can you manage?' he asks, concerned.

'How else will I get up there?'

I'm joking, but he says, 'I can carry you.'

Good Lord, I think. He would, too. I rather like the idea, but flush wildly and lean on the banister, heaving myself up one difficult stair at a time. Justin doesn't insist on carrying me, but he does put a strong arm around my waist, taking my weight. Unlike men like my father and Cathal, his true strength is hidden beneath a mantle of sophistication, all the more powerful for being so.

At the door to my room, I admit, 'I'm totally exhausted. I mean, it's bizarre, isn't it? I'm going to wake up and find it was all a dream.'

He cocks an eyebrow. 'The law of unintended consequences. They do have a habit of making life a bit more interesting, don't you think?'

I laugh with him. 'Well, I think I've had enough surprises for a while. In the morning, we'd better get back to Roone Bay and see what unfolds. I'm going to tell the solicitor I'm not going to fight the will.'

'Are you sure? You're certainly owed something of the inheritance for your loyalty, and I'd like to see Mark get his just deserts.'

'All that effort for revenge? I don't think so. Let's put our efforts into finding out what happened to your granddad, then we can both get on with our lives.'

'You still want to help me with that?'

'Of course,' I say, surprised.

I tell myself it's because I'm curious – which I am, of course – but deep in my heart I know it's because I want to spend as much time as I can with Justin. He doesn't see my disability as something to be ashamed of. He lifts my spirits. He makes me feel all the things I should have been feeling as I was growing into a young woman: interesting, intelligent, desirable even. He's going to walk out of my life as suddenly as he walked into it, and I want to hang on to this moment for a little longer.

I haven't told Justin what Turlough told me about the rebels hanging his granddad. I don't want to, in all honesty. Let him hold on to the dream. 'If we don't find out the truth,' I suggest, 'maybe we could still lay a wreath up on the hills, near the old standing stone. There's a kind of closure in that.'

He holds my gaze intently for a moment, his smile broad and sincere. 'You are a wonder, Hannah Barry,' he says, and after a tiny hesitation, he leans forward and pecks a kiss on my cheek. 'Sleep well. I'm really happy for you.'

32

JACK, 1920

As often as he could, Jack walked up the hill behind the barracks in the hope of meeting Aisling. From the frequency of their accidental meetings, he was sure she was seeking him out equally as determinedly. His colleagues said he was a fool for going out on his own, that they were supposed to work in pairs, that he would get himself shot by some vigilante rebel, but he said he needed the freedom, the fresh air, after the traumas of the war. Knowing nothing of his fairy woman, they shrugged. If he got shot dead, they grumbled, he couldn't say he hadn't been warned.

Jack didn't have to walk far to be out of sight of the barracks, and once there, he would keenly peruse the landscape, seeking Aisling. He never saw her before she saw him. It was a game he would never win. She would rise from behind some rock or other, like a child with a toy gun, and say, 'Bang, you're dead!' which made him smile every time. He felt gauche and clumsy in her presence, not able to jest in response. He was simply too entrenched in his internal conflicts to play pretend games. He wondered why she sought him out; surely he was the most boring man on the hill. But he found comfort in her secret presence, and he knew she felt the same.

Sometimes they would simply walk together without talking. She would point out the sun's path over the sea, a seagull overhead, a rainbow in the mist, a hare on the mountain, and he would see beauty through her eyes. He knew that one day his secret would get him killed. He was falling in love with this tempestuous girl, with her ragged clothes and tousled black hair. No, there was no doubt about it: he had fallen in love in the most absolute way possible. He tried to rationalise his own actions, tell himself that it wasn't real, that he had just been in the army too long and any girl would have made his body sing the way it did when he saw her. But he knew that wasn't true. Whenever he closed his eyes, it was Aisling's face he saw, Aisling's laugh that rang inside his head and Aisling's trim young body that he yearned to hold.

It was Sod's Law, he told himself – or Murphy's Law, now he was in Ireland – that he had to be on the other side of the fence from the girl he fancied. No, not just fancied; wanted with all his being. He had little flights of fancy about making love to her, but his emotions ran deeper than that. He wanted to hold her close to his heart, show his love every day with presents and flowers. He wanted to marry her, to hold her, until they faded into old age and death.

He had married Rose simply and selfishly because he didn't want to go off to war a virgin, but once a child came along, he felt trapped. He tried hard to recall Rose's face, to impose it on his dreams, but he could not. All he could see was Aisling, her vibrant love of life, the practised way she handled the rifle and the dreadful clothes she wore: half male, half female, with the too-big boots. He'd never met a woman like her. In comparison, his English Rose quite simply paled into insignificance.

He'd told Aisling about Rose, about his son, about his narrow vision of life before the war.

She'd told him about growing up in a small community, with all the restrictions and expectations of being a pretty girl destined for marriage and an endless string of children. It wasn't *if* she would marry, she'd said, but which young man and when. The girls were lined up like wallflowers in the dance hall, waiting to be asked.

'Why?' he'd asked.

'Because that's just how it is,' she'd explained. The boys ask and the girl is expected to choose. And from that point, she is no longer in charge of her own body.'

'That's kind of mediaeval.'

'It's not the same in England?'

'Not quite that bad.'

'So,' she'd said, 'I decided I would never marry.'

'And now?'

Her eyes had met his seriously. 'Things would need to change.'

'They would.'

But he dreamed. There was something magical growing between him and Aisling. When the war was over, would he be able to go home and take up the reins of a normal policing job in Somerset? He doubted it. Instead, he imagined Aisling living with him in his old cottage in Somerset. He imagined them having children together, and drafted all sorts of daft notions in his head about Rose being unfaithful to him so that he could blame her and legally divorce her, so that he could marry his love, his wild Irish fairy woman.

Daytime, however, brought cold reality. He was married, with a son. The letters he received from Rose and his mother were loving and kind and hopeful for the future, making him feel like a real cad. He was told how well his little boy was doing, that they'd told him he would soon meet his father, and his father would live with them in the house and never have to go off to war again.

He replied with guilty lies about how much he was looking forward to going home to be with them again and felt ashamed at his own deception. But how could he tell Rose, who had waited faithfully for several years, that he had fallen in love with someone else?

He tried to believe his relationship with Aisling was platonic, but he yearned to touch her. Sometimes his hand would involuntarily brush the air towards her, but he always managed to pull himself to task before completing an action he couldn't take back. He wondered if she noticed how difficult it was for him to restrain himself. Maybe she felt the same way but was wise to the repercussions of being with a man. A man could always walk away from a thoughtless liaison; a woman would bear the shame and social disapproval forever.

Then came the day everything changed.

He met Aisling once again in the secret grotto by the ancient spring and discarded his sand-coloured jacket as had become habit. When they rose to part, her to disappear into the landscape, he to trudge back to the cold and unwelcoming barracks, she bid him goodbye with a cheeky smile and a flash of her dark eyes. She unexpectedly put her arm around him and gave him a hug. Almost involuntarily, Jack pulled her close and was kissing her fiercely. A long moment later, he realised she wasn't responding but struggling fiercely, trying to free herself. He instantly released her and with the shock of self-loathing sank to his knees by the silent moss-rimmed pool.

She leaped up and ran.

Head in hand he stayed there a long while, on his knees, repeating, 'I'm sorry, I'm sorry, I'm sorry...' as if it would turn the clock back. In the lonely silence, he gathered his jacket, buckled everything smartly in place and stumbled back to the barracks. He didn't think he'd ever see her again. There was no saving him. War had unmanned him. If the rebels killed him now, he'd accept their sentence with the knowledge that they were right. It would have been better if he'd died in the trenches of France.

33

HANNAH

On the way home, I find myself saying, 'What Mam did, it wasn't right.'

'I'm guessing she must have been consumed by grief. If she did it on the spur of the moment, she maybe couldn't find a way to undo it without causing grief to the rest of her family,' Justin says. 'She must have learned to love you.'

'Maybe Mam was so lost in grief for her dead daughter that she didn't know what she was doing. But a different child can't replace the one who died.'

'No,' he agrees.

I'm still stunned by the revelations. 'I mean, how *could* she?'

'But there was kindness, wasn't there? It wasn't all bad?'

'There was, when I was small, but mostly I recall Mam being tired and ill. I was a teenager when she passed. I think Dad blamed me for that, in some peculiar way. He told her once that he couldn't bear the sight of me.'

Justin is clearly shocked. 'No, really?'

'He didn't know I could hear him. I guess the truth just slipped out. Before that, I overheard him say to Mam that she should never have brought me home from the hospital, that I was just a useless mouth to feed. At the time, I thought it was because of the polio, but it must have been because I wasn't their child. He also said if I was an animal, he would have had me put down. That's not something you forget, is it?'

'It was a horrible thing to even think, never mind say out loud.'

'He grew up in hard times.'

'So did you,' Justin says dryly. 'You can't justify your father's actions. He was a fool. You've grown into this kind, beautiful, wonderful person despite him. You see yourself as disabled, but no one else in Roone Bay sees you that way.'

He casts his eyes at me briefly.

'You've been talking about me to people in town?'

'Not exactly. I was seen with you on the donkey cart, so it became a national scandal. I think I was being warned off, in case I meant you harm.'

'It's amazing what I'm learning in hindsight. It would have been nice to know that people cared about me,' I say testily.

'Better late than never.' His lips quirk in a faint smile. 'When I was trying to get people to talk about the past, in the last couple of days, all they wanted to know was what my intentions were towards you. No one ever asked if I was talking to Hannah, the disabled girl. All I heard was, *Hannah, such a loyal daughter, Adrian really didn't deserve her.*'

I don't know how to answer that. Dad always called me a cripple, if he called me anything at all, so I assumed that's what everyone said. Justin might be lying, but if so, it's kind lying. The kind of lies, Mam would have said, that the good Lord would forgive a body for.

Instead of driving through the tiny, winding passes over the mountain, Justin chooses to take the easier route to the south, via Kilmichael, where the narrow road winds through rugged, scrubby hills down to Dunmanway. This is ancient landscape, untouched by farming, where huge rocks litter the ice-scoured bedrock, and a thin smatter of soil supports a messy forest of stunted trees. We pass a monument to an IRA ambush in which a group of Black and Tans were all killed. It's not hard to imagine the IRA disappearing into these hills after their guerrilla activities, harassing and disrupting the Black and Tans' military strategies.

I point out the bleak grey cross that rises through a surrounding thicket of untamed shrub. 'That's where the Irish flying column ambushed a brigade of Black and Tans, in 1920, and killed twenty of their men. You know *kil* means church in Irish? It doesn't refer to the men who died.'

'I do,' he answers. 'Kilmichael, the Church of Michael. Called so by the Scots who first inhabited this area. You aren't the only one who reads, you know.'

I laugh. 'I'm the only one here who's done little else.'

'Well, that can be remedied.'

He slows and peers up. 'I read that the rebels lost a couple of men themselves.'

'They did, but they became martyrs. It was a great victory for Ireland. It boosted the morale of the Irish people who were fighting for the cause.'

The drive back to Roone Bay is all too short. We slide into companionable silence. I'm mulling over the strange outcome of our visit to Macroom, and I suppose Justin is consumed by his own quest. We're back in Roone Bay by midday. He drives us up to Noel's house and insists on walking me up the steps to the front door and ringing the bell as though I'm not capable of doing it myself. Mrs Weddows opens the door wide, inviting us in. 'Noel is in the lounge,' she says. 'He said for you to go on in.'

'I just need to collect Old Grey and hitch the cart,' I say. 'I don't want to trouble anyone.'

She gives a pursed-up smile that could be annoyance or

amusement. 'Noel's curiosity will be the death of him. I'm not to let you away until he has the whole story.'

I exchange a laugh with Justin, and we both dutifully make our way into the impressive room, to find Noel lounging before a blazing fire, Caitlin in an easy chair beside him, knitting something in violent shades of purple and orange. She casts her knitting aside, while Noel rises to greet us, waving effusively towards a sofa, saying 'Come, come, come, sit and warm yourselves. So, what's new or strange?'

Caitlin laughs. She has a welcoming aura, pulling us towards her in some indefinable way, making us feel at home. 'Give them a chance to get in through the door, my love.' Then to me: 'You might not want to go on up to the farm at all.'

'Why wouldn't I?'

'Grace told me that Mark has left the hotel and moved up into *his* farm in your absence.'

'Oh.' I suspect his finances are being stretched by an extended stay. 'He thought he could just come over, put the farm in the hands of an agent, and go back to America and wait for it to be sold,' I say.

Noel nods. 'But the solicitor told him that nothing will happen, this year or any other year, if the deeds don't make an appearance.'

'So, until we know the whole story, you will stay here,' Caitlin adds, picking up her knitting again. The needles move almost of their own volition, so familiar is the action to her.

I'm too tired to argue. 'What are you making?' I ask as we sit.

'Best to ask what she hasn't made,' Noel jokes, rolling his eyes.

'A blanket,' she says, pulling the complex pattern across her knee for me to view. 'Grace is presenting us with a great-grandchild soon.'

'That's beautiful!'

'She doesn't hold with baby pastels – she wants this child to grow up with as much colour in its life as possible, to use her own words.'

'Is that your first great-grandchild?' Justin asks.

'Oh, no. Grace has Olivia, from a previous marriage.'

I knew this, of course. Everyone in Roone Bay knows how Grace ran here from England to escape a controlling husband, only to discover true love and quite accidentally reunited her grandmother with Noel, who had been her first love half a century before. There's something quiet and beautiful about their relationship, probably the result of a couple able to bypass the roller coaster of marriage, work and children, and go straight for twilight contentment. But Caitlin, despite her age, still betrays hints of the vibrant beauty she must have once been.

I try not to be envious. I can only dream of such love. Clumping about in my thick-soled shoes, my dead legs and twisted feet aren't likely to make me the recipient of anyone's romantic desires. I don't realise I've sighed out loud until Caitlin leans forward. 'Is everything all right, *a chara?*'

I laugh away my discontent and glance at Justin, brows raised in query. 'Actually, everything is amazingly all right.'

Noel and Caitlin wait, expectantly, for more.

Justin smiles and leans back comfortably, a little wave of his hand offering me the stage. 'Go on, tell them. It's your story.'

It falls from me in a rush of words, accompanied by exclamations of astonishment from Noel and Caitlin.

'So, Adrian and Esther weren't your real parents at all.' Caitlin's statement is filled with satisfaction. 'And that horrible man, Mark, is not your brother. When I learned what he was about, I was tempted to go up there and give him a piece of my mind.'

'She would have, too,' Noel says with a laugh. 'But I asked her not to interfere. People need to find their own path, make their own decisions.'

'Says the man who has a finger in everyone else's pie,' Caitlin says, casting him a fake frown.

'I do not!'

'Great fool!' she mutters. 'So, Hannah, my dear, what will you do now? Your birth mother has offered you a home – why wouldn't you go there?'

I grimace. 'I don't know how her family would react. They might be the kindest people in the world, but I'd still feel like a duck in their henhouse.'

'It was a donkey in a field of thoroughbreds yesterday,' Justin reminds me.

'Well, you know what I mean! I do want to get to know her, and my sisters and brothers, but to go there to live, well, it would be like accepting the charity of strangers. I can't just plonk myself on them and expect it to work out, can I?'

'Sure it will!' Caitlin says vehemently. 'But if you don't go there, where will you go?'

'Well,' I say, 'I'm thinking I'll go to London, to be with Aine, after all. I'm sure I can find work of some kind.'

'But would you be happy in London?' Caitlin asks softly.

'She wouldn't, of course,' Justin answers for me. 'But there are other options. With her father gone, and the farm stolen out from under her, she can finally get out and discover a life for herself.'

He reaches over for my hand and pats it companionably. His eyes meet mine, and his smile seems to be for me alone. Does he like me, truly? Am I imagining it? After all the excitement of the last couple of days, I find myself fighting off tears. It's not fair of him to make me feel wanted in that way when I know he's going to waltz out of my life as easily as he came into it.

Caitlin's shrewd glance makes heat rise in my cheeks, and I pull my hand from Justin's and tuck it into my lap. 'So,' I say brightly, focusing my gaze on Noel, 'did you find out anything about Justin's granddad while we were away?'

Before he can answer, there's a soft knock, and Mrs Weddows puts her head around the door. 'There's someone here asking after Hannah.' My fleeting dismay that it's Mark is dissipated by her following words. 'It's her sister, Aine.'

'Well, show her in!' Noel exclaims.

But I'm already rising cumbersomely to my feet with shocked pleasure as Aine erupts into the room like a whirlwind, reaching for me, her whole face alight. I burst into tears. She seems taller than ever and thin as a whippet, but the strength of her arms around me is solid and familiar.

'Oh my God, Hannah,' she says finally, pushing me back to stare at me through her tears. 'Look at you! You're all grown up! I was so afraid... I came as soon as I could and found you gone from the house, and Mark with no clue where you were. What a langer he is! He's more like our father than ever.'

She pushes me back and looks me up and down. 'You're coming home with me, Hannah. I'm not standing for any arguments. We have our own flat now, and—' She stops suddenly and turns to a man who's followed her, somewhat hesitantly, into the room. 'Oh, ah, this is Danny, my fiancé.'

Danny has to be the widest man I've ever seen. He's shorter than Aine by half a head, and he's mutilating a hat of some kind between massive hands, a smile lurking below a nose that has probably been broken more than once.

'Come on in, Danny. The more the merrier,' Noel says, obviously amused, and pulls a couple of upright chairs closer to the fire.

'Engaged?' I squeak. 'Oh, Aine! You should have said!'

'I wanted to tell you myself. And after that last letter you sent, about Mark and the inheritance, and Cathal, I had to come and make sure you were all right. I was afraid I'd find you gone and no trace... I'm so mad with Mark, I could kill him.'

She steps aside to let Danny greet me, and my hand briefly disappears inside his. 'She's told me about your ma and your da, and everything,' he says in a voice that rumbles gently in low gear, like an old tractor. 'I just want to say, you must come and live with us. Plenty of room.'

Noel introduces Caitlin and tells them that Justin is a doctor, come over from England in search of his past. Aine's eyes flit between me and Justin questioningly. I give a tiny shake of my head, but I don't think my denial is very convincing.

'Well, sate yourselves down,' Noel says.

Mrs Weddows is standing by the open door, waiting for a pause in the dialogue. 'More tea?' she asks.

'If we're not intruding?' Danny says deferentially.

'Lord, no,' Noel exclaims. 'Distraction is what we all needed! Come on – take a seat. Make yourselves at home. And what do you do for a living?' Noel eyes Danny curiously as we all settle, unconcerned by the jab in the ribs provided by his wife.

'Sure, let the man in the door!' Caitlin admonishes.

'Boxer,' Danny says. 'Middleweight.'

Noel's face lights up. 'Successful?'

'Moderately,' he says modestly, but Aine's having none of it.

'He's, like, famous, on telly and everything,' she informs everyone proudly.

Noel beams. 'Thought I recognised your face.'

'Not forgettable, eh?' Danny says, his smile relaxing somewhat. 'I've had a few makeovers in my time.'

Within minutes, Noel has Danny talking about his latest fight, and they both cut the air with hands that illustrate punches, counter punches, uppercuts and hooks.

When Mrs Weddows brings in a huge tray, Danny jumps up to take it from her and places it on a small table, asking, 'Shall I be mum?'

For some reason, that incongruous statement makes us all

dissolve into laughter. As the cups are handed around, Noel tells Justin that Turlough turned up briefly while we were away.

'Oh, I missed him!' Justin exclaims, disappointed. 'So, did you get to talk to him at all?'

'Not me. Sure, I think he has a fear of the Big House, deep-seated from the past. But he stopped Jane in the street down below.'

'And? What did he tell her?' Justin leans forward eagerly.

'It was difficult to work out, but the gist of it seems to be that there was some kind of scandal.' He glances at Justin with a hint of apology. 'Apparently, Jack took a fancy to a local girl, Aisling Crowley. Her family are still here, in Roone Bay. They won't say anything at all, him being a Black and Tan, you see.'

'But he was married,' Justin says, surprised.

'He was a man, just back from war,' Noel counters with a faint smile. 'Apparently, she was a feisty girl, handier with a rifle than a needle. Turlough said she worked with the IRA. He didn't say in what capacity, but I doubt the Black and Tans would have suspected her. It would have been unusual for a woman to be involved, but it seems she was quite a character, almost a local legend. Even so, it certainly would have been a scandal for a woman to be interested in one of the enemy soldiers.'

'They weren't soldiers, and they weren't all bad,' Justin says defensively.

'Maybe so, but they were difficult times. I doubt such a liaison would have gone down well with either side. But I think what Turlough was trying to tell us was that Aisling moved away to Kerry after the barracks was burned. If she's still alive, and if you can find her, she might be able to tell you what happened to your Jack.'

The words dangle in the air like bait, and Justin exclaims,

'Trumped! I was about ready to go back to England, but it seems I'm off to Kerry. I hope it's not a wild goose chase.'

'Turlough is a little, ah, different, but I'd say if he told us that, it would be with good reason.' Noel looks down at his hands. 'He travels widely, you know. It wouldn't surprise me to find he knows more than he's saying.'

I know he does, of course. I wonder if this Aisling is the girl he raped. Part of me doesn't want Justin to find out the hurtful truth.

'She might be alive, then, this Aisling?' he suggests with bright interest.

'She'd be younger than me, and I'm still around,' Noel says.

Justin laughs. 'Okay. But Kerry is a big county. Did he give any clues where I would start looking?'

'Well, I asked around a bit. The Crowleys aren't talking, but I found out they have family in Killorglin, so that might be a good place to start.'

'Where's that?'

'Just a moment.'

Noel hops up and disappears, coming back a moment later, wrestling open a large Ordnance Survey map, indicating for Justin to join him at the big table. A moment later, they're both engrossed in working out the best routes.

At this point, Caitlin decides to take her leave. 'Excuse me. I'm not being rude – I told Grace I'd help cover the hotel reception,' she says, then turns to me. 'How about you and your sister catch up, then you can all come over to the hotel for a meal?'

'I don't want to be a nuisance…'

She laughs. 'Sure, won't it give the chef something to do? It's fair quiet at the moment.'

When Caitlin is gone, Aine turns to me, her hand tucked firmly in Danny's. She radiates happiness. 'So, will you come and live with us? Really. You can't stay here on your own.'

I shake my head, not so much in negativity as indecision. A

few days ago, I didn't know where I was going to live if I didn't marry Cathal and keep the farm, but now I've been offered a home by Mickey Hoolihan, Noel and Caitlin, Aine and Danny, and my birth mother. My life seems to be filled with people who care. How very strange that seems.

I change the subject. 'So, how did you two meet?'

Aine embarks on a convoluted story about a mix-up during a date in which she was asked to make up a foursome, and somehow the couples swapped partners in the course of the evening, after which Danny came around to ask her out. 'I wasn't sure, to start with,' she says frankly. 'Because of the boxing, you see. I don't like that kind of thing, never did.'

'But I wasn't having no for an answer,' Danny says. 'I knew she was all right, the moment I saw her.'

'And he's going to give up boxing when we start a family. I don't want our children to have a brain-damaged father.'

'No, I'm not,' Danny states. 'I'm a boxer. It's what I am.'

Aine sighs. 'Well, I tried.'

They exchange a glance that says everything. She's proud of his success and afraid for the future at the same time. But sometimes you don't choose – fate chooses for you.

She turns the conversation back to me. 'I'm really angry at Mark, thinking to sell the farm out from under you. He can't just turf you out of your home,' she says. 'My Danny will go and sort him out.'

'No, I won't,' Danny says placidly.

I cast him a conspiratorial smile. This isn't something that can be settled with fists, no matter how handy he is with them.

'He's inherited the farm, Aine,' I say. 'So be it. Actually—' I look down at my hands and pause, realising that I'm telling myself a truth that's been long hidden. I never thought I wanted to leave Roone Bay, but now I find I don't want to stay; my whole life, it seems, has been a lie. 'I've been vegetating here too long already. I don't know what I'm going to do, but it's time I moved on.'

'So, you'll come to London, then,' she states.

'I don't know. But Dad leaving the farm to Mark, and everything else...' I nearly blurt out everything, but the time isn't right. 'I've been constrained by these...' I tap the ironwork on my legs.

'Don't use that as an excuse. It was that stupid promise you made to Mam!' she snaps.

'You're right. Mam should never have asked it of me.' *Especially knowing what I know now*, I think. 'But being bitter about what can't be undone is self-defeating. I could maybe get a job as a librarian. I've certainly had enough experience there.'

Justin and Noel rejoin us at the fire.

'It's settled, so,' Noel states. 'Justin is going to drive over to Killorglin, see if he can't find this Aisling Crowley, if she's to be found at all.'

'I've been steamrollered,' Justin says, turning to me. 'Will you come and keep me company? It would be useful to hide behind your Irish accent when asking questions about the Black and Tans.'

I'm torn. Justin's right that people are more likely to talk to me than him. I don't want to lose the chance to spend a couple more days in his company, but my sister, who I haven't seen for too many years, has made the effort to be here for me, so I feel obliged to stay. 'I'd love to, but I don't think it will be possible...'

Aine casts me an amused glance, as if she can read my mind. 'Right,' she says. 'We'll come, too. Danny has never seen Ireland, and I've been told the Killarney lakes are worth a look, even in winter. I'm sure there will be a hotel with rooms at this time of year.'

'Sure,' Danny agrees. 'We can all go in my car.'

'But the cost!'

'Hannah, dearest,' Aine says, 'I can afford a hotel for a couple of nights!'

'Right popular, she is,' Danny says complacently. 'Going places, you know. Though I'm trying to persuade her we should start a family as soon as we're married. Like me, she ain't getting any younger. You'll come to the wedding, of course, in June.'

'Danny!' Aine exclaims, blushing, but her glance is full of love.

It's strange to me that she's ended up with a boxer, knowing her dislike of violent sports. But we don't choose who we love, do we? And we don't always make good choices. I made a dreadful mistake with Cathal, but thank goodness I realised in time. I am pleased for Aine, I really am – that one of us at least has found true happiness. But I can't help wondering if I will ever find that too.

34

HANNAH

The next morning, Caitlin states, 'When you come back, you'll stay with us, of course, at least until Mark has taken himself away to America, and no argument! Seems he takes after his father, with the drinking. That man is a danger to himself and everyone else at the moment.'

It never occurred to me that Mark might become violent towards me, but it's a relief not to have to face him at this time, knowing what I now know. He has the vindication of knowing I have no inheritance rights at all on the property. If he's up there tearing the house to shreds looking for deeds that have mysteriously vanished, at best he isn't going to be pleasant company. I nod, still bemused by the unexpected concern of people I'd barely said hello to before Dad died. 'But what about my chickens? Mark won't think to feed them.'

'As it's unlikely that you'll be going back there to live, shall I ask Mickey Hoolihan to bring them away?' Caitlin suggests, then without waiting for my answer, says, 'I'll phone him. He can just nip away over with his truck and fetch them to his own barn.'

'What if he doesn't want them?'

'Sure, he'll want them,' Noel jokes. 'He wouldn't dare say no to Caitlin.'

I laugh. Well, chickens don't cost so much to keep, and more eggs won't go amiss in a big family, and it's one worry from my mind.

After breakfast, Aine and Danny arrive at the Big House, and I learn that Aine has decided to take me to the shops.

'It's time you had some decent clothes. You look like a waif kicked out of an orphanage.'

'But I haven't—'

'No point arguing when she's made up her mind,' Danny says placidly. 'Trust me, I know. She has a habit of being right, but she could have found a nicer way to say it. From what I've heard, your dad didn't treat you well.'

That doesn't quite describe it, I think.

'Well, Hannah, we're going to put that right,' Aine says determinedly. 'We're going to make you look beautiful for that man of yours.'

I flush violently, wondering if there's been talk about me and Cathal. 'What man?'

'The English doctor, of course. Sure, isn't he lathering himself over you?'

'I, ah—'

'You didn't realise?' Aine chortles with delight and starts to hum the wedding march.

'Stop, love, you're embarrassing your sister,' Danny advises.

'Sure, and I didn't mean any harm. Well, if it's for him or for yourself, it's time you had a care to your appearance. Ye look like something dragged from the bog, so ye do.'

I don't quite agree with that statement, and it's hard not to take offence, but this is Roone Bay, where people are used to me. She would be ashamed of me in London, no doubt. I've never worried about my appearance, because no one ever notices anything except the callipers, and their eyes slide away in embarrassment. Nice clothes aren't going to change that at all. I think about the minimal clothes I have up at the farm, the skirts made from tough, serviceable fabrics that I've mended many times over. There's little enough I'd go back to pack, in all honesty. 'I could do with some new clothes if I'm to go to England,' I admit on a sigh. 'I'll pay you back when I get a job.'

'Ye won't. Ye've suffered long enough at the hands of our father. Buying you some nice things is my way of making up for having left you with him in the first place. I'm glad he's dead!'

'Aine!'

'No, but I am. He didn't love anyone except maybe Mam, a long time ago, and there's no one will disagree with me.'

She's probably right there, but a pang of guilt hits me in the gut that I'm still withholding so much from her. I just can't bear to tell her that she's not my real sister. I don't think I could cope with her knowing that.

'Will ye come shopping with us?' Aine asks Danny.

He winces theatrically at the suggestion. 'Me and Justin is gonna take a walk down the road. According to Noel, there's a nice little bar down the way.'

There's only one shop selling clothes in Roone Bay, and by Aine's dismissive expression, it's madly out of date. Still, what she buys me is a draper's yard better than what I already own. I absolutely refuse to let Aine buy all the fripperies she wants me to have, though. What use have I got for perfume, silk scarves and embroidered handkerchiefs? I agree to two skirts, longer than is the fashion but shorter than the ones I presently wear, two blouses, two cardigans, a smart coat and some new underwear – a secret pleasure! But below that I still have my clumping black shoes and ironware.

I submit to sitting in the hairdressers to let the girl cut the front into a thick fringe, but that's the limit of my tolerance. The pictures on the walls in the salon make girls look as if they've had electric shock treatment, and even through Aine's pleading – she'd have her hair done like that in a heartbeat if she was lucky enough to have hair like mine – I stand my ground. She looks chic with her blonde straight fringe, but my unruly mane only looks tidy when plaited. When we were girls, we used to wonder why we looked so different in just about every way. It never occurred to either of us that we weren't actually genetic sisters.

We walk past the quay on our way back to the hotel, clutching carrier bags full of shopping. Aine stares at the sullen, dark water and the rocks on the shore black with winter damp. I think she's having a moment of nostalgia, but when she turns to me, her lip curls. 'I don't know how you can stand this place, Hannah. Everything is so bleak, so ancient, so, oh, lost in the past.'

That's what I've always found comforting about my surroundings, but seeing it now, with her eyes, I wonder if I've just kept myself tucked into this small community because I'm not brave like her. I'm afraid of stepping out of my comfort zone – not that it's been comfortable in any way – because people here know me, and going to a new place means meeting new people who would ridicule me for my disability.

Aine has never known that lack of self-esteem. She's always been vibrant, beautiful and self-confident, something that has shone through all her letters to me. She's always been loyal, too. The only one of my siblings who has ever kept in touch with me, and just here and now, I am grateful for that.

'So,' she says, turning from the sea abruptly. 'We'll go back to the hotel and plan our trip to Kerry. Danny and I talked about that last night. Justin needs to settle his mind about the past before leaving, or he'll always be wondering about coming back here, and he needs to be focused on the future, on making you happy.'

I blush but realise she's already back in London in her mind. She left Roone Bay many years back and no longer fits into this tight community. She's more at home in the Big House or the new hotel, with their comfortable furniture, bathrooms and endless hot water. If she thinks Justin wants to take me back to England as his blushing bride, she's way off the mark. He's being nice to me now, but will he be so nice when he learns that I'm not the sweet, unsophisticated virgin he believes I am?

The priests would call me a fallen woman.

I'd never before been told I was beautiful, that I was loved, even though I'm well aware that Cathal was simply throwing me a line. I knew he wanted to marry me for the farm. I accepted that truth for its blatant honesty. But I had fallen for the oldest tricks in the book... sweet words coupled with the suggestion that if I didn't lie with a man, was I frigid? Was I able? As we were getting married, why would I deny him? He wanted to know that we could make children. As if that was something beyond me.

I wonder now whether Cathal, knowing that I'm not inheriting, has betrayed my foolishness. I imagine him and Mark sitting over their pints laughing at my naivety. I will no longer be able to drive through Roone Bay without being fearful of seeing Cathal and wondering what stories he's spread about his conquest of the weird disabled girl. I sigh. I wonder who, out of those people who have offered me a home, would truly want to take me in once I begin to show.

I can't go along with all Aine's plans, knowing what I know now. I take a deep breath. 'Aine, there's something I need to tell you.'

She's quick to realise that this is important. 'Let's go back to the hotel and get a pot of tea. It's too cold out here for intimate discussions.'

She takes my hand and leads me back up the hill. I clutch

her hand with desperation, wondering if she'll even want to know me after.

When we're seated in the lounge area of the hotel with a pot of tea between us, she says, 'Come on – spit it out.'

'You recall what I wrote, about Cathal Carrol, that things didn't quite work out?'

'Sure I do. Why do you think I'm here? He's a langer if ever I saw one, and I wanted to make sure you didn't—' Her eyes widen. 'Oh, Hannah, you didn't...?'

I grimace. 'When you left, he was a skinny lad, but he grew up well.'

'I remember he stole money out of the poor box when he was a wean.'

My eyes widen. 'I didn't know that.'

'At school he couldn't write for a week. The priest nearly broke his hands with the ruler. He swore he'd get the priest back' – she gives a wry grin – 'but his dad said if he did anything of the sort, he'd get the same and more from himself. He's not like the rest of his family.'

Everything she says makes me feel more of a fool, but my secret is burning a hole in my mind. 'I was going to marry him, Aine. I knew he wanted the farm. I... I'm having his baby. And now I don't know what to do.'

'You're pregnant?'

I nod woefully.

'Oh, Hannah.' She sighs. 'Well, it's no matter. You can get rid of it when you come to England.'

'Aine! No, I can't.'

'I didn't think you would.' She pops a grimace. 'It was worth the asking. But you can still come and live with us.'

'But Danny...'

'Danny loves children. He was an orphan himself. He'll understand. But, listen. Tell Justin. He's besotted with you. If he doesn't want you just because you're pregnant, it's his loss.

You're beautiful and kind. You'll be a great mam. He'd be stupid to lose you.'

'Get away – you were always the beautiful one. The boys were all over you at the dances.'

'So they were, but there were more boys than girls! I was skinny; too tall and thin, and there you were, with a face like a model, and I was so jealous of your voice. I loved to hear you sing, and there's me sounding like a frog joining in the chorus.'

I'm taken aback at how vastly different our memories are.

'You daft girrul,' she says, giving me a hug. 'You always put yourself down more than anyone else did. I don't know where that came from. So, you slept with Cathal?'

'I was afraid if I didn't, he wouldn't want me.'

I thought she'd be shocked, but she just rolls her eyes. 'Sweetheart, if he'd had the least bit of care for you, he wouldn't have done that. Not in Ireland... So, he was going to marry you for the farm. Does he know about the will?'

'I think Mark has told him. They were chummy in the bar, apparently. He asked was I going to fight it? I guess he thought he was still in with a chance. But now, I imagine everyone in Roone Bay will be looking at me, thinking what an idiot I am.'

She grins. 'They'd be right there. The biteen of a farm was never worth that kind of sacrifice!'

I'm laughing through my tears. 'But, Aine, what can I do? Justin won't want me if he knows.'

'Do you love him?'

'Is it possible to love someone you barely know?'

'Sure, it is.' She puts an open hand on her breast. 'I loved Danny instantly. Even discovering he was a boxer didn't change that. You have to tell Justin.'

'I can't!' I exclaim in panic.

'Well, you don't have to blurt it out. Not yet. Let's see what tomorrow brings, eh? But I tell you one thing for sure. If Justin loves you, he'll understand. And if he doesn't, then he's a fool.'

'He's no fool.'

'No, I don't think he is. So, your secret is safe with me, for now. But what you can't do is leave him in ignorance if he's interested in you. And you can still come to London with me if that falls through. Don't you worry about that now.'

'Even if I've conceived out of wedlock?'

'All children are innocent of what went before. I think your Justin, being a doctor, would agree with that more than most. All that blather about sin... I mean, the concept of sin was invented by men, wasn't it?'

I chuckle. 'But, Aine, I'm scared.'

'You have our mam's strength, even so. We'll cope. Let's go to Kerry as planned, see if Justin can find out what he came here for. When that's done, we can make plans to go back to England. Whatever happens between you and Justin, you'll always have a home with me.'

I bury a sense of guilt for keeping the truth from her, but I can't bear the image of her turning away from me when she knows I'm not even her real sister. And when I finally do, will she be less keen to offer me a home, especially now I'm carrying Cathal's child? But somehow, the burden of my pregnancy is slightly less frightening for having shared it.

35

HANNAH

I'm seated in the back of the car, squeezed in beside Justin. As we drive off, he smiles at me in a way that sends my heart flying in two ways: into the heavens of happiness and to the depths of depression. Is that look really for me, or is it just because he's enjoying the road trip? I smile back, betraying nothing of my inner turmoil.

The drive is stunning, even in the rain that is presently sweeping across the landscape in sheets. The charm of Kerry lies not in sunshine but in the scudding clouds, the black rocks and the narrow roads that wind through the mountain passes. We pass through Bantry and Glengarriff and wind up and over the narrow Caha Pass that zigzags around the mountainside. The cloud base is low, obliterating the mountaintops, but we gaze in awe down into valleys where fields are a green patchwork quilt, the boundaries stitched by ancient stone walls. The roads below lie like a tangle of abandoned threads, the scattered farmsteads like dolls' houses far below, with thin wisps of smoke drifting up from their ragged stone chimneys.

Sheep are dotted all over the landscape, splashed with red

or blue paint. They forage for grass wherever it can be found, often along the roadside having broken through rusting wire fencing. At one point, we find ourselves following a scraggy ewe with two fat lambs in tow. She ambles along happily, snatching at the longer grass in the verge, while the lambs grab a quick suckle each time she stops. Aine gets out and tries to manoeuvre them to one side, and we all laugh as the ewe neatly sidesteps her and trots calmly on. We trundle slowly behind the ewe until she reaches into a gateway for some extra-luscious titbits, allowing us to squeeze carefully past.

The road then swerves down the other side of the mountain, through dripping tunnels blasted out two hundred years previously, and down into Kenmare. There we stop for lunch and pore over the map. I thought Roone Bay was remote until we set out on this journey. It doesn't matter which route we take – there is no quick way to Killorglin.

'It's about an hour from here. We won't see the best of the Killarney lakes,' Justin says sadly, seeing the low-lying cloud base sitting just above our heads. 'But, hey, I've seen more of Ireland than I ever expected, and we can always come back for a holiday.' He puts his arm around my back and gives me a brief hug and a smile as though to include me in that statement.

'Me, I'll be glad to get back to London,' Danny mutters, and I don't think he's joking. 'These roads give me the jitters. Might be in Timbuktu. These wiggly roads are scarier than that time I went up in a hot air balloon!'

'Ah, ye woosie,' Aine says lovingly. 'We'll be back there soon enough, and ye'll be bragging in the pub about having been on a jaunt to the wilds of Ireland.'

The road flattens out after the mountain pass and remains steady all the way to Killorglin, which turns out to be a compact town of brightly coloured buildings rising from an arched bridge over the River Laune. We discover a central row of business premises harbouring more bars than shops.

Danny parks the car, and we climb out into a lull between showers.

'Us men'll search the bars for news of this Aisling woman, while you ladies ask in the shops,' Danny says with a wink.

Aine slips her arm into his. 'No way, buster. We go together or not at all.'

'Spoilsport.'

'Besides, you're driving.'

'Perhaps the telephone directory would be a good place to start,' I suggest. 'Maybe there's a post office?'

'What was her name again?' Justin asks.

'Crowley,' I say. 'Aisling Crowley.'

'She'd be in her eighties or near, if she's still alive. Maybe she married and changed her name?'

'Even so, if she had family – parents, brothers – there might still be a line of them here. Someone would remember.'

I stop a young woman who's striding down the street. 'We're looking for a family called Crowley – do you know of anyone by that name?'

She shakes her head. 'Sorry, I'm new here. Try the post office at the top of the street. Postmen usually know everybody.'

'In Ireland they do, anyway,' Aine says.

The man behind the counter in the post office, however, isn't so obliging. He thrusts a telephone directory at us with a shrug. There are, in fact, quite a few Crowleys. I write the names and numbers on a pad, and Aine and I take turns in phoning from the call box, saying we're trying to trace a woman called Aisling Crowley who had once lived in Roone Bay. Most people just say sorry, they don't know anything, but eventually my request is answered by a silence and a question. 'Who wants to know?'

'My name is Hannah Barry. My granddad was with the freedom fighters in Roone Bay, and I'd like to talk to someone about what happened at the barracks in 1920.'

There's another silence. 'Why?'

'Can we meet? We aren't after making any trouble; we just want to speak to someone who actually knows what happened.'

The phone goes dead. I pull the handset from my ear and hold it out for everyone to hear the dial tone. 'I think that's our contact,' I say.

I dial the number again. 'Please, will you—'

The phone is disconnected.

'Right,' Justin says. 'Let's find out where Bridge Street is.'

'We're parked on it,' Danny says.

'Oh. Right. So, it's number forty-six.'

We trawl back down the street and find a tall, thin town house painted in buttercup yellow with a red door. I knock, and eventually it's opened by a smartly dressed woman who looks decidedly annoyed.

'Hello,' I say. 'We're looking for Aisling Crowley. I just—'

'Please just go away,' she interrupts. 'Leave the past alone. Mam doesn't like to speak of those days, not any longer. She's too old, and your telephone call has upset her.'

'We don't mean any harm,' Justin says softly. 'I'm just trying to find out what happened to Jack Sanders, my granddad.'

She gave a faint indrawn breath, betraying knowledge that she's withholding.

'Please,' Justin says. 'I think he was executed by the IRA because he was with the Black and Tans. I don't blame anyone for what happened. I understand. It was a war. I'd like to know what happened. And I promised his mother I'd put flowers on his grave. But no one seems to know where that is.'

'Who is your great-grandmother?'

'Kyra Sanders. She died nearly ten years ago. I was training to be a doctor, and I've only just managed to take the time out.'

'You came all this way, even though she's passed?'

'A promise is a promise.'

'Just a minute.' She closes the door and we wait. After a while, the door opens again. 'Come on in.'

We're shown into a small living room. Against one wall is an enormous dresser cluttered with a pretty bone china tea service. She indicates the chairs. 'Please, sit.'

Eventually the door opens again, and an old woman walks in. She's leaning heavily on a stick, and has pure white hair that is plaited and wound into a knot at the back of her head.

We all stand, and she walks towards Danny, who is standing in front of a wing-backed chair. 'I hope you don't mind if I take that seat? I'm not as spry as I once was.'

'Sure thing,' he says and moves aside.

'Well, sit down,' she says testily. 'You're cluttering up a small room.'

When we're all seated again, she says sharply to Danny, 'You're the Englishman?'

'English is as English does,' he jokes. 'But it's Justin, here, who's looking to find out about his granddad.'

She looks long and hard at Justin, and finally nods. 'Yes, you have the look of Jack about you.'

Justin's eyes widen, and he edges forward on his seat. 'You're Aisling Crowley?'

'I am.'

His whole face lights with excitement. 'Wow. I really didn't think we'd find you, to be honest. And you were there that day, when the IRA burned the barracks?'

'I was.'

He sighs. 'Will you tell me what happened? Really, I'm not trying to cause trouble. I just want to know where he's buried. I promised my great-grandma I'd pay my respects.'

Her lips curls. 'Really? You came all this way to lay flowers on a grave?'

'It was a good excuse, anyway.'

She gives a short laugh. 'That sounds like Jack. He said he had a son called William. That would be your father?'

'No, my father was called Walter.'

Aisling's mistake, I'm sure, wasn't so innocent. She's testing Justin, to make sure he is who he says he is.

'So why you, why now? Walter didn't come to find his father.'

'No, his mother, my grandma Rose, married again, but my father kept Jack's surname, Sanders. He wasn't at all interested in finding out about his birth father. All he knew was that Jack was killed by the IRA after taking a job as a Temporary Constable in Roone Bay after the war.'

'Why would you be interested in what happened all that time ago?'

He doesn't let the abrupt inquisition fluster him. 'I promised Great-Grandma, but it's more than that. When Kyra died, my grandmother cleared out her house and found some correspondence Jack must have sent home during the war, and a couple from his time with the RIC in Ireland before he disappeared.'

She looks shocked more than surprised. 'His mother kept his letters?'

'Some; most were from France. My dad – Walter, that is– wasn't interested in old letters, so Grandma Rose gave them to me, mostly because of the envelopes. I collect stamps, you see.'

'And you read them?'

He looks guilty. 'Well, I didn't think it would hurt, Granddad Jack being dead such a long time.'

'And what did you think of this Jack Sanders, from reading his letters?'

I think it a strange question, but Justin answers simply. 'I know the Irish want to believe all the Black and Tans were bad people, but he sounded like a straight-up gentleman caught up in terrible circumstances. He went straight from the First World

War into the Irish conflict. He was probably a very confused young man.'

'But you know what happened, don't you? The barracks was burned. The Black and Tans were executed.'

'That's the story.'

Her bright eyes snagged his. 'What do you mean?'

'It wasn't the letters that were confusing; it was the envelopes. The strange thing was, one of them, with just a birthday card inside, had a stamp on it that was issued maybe two years after Jack's death. Before my great-grandma died, I promised her I'd one day come over here and find Jack's grave, but seeing that stamp, well, it was peculiar, to say the least. It tickled my curiosity.'

'I guess it would have.' She gives a sideways smile but betrays no sign of surprise.

'So, the thing is, can you – will you – tell me what actually happened? I heard a rumour that Jack had, ah, raped a girl and was executed for it. I find that hard to believe.'

I jolt, surprised. How had he found that out?

She mulls over that for a moment, then says. 'Well, I suppose you deserve to know, after making the effort to find me. Jack didn't rape anyone. It was another man, Billy Devon, who did that. They hanged him for it, up at the standing stone.'

Justin sighs and closes his eyes briefly. 'Thank you. Even if I don't find out anything else, that has made the trip worthwhile. So, you knew Jack?'

She smiles. 'I knew him well. I suppose you deserve to know the rest of the story.'

We all lean forward a little.

'I met Jack by accident, out on the hills one day. It was hard to get my head around the fact that not all the Black and Tans were evil thugs, which is what I'd been told. But there he was, sitting on a rock, crying, torn up about the war, about the killing. I could have shot him, there and then, but instead' – she smiles softly in recollection – 'I fell in love with him. Then Billy Devon, one of the Black and Tans, raped a local woman. The men had already made plans to take out the barracks and commandeer the weapons. They took to arms in anger, intending to execute everyone in the barracks.' She grimaces in recollection. 'I ran up to the barracks to warn him, but things didn't work out quite as I'd planned...'

'Go on,' Justin whispers, knowing he's about to learn about Jack's final moments on this earth.

36

JACK, 1920

For a long while, Jack didn't go out on any walks on his own. He stayed close to his comrades, fearful that Aisling would spread the word of his aggressive advances and that he would be targeted for assassination. He had acted on impulse, thinking she felt the same way, but it would be no use protesting his innocence. The climate was seething with resentment of Irish treatment at the hands of the English, and he'd been stupid enough to ruffle their already outraged feathers.

The following fortnight carried on much as it had before. They took turns in trawling the countryside, visiting local farmsteads in the Crossley Tender, seeking out the elusive IRA soldiers. Arms at the ready, they were mostly greeted at doors by closed-faced women, the men noticeably absent. They searched houses, barns and outbuildings, and Jack always had that tingling between his shoulder blades, the one he got in the trenches while waiting for the final bullet.

Then came the incident Jack guessed he'd instigated, albeit by accident; the incident that changed everything. Early one morning, there was a ruckus outside and Billy Devon barged backward in through the half-open door, dragging a sodden, struggling figure into the barracks.

Recognising Aisling, Jack jumped to his feet.

'Caught her sneaking around outside, spying,' Billy said.

Johnny Crowley snarled, 'Get your hands off that woman.'

Billy dumped Aisling onto a wooden chair. 'Fetch me some rope. I'll find out what she's about. Then we might as well have a bit of fun with what's left.'

The way Billy spoke sent shivers of apprehension down Jack's spine. 'Don't touch her,' he said in a low voice.

Aisling's wide eyes caught his, but she said nothing.

'Don't be daft, man,' Billy said with a laughing sneer. 'We'll get a medal for this; you wait and see. And there's no point wasting a bird that landed herself in our nest.'

He turned to Aisling and grabbed her chin. He turned her face this way and that, stuffing a finger between her lips and running it along her teeth, as if assessing a prize dog. The rest of the men were still locked in an almost terrified silence, out of their depth, not knowing how to handle the situation.

'So, you IRA tart,' Billy asked, 'what were you doing out there, eh? Listening at the door for our plans? Going back to tell your rat's nest of traitors what we were going to do this morning? Well, our plans just changed.'

Billy released her chin and turned to face the men, his triumphant smirk betraying delight at having captured one of the rebels when everyone else had failed.

Aisling spat to clear her mouth of his foul touch. But her defiant, scathing glance alerted Jack to the fact that something was off-kilter. When Billy's back was turned, Aisling flashed Jack a meaningful glance, mouthing the single word that he lip-read clearly: *Run!*

'Incoming!' he screamed as the windows were smashed in with rifle butts. Shots spattered into the room. Even as Jack was diving to the floor, one of his colleagues was hit, and blood exploded from his chest.

Billy grabbed Aisling as a shield and was backing with her towards the bunkroom, the rest of the team scuttling in behind him. Aisling was fighting him, legs and arms flailing, but despite his small stature, she was no match. Jack crawled rapidly after them as the main door shuddered under a physical battering. He managed to get his shoulders through the door just as it was being rammed home, his comrades looking after their own skin rather than waiting for him. When inside, he jumped to his feet, slammed the door and threw the bolt just as the outer door lost the battle and was flung open.

There was a sudden silence.

The spit of bullets had ceased almost as quickly as it had started. That had been no indiscriminate spray of fire but carefully targeted shots that might have killed more men had Jack not shouted. Inside the bunkroom, windows had been nailed shut, leaving small apertures through which the RIC men could shoot, but right now it had become a trap.

'Come on out,' a voice called. 'If you put down your arms, we won't kill you. We just want the girl and your guns. You'll be allowed to leave.'

'Listen to them,' Johnny Crowley urged. 'They just want our rifles and handguns. We can get out of this alive.'

'Like hell,' Billy muttered, eyeing Johnny with suspicion. 'Whose side are you on, anyway?'

'If we have to break this door down, you'll all be executed,' a calm voice promised from the other side of the door.

'Murdered, you mean, you traitorous bastards,' Billy yelled back. He held his knife to Aisling's throat. She closed her eyes and froze in his grasp. 'I've got a knife. If you break that door, I'll slit the tart's throat.'

'If you harm the girl in any way, I promise, you'll be begging for death.'

Jack stepped towards Billy. 'Come on, man – we don't make war on women,' he said. 'Put the knife down.'

Billy glared at Jack. 'Who put you in charge? Are you stupid? Don't you realise she was a decoy? The bitch would have no problem sending us all to the devil.'

There was a terrific thud at the thin internal door, which would survive only seconds under that kind of force. Billy jumped, startled, and Jack dived at him, grabbing the hand with the knife, twisting it away from Aisling's throat. Released, Aisling ducked instantly, grabbing the handgun Jack dropped, just as the door burst open and a tight cluster of rifle barrels preceded a small band of men into the room. Jack backed away; hands raised. Aisling rose to her feet and dusted herself off, putting a tentative hand to a thin line of red that had blossomed on her throat.

One man, obviously the leader, was dressed in a pseudo uniform that was worn thin, but his eyes were sharp, his tone commanding. 'Are you hurt?' he asked.

She shook her head.

He turned squarely to Johnny and held his hand out for the rifle. 'Either join us or take your family and leave Roone Bay.'

Jack had wondered, briefly, whether Johnny had been with the IRA all along, party to this ambush, but now gathered that he wasn't. Johnny cast a silent apology to Jack, who nodded in silent agreement. The Irish didn't want to kill one of their own, which is certainly what was going to happen to the rest of them. Johnny handed over his rifle and sidled out.

'Which man cut you?' the IRA officer asked Aisling.

She pointed at Billy, who backed away, spitting foul language.

'Not so brave without a girl to shield you,' the IRA officer said in distaste, then to his men: 'Tie their hands.'

Jack and the other two Temporary Constables obediently turned and allowed their hands to be tied, knowing that this was the end of the line. He watched without expression as Billy fought and was taken to the floor violently, screaming obscenities. He had never before met a man who emanated a dark and loathsome aura that physically repulsed him, and felt no outrage as Billy was hauled to his feet and dragged outside. By the time Jack and his two comrades were prodded at gunpoint out into the fresh air, Billy and his captors were nowhere in sight.

The IRA leader assessed them and glanced at Aisling. 'Which one?' he asked.

She indicated Jack, who gave an apologetic half-smile and shrugged in resignation.

'Right,' the leader said to Jack's companions. 'You two can start walking. I suggest you go home to England. Leave Ireland to the Irish. That's all we want. If your faces are seen around here again, you'll not be given a second chance.'

As the men left, on foot, in the black-and-tan uniforms with their hands tied and no guns, Jack wondered if they would even make it to Cork city, let alone England.

The leader turned to Jack. 'You, come with us.'

He turned towards the hills, and Jack followed awkwardly, his wrists tied, a handgun prodding his back. If they intended to torture him for information, there was little he could give them. But he was sure about one thing: he wasn't going to leave this country alive.

When he had arrived in this place, he'd seen nothing but the yellow winter grass straggling over the damp grey rocks that were scattered up to bite the grey skyline, but now, stumbling along a goat path, a man's hand on his upper arm steadying him, he drank in his last glimpse of the rugged landscape. There was a hint of blue between the tumbling clouds and shoots of fresh green springing up through the winter foliage. He wished he could tell his mother that he found her beloved Ireland after all. He just hadn't known how to see it.

He glanced back as the barracks was torched. Flames roared, sending black smoke signalling into the sky. To the left, the Atlantic looked on impassively, as uncaring as death itself. Jack was strangely calm. Death would almost be a relief. The war had eaten into his soul and destroyed the man he might have been. The man he was now just wanted peace, and it seemed he was about to find it.

Jack was ushered up a narrow path by the men with guns. He stumbled awkwardly through a maze of wind-scoured boulders and was steadied more than once as he lost his footing. Eventually, they reached a small stone-built cottage nestling in a valley. He ducked his head, entered and was pushed towards a rough-hewn seat.

The leader grabbed another chair, turned it and straddled it the wrong way, folding his arms over the back rail. 'So, English, what are we going to do with you?'

Jack sensed that his answer would decide his fate but was too tired to lie. 'I don't know,' he said honestly. 'I thought I was going to help calm an insurrection. I didn't understand.'

'But you understand now that it's not an insurrection; it's a rebellion, a war? The invaders have kept us poor for too long.'

Jack nodded. 'I'm sorry for what the Irish have been subjected to, all through the ages. You will execute me, I know. I forgive you.'

'You forgive us?' The rebel's eyes widened in astonishment.

'I mean it,' Jack said earnestly. 'I don't blame you. If my death can cancel out some of the wrongs, I'll go willingly.'

'Like Jesus on the cross, you'd die for the sins of your countrymen?'

Jack gave a crooked half-smile. 'I don't put myself in that category at all.'

'You seem very calm, for a man in the hands of the enemy. Aren't you afraid?'

Jack thought about that before answering. 'I'm not afraid of dying. Once, maybe, but not any longer. I've seen too much... But if you think to torture me, then yes, I'd be afraid of that. I'm not brave.'

'Have you any knowledge that would benefit us?'

Jack shook his head.

'Then it won't come to that. I'm leaving you here with Aisling. It would be best if you don't try to leave. There are those who would shoot you on sight in that uniform.'

Jack froze, then his eyes widened. 'You trust me?'

'Not at all, but Aisling does. What happens next is up to her.'

The IRA officer sliced the bonds, and Jack rubbed life back into his rope-burned wrists. He didn't say anything but surveyed his captors in turn, confused by their lack of aggression. One by one, they turned, ducking out through the entrance, and were gone.

Jack glanced at Aisling, who was standing to one side, her arms crossed, assessing him with a faint smile on her lips. 'I don't understand. Am I not to be executed, then?'

'Only if you want.'

He shook his head, smiling slightly. 'I, ah, I'm sorry for what I did. I've never—I just... When you ran, I wanted to die. I thought I'd lost you forever.'

'I was worried that someone might have been watching. I was worried for you. I couldn't allow anyone to see that I wanted you to kiss me. Not then – it was too dangerous. I was afraid the men would not have understood.'

She walked up to him, put her hands on his shoulders and kissed him squarely on the mouth. He froze, wondering if it was some kind of trick or test.

She stepped back, frowning at his lack of response.

He rose and ducked outside. There was no sign of the rebels. They really had left him alone with Aisling. The roiling clouds were being driven by a cool breeze from the south, leaving a clear ribbon of blue above the mountains. In the distance, a silver sliver of water made its way down the mountainside. It was so beautiful, he found himself crying, the tears pooling on his unshaven stubble. He lifted his hands and smeared his cheeks. He sensed her behind him.

'Will you join us, Jack? Help to free our beleaguered people from the English tyrants?'

He turned to face her. 'So, they left you here to turn me? Is that it? The soft touch first, then the hot irons? The answer is, and always will be, no. I won't turn traitor. I won't betray my country.'

'I told Conal you wouldn't.'

He asked bluntly, 'What did they do with Billy?'

Her mouth compressed. 'That one is gone. Don't ask again. It seems I'm the one to decide your fate. If I tell the men to kill you, they will. If I say to free you, will you go back to your wife in England?'

He thought about it for a long moment, then sighed. 'I don't know what I'd do, but I can't go back. I've seen too much killing, too many deaths, too much misery. I'm not the selfish youth I was when I left to go to war. That can never be undone. I can't be a good husband to a wife I don't remember, and if she remarries, my son will be better off without me.'

He mused on what he'd said. It was strange how the words had come tumbling out, rationalising things he hadn't known he'd been thinking.

Resignation weighed heavy in every line of his body. 'And another thing. The other RIC officers will tell our people how Billy and I were taken away for questioning. If I go back, they'll wonder why the IRA let me go. They'll wonder what I told them. I'll be labelled a traitor and would likely be executed by the English, especially now, because I'm alive and there's so much anger for a whole generation of men lost to the war.'

'So, what will we do with you, Jack? You're sitting on the fence.'

'No, I'm executing my right to remain neutral.'

She laughed at his gallows humour. 'You and your oh-so-British honour present us with a problem.'

He shrugged. 'I haven't a clue. Do with me what you will. I'm a dead man, whichever way you look at it.'

'Or,' she said, 'you could move over to Kerry and take a different name. You can either start a new life or spend the rest of your life feeling sorry for yourself. Your choice.'

His mind quietly churned over the possibility of this unexpected future, and finally he asked, 'If I go to Kerry, will you go with me?'

She smiled and reached up to kiss him.

'Maybe I will,' she answered eventually.

37

HANNAH

We're hanging, spellbound, on Aisling's words, when Justin, wonderingly, says the obvious. 'He wasn't executed? He came to Kerry with you?'

She gives a wry smile. 'And lived happily ever after. Do you hate me now, Justin? He changed his name to Jack Crowley and we lived as man and wife. He didn't love Rose, but he did love me.'

Justin is struggling with this exposé. 'He didn't come back for his own son?'

'He was traumatised by the war. Changed in ways it would be hard to explain. He saw dreadful things. He did dreadful things that he had to live with. When the IRA came for him, he was ready to die. Sometimes I'm not sure if I saved him at all. He didn't go back because he didn't want to ruin Walter's life. Can you understand that?'

'I'm trying,' Justin murmured after a long moment. 'But that means my grandmother wasn't divorced when she married again? She was a bigamist?'

She shrugs. 'She didn't know that. She thought she was a widow. Marriage is an artificial institution propagated by those in power; what Rose didn't know didn't hurt her. She believed she was honestly married.'

Justin runs his hand through his hair. 'Well, I'll be darned! My poor great-grandmother, though. All that time, she thought her son dead.'

'No, she knew he was still alive. They wrote to each other for years. When her letters stopped coming, we knew she'd passed.'

Justin's face pales. 'She knew Jack was alive? All that time?' he whispers.

'We asked her to visit, but she wouldn't. To start with, she was afraid Jack would be treated as a traitor if anyone found out he was still alive. He might have been imprisoned or even hanged. But as time went by, she didn't want to hurt Rose and little Walter. If Jack had simply arisen from the dead, it would have ruined other lives. You see, his mother's sacrifice was the ultimate one. She never saw her son again, to keep everyone safe. So, now you know. Now it can't harm anyone, it's not such a big secret any longer.'

'What an amazing woman my great-grandma was,' Justin says in awe.

'She wasn't daft, either,' I say. 'I wonder if she told you to come and place a wreath on Jack's grave so that you would find all this out?'

'I wonder that myself.' Aisling assesses me, then addresses Justin. 'Is Hannah your wife? You didn't say.'

'Not yet,' Justin says. 'But I'm hoping she's considering it.'

Aine gives a little squeak of happiness, while my embarrassed flush radiates wildly down towards my chest. I find I've totally lost the power of speech.

Aisling's lined face softens, perhaps with the recollections of a love stolen by age.

There's a knock, and the woman who had first answered the door comes in. 'You'll be tiring, Mam,' she says.

Aisling asks Justin, 'You'll be staying overnight in Killorglin?'

'We haven't found a place yet. But it's too far to go back tonight.'

'There's a hotel just down the road. I'm sure they'll have free rooms at this time of the year.'

Aisling grabs her cane and heaves herself laboriously to her feet. I sense Justin holding himself back from running to assist, but despite her age, she radiates independence with an almost physical aura. I can imagine her as a young woman running around the hills with a rifle, as strong-willed as any man. 'So, you'll be going back to England soon? Will Hannah here be going with you?'

He smiles at me. 'I'd like her to, if she'll have me.'

She casts me an amused glance. 'She'd be a fool not to.'

'But before we leave,' he says, 'can we visit Jack's grave, as I promised his mam I would?'

'Sure, you could,' she says, 'if he was in it at all.'

38

HANNAH

The evening passes with Justin in a strangely discombobulated state of mind. He had come to Ireland to find his granddad's grave, only to discover that Jack had not died at all.

It turns out that Jack had asked Aisling to sound out Justin's reaction on discovering that his granddad was still alive. If Justin had been upset or angry to discover that not only had Jack not died all those years ago but had three generations of offspring, it would have ended somewhat differently. Justin would have been sent on his way without ever knowing Jack was still alive. But now, Justin is to meet with him tomorrow.

We book into the tired luxury of a hotel that has settled quietly into old age, but the meal is good, without frills, the rooms clean and tidy. Over dinner, Justin tells Aine and Danny what he knows about Jack's years in the war, of his experiences in the trenches and why Jack had ended up in Ireland. He says he'd grown up *knowing* that his granddad had died at the hands of the IRA; it had never been in question. He ruefully admits that his great-grandma – Jack's Irish mother – had been lying to him and his father all their lives. She'd known he hadn't died.

She had known Rose was still legally married to Jack when Rose married her second husband.

'What a woman,' Aine says, in evident admiration. 'I thought I was bucking convention, running off to England to be a dancer rather than get married in Roone Bay, but she beat me hollow.'

'And Aisling and Jack lived sinfully in Ireland as if they were legitimately married,' I add. 'It's a good job the priests didn't know that!'

'It wasn't a sin if they loved each other,' Justin says gently. 'There are a lot of things that don't make sense in our society. Like women having babies out of wedlock being treated badly. It's unfortunate that women get blamed the world over for something so fundamentally normal. Thank goodness such views are changing in England. It's a shame Ireland can't catch up. It takes two to make a baby, so I don't get why women receive all the censure.'

I wince. It's not the first time he's said this, and I wonder whether he's somehow worked out that I'm pregnant.

Aine claps her hands in delight. 'Justin, if I didn't love Danny, I'd marry you!'

'It's because men still rule the world,' Danny says, puffing out his chest manfully. 'Rightly so, when you think about it.'

Aine clouts him playfully. 'If there weren't women, there wouldn't be any men, yeh daft sod.'

Justin is watching their repartee with a tiny grin on his lips, and I resolve to admit that I'm pregnant. Whether he has guessed or not, at least it will be out in the open. I can't wait any longer. I wouldn't want to start a relationship with lies, any more than he surely does.

As we retire for the night, Aine gives me a hug, her eyes bright with happy tears. 'I'm so happy for you; he's lovely,' she whispers, and I have to agree. Everything in my garden would appear to be rosy – except that his notions of culpability versus convention are about to be sorely tested.

After Aine and Danny have disappeared into their room together, obviously flouting convention, there's a faint knock on my door. I've been half expecting it.

'Can I come in?' Justin whispers.

'I'm still up,' I say.

He slides in and closes the door silently behind him. He indicates the bed I'm sitting on. 'May I?'

I nod, and he sits beside me, his weight pulling me towards him.

He takes a deep breath. 'I didn't mean it to come out like that, in front of everyone. I've been trying to find a way of telling you how I feel about you. I need to know that my, ah, inclinations are reciprocated before making a fool of myself. You're very... reticent to betray your emotions. Do you think you could like me that way?'

I choke back a laugh at the antiquated sentence.

'*Like* you?' I say lightly. 'Of course I like you. How could I not? You appeared to me in my hour of need, like some kind of visiting angel. I was just afraid that you would disappear back to England as suddenly as you arrived, and that all my hopes and dreams would be gone with you.'

He puts a hand to my cheek and turns my face towards him. 'I'm sorry. I didn't mean to... I'll go. We can talk in the morning.'

'No!' I speak too quickly, then lower my voice. 'No, don't go. It's just that...'

He pulls me towards him and is kissing the tears from my eyes and cheeks, and for a while I find myself overwhelmed by emotions I have no control over. I lift my face and find his lips with my own. Cathal has kissed me, possessively, intrusively, but I've never kissed a man like this before, wanting with all my being.

After a while, Justin pushes himself away, but his eyes are heavy with desire.

'I need to go, my love,' he says. 'Before I do something that's going to jeopardise all my good intentions.'

I smile. 'You're such a good man.' I distance myself from him slightly. 'Justin, there's something I need to tell you. You have to know, before you go any further. You might not want me after all.'

'Goodness,' he says calmly. 'Did you murder Mark? I don't blame you. I'll visit you in prison, I promise.'

I giggle. 'Tempted, but no. The thing is...'

I suddenly find I don't want to say it, to ruin a moment I want to hold on to for the rest of my life.

'Hannah,' he says, 'I know why you're upset, but you don't need to be.'

'You do?'

'You think I shouldn't tie myself to someone who's disabled? Your word, not mine, by the way. I think your family – your father, that brother of yours – have made you feel worthless, but can you try to fight it for me, please? You aren't defined by the polio. It wasn't your fault. Your callipers make your life difficult in ways I can't imagine, but it just makes me realise how lucky I am not to have suffered in that way, and what strength it has taken for you to keep going. I want to marry you. I want you to be my wife. I want you to come to Somerset with me, live in my cottage and have children with me.'

I wince at the mention of children and cast my mind around for other excuses. 'We barely know each other.'

'I know you as if we've known each other all our lives. I knew you the moment I first saw you sitting on that donkey cart. I think you're beautiful inside and out, and I have no doubts whatsoever. I want to marry you, but you must want that, too.'

'I, ah—'

He smiles, comfortable with himself. 'I can wait. If you have doubts, if you need time to get to know me, I understand.'

I stand and limp anxiously to stare at the darkness beyond the window.

Justin rises, increasingly worried. 'Hannah? What is it?'

'It's that Cathal and I...'

He jolts, shocked. 'You're not in love with him, are you?'

'No,' I say shortly. 'I never was. Aine's right; he's a langer. I think I already knew that. It's just that...' Finally, I blurt it out: 'I'm pregnant.'

He's totally still for a moment, and I think, *Well, that's it. I've said it. He'll leave now.*

He takes both my shoulders and turns me fully towards him, his face the picture of concern. 'Hannah, did he force himself on you?'

'What? No, of course not. It was just that, well, we were going to be married, and...'

'He made you think that as you were going to be married, it was all right? Or, worse, if you didn't allow him to have sex, then you were frigid or something?'

'Well... a bit of both, really.'

'In Ireland, too. What a cad!' He's silent for a moment, but I don't see the disgust I was expecting. 'So, do you want to keep the baby?'

'I'm sorry.' Tears gather. 'It's a baby, Justin. Aine said I could get rid of it in England, but I can't do that.'

'And nor should you,' he says. 'Right. If you agree, if you want to, we can get married the moment we get back to England, and no one needs to know the baby is not mine unless you want to tell them. We would have to tell the child, though, some day.'

'Really? You don't hate me?'

'Hate you? Come here.' He moves close and holds me tightly. 'Hannah, I meant what I said at dinner. It's always the woman who takes the fall. I didn't know you were pregnant, or I'd have been more careful with my words, but I want to spend my life with you. Your child – our child – will be loved, the same as I love my sister's child, and the same as I'll love any children we have together.'

I find I'm crying, but they're tears of relief and happiness.

'But there is one thing,' he says slowly.

Something in me goes cold, but I lift my head to see a quirk of amusement.

'You haven't actually accepted my proposal yet.'

I chuckle. 'Oh, Justin. You have no idea how much I've wanted to tell you yes, long before you even asked.'

'Everything is going to turn out all right – you'll see.' He pecks a soft kiss onto my lips. 'It will all work out. Sleep well.'

'I think I might.'

How foolishly, how desperately, I had given myself to Cathal and almost blighted my own future. How lucky I am. My heart sings to know that Justin sees the real me and loves me, and to know my child will be loved.

In the morning, Justin slips out to walk along the river while we take breakfast. It must be hard for him to face the concept that his granddad is alive, after a lifetime of believing he had died all those years ago. Danny makes himself absent after breakfast, too, leaving Aine and I to have some time to ourselves.

'Danny's gone to bet on the horses,' Aine says. I must look shocked, as she laughs. 'It's about enjoying the race, not desperately hoping for a windfall.'

'I'm relieved to hear it,' I say dryly.

'I'd rather have him lose a few bob at the races than turn to drink, like Dad. So, tell me about Justin. Has he asked you to marry him?'

I blush. 'He did, last night.'

She squeals with excitement and jumps up to do a neat pirouette before sitting again and putting her arm around me. Then she asks seriously, 'Does he know?'

'He does. I told him.'

'And he's okay with that?'

'He's amazingly okay with it. He already has a child at home. Paul, who's three years old. His sister's child, not his.'

Her voice snaps, 'She abandoned her child?'

'No, she died. I don't know the details.'

Her fury fades. 'Oh, sad. But Paul is lucky, you know. He's got a man to be dad to him, and now he's going to have a mam and a baby brother or sister.'

I pause and suddenly realise I can't leave Aisling in the dark any longer. 'Ah, talking of sisters, I've, ah, got something I must tell you.'

She is instantly still, sensing the import behind my words, and as I give her the abbreviated version about my childhood, her jaw gradually drops. I finally grimace and add, 'So, you see, we're not really sisters at all.'

She sits back and eyes me curiously. 'So, why are you only telling me this now?'

'I was afraid,' I admit.

'Afraid of what?'

'That you wouldn't want to, ah, know me any longer.'

She puts an arm around me and hugs me tightly, as close to tears as I am. 'Don't be daft, Hannah. You're my sister in every way that matters. I'd feel the same if you were my real sister, or if you had been adopted. Let's face it, if I didn't have you, I wouldn't have a sister to call a sister at all! I love you, Hannah, and I always will. So!' she says decisively, 'that's got that out of the way. Now we can move on to more important things, like you getting married and coming to England after all.'

And all my anxiety flies away as if by magic. I smile. 'England but not London. He lives by the sea, and it sounds a bit like Roone Bay. A small fishing community.'

She shudders dramatically, laughing at the same time. 'Well, it looks as if I'll have to visit you, then, if you won't visit me. But I just want you to know that if it doesn't work out with Justin, you can still come to live with us, baby and all. Danny's okay with that.'

'He's a good man, your Danny.'

'He's sound, all right. For a boxer.'

'I'm so happy for you, Aine.'

'Well, it was time I got lucky in love. I've been dancing for several years now, and you wouldn't believe the number of indecent proposals I've had. It's kind of nice not to worry about going home after a gig, afraid that some nutter is going to follow me. I used to have to walk, but now if Danny can't come and walk me home, at least I can afford a cab.'

'You never said in your letters that it was dangerous where you are!'

'I wasn't going to worry you, was I? It's always dangerous for women who do that kind of work. Inviting trouble, people say. But I just like dancing. It's not exactly a sin, is it? Anyway, I get good gigs now. I have an agent and do backing work for musicals and pop groups rather than nightclub gigs.'

'I've never seen you dance like that.'

She giggles. 'You must! Mam would turn in her grave at the outfits and the moves.' She rolls her eyes. 'But times have changed, you know.'

'Not in Ireland. Convention is still king. If the priest in Roone Bay had known I was pregnant, he'd have me married off to Cathal in an instant.'

'Or he'd call you out from the pulpit, and him probably banging underage boys.'

'Aine!'

She grins. 'Well, priests are sexually confused, aren't they?'

'Cathal wouldn't marry me without the farm, anyway. He'd have done a runner, rather.'

At that moment, Justin and Danny walk back in, companionably. 'We met in the high street,' Danny says, leaning down to plant a kiss on Aine's lips. 'Won a couple of bob on Angel's Delight. So, what's happening, girls?'

I laugh at being included in this phrase.

Justin says, 'Well, I have an appointment with the past after lunch.' He glances at his watch. 'But I don't think I could eat, I'm so wound up. Will you come with me, Hannah?'

'Moral support?' I ask.

'Maybe a little. But I want Jack to meet you, and I'd like you to share this moment with me.'

I cast a quick look at Aine, feeling guilty, but Danny beams at Aine and nudges her. 'Come on – let's leave these lovebirds and see if we can't buy you something nice with my winnings.'

She laughs. I love the easy way they have with each other.

'Give us girls five minutes,' she says. 'We'll just freshen up and fetch our coats.'

39

HANNAH

When we knock on Aisling's door, she opens it herself. 'I was wondering if you'd come back for the rest of the story, or go home feeling justifiably betrayed,' she says, slowly leading the way in.

Justin shakes his head. 'Not betrayed, no. I haven't slept a wink, but every way I've thought it through, it makes sense – what Jack did, I mean. But I have so many questions for you both.'

She smiles openly, and behind the paper-thin, wrinkled skin I see the strong-willed girl she must have been. 'I'm pleased you see it that way. I know you have questions. I have some, too. I'm curious about Hannah.' She directs her words to me. 'You're Irish through and through, yet here you are, with Jack's grandson.'

'We only met recently,' I say quickly. 'Justin came to Roone Bay asking questions about his granddad, and no one would tell him anything. He asked me to help.'

'Sure, there's still bad feeling about the Black and Tans. And the IRA are still at their shenanigans up north, trying to unite Ireland into one country, but I'm not going into the rights and wrongs of the way they're going about it.' She shakes her head. 'You said your granddad was with the rebels, back in the day?'

I nod.

'So, who was he?'

'Conor Barry.'

'Oh, yes, I remember him. He was a bold one, sure enough. He hung around with Turlough, who was always a strange twig of a lad, even then. They ran messages for the rebels, all right. It's strange to think of Conor grown up and married.'

'Granddad Conor passed a long time back, but apparently he and Turlough were following the rebels when the barracks was raided. Turlough thought he saw the men hang Jack on the big stone, but it was Billy Devon they hanged, wasn't it?'

'If the boys saw that, I'm sorry. It wasn't quick. It wasn't a sight for children. It wasn't undeserved, though. Billy Devon was pure evil. He'd boasted to Jack of doing horrible things in the war. He might have hurt more than one woman in Roone Bay, too. If he did, they didn't say. Women wouldn't have, back then. But that one, she told her husband, though Billy had threatened her children if she spoke out. That was brave enough. But that was why the rebels burned the barracks. Our local copper was let leave. He moved up to Rathmore, I heard. A couple of Black and Tans were let to walk to Cork city.' She smiles grimly. 'I don't know how far they got. There wasn't a body in the county who would have helped them.'

'Granddad Conor died about the time I got polio, and Dad never told me any stories about the past. All I know was what I found in the library.'

At that moment, the door creaks open. The bent old man who comes in, leaning on a stick, bears no relation to the tall, upright soldier I'd been imagining. He has no weight on his bones, liver spots on his gnarled hands, and fine wisps of white hair. But the sunken eyes that gaze piercingly from under his lined brow are Justin's.

Justin stands and holds out his arms. 'Granddad Jack?' he says.

There are tears in Jack's eyes as his grandson embraces him. He's obviously at a loss for words, so Aisling says, 'Well, I think this calls for a wee drop of the pure, don't you? It's a celebration, not a blooming funeral. Not yet, anyway.'

I shake my head. 'My dad was an alcoholic. I don't drink.'

'Ah. No bother. We'll have tea, then.' She slips out.

Jack gives a laugh that sounds like a hacking cough, and I realise that he's an ill man. 'Tea? The woman's been waiting to see me underground for years. She'll get her wish soon enough without depriving me of my tipple.' But he casts a grin that takes accusation from the words.

'Will we sit?' Justin suggests, ever the doctor.

'So,' Jack says, 'Mama left an envelope for you to find. Or for someone to find, anyway. She wasn't daft enough to do that by accident. If there was just one, the others must have been binned. Sneaky Mama. I didn't expect this, not after all these years.'

'Great-Gran was a canny one,' Justin agrees. 'I hope you don't mind, but I read all your letters. I wouldn't have, if I'd known you were still alive.'

'It's too late to go minding, son. I'm sorry I didn't get to see Mama before she passed, but we wrote often. Maybe it's possible to put things in letters that you can't say in person. Maybe we were closer for all that the Irish Sea was between us. When I die, Aisling will give you all Mama's letters to me. Then you'll have the whole story. She was a wonderful woman, and the more I know, the more I realise how wonderful she really was. And my son, does he know?'

Justin shakes his head. 'I'm not sure it would be right to tell him. I guess he'd be hurt and offended at learning his real dad had been alive all this time and didn't want to know him. And Grandma Rose would realise that she's never been legitimately married. It would open a real can of worms.'

'Sure it would, sure it would,' he agrees.

He turns his gaze on me. 'And how does Hannah fit into the story?'

'She's going to be my wife.'

'Ah, history repeats itself. Another Irish lass off to England. We'll win the war yet, just by populating the planet.'

We laugh, and Aisling comes back in and sets the tray on the table. Her gaze settles on Jack with a depth of love that hasn't died over the years. She takes a deep breath. 'So, Justin, you want to know about me and Jack. We had four children, all boys. They grew up and married. Two of them are still local, one is in America, one in the north. We have a bundle of grandchildren, and another on the way.'

Jack gives an amused smile. 'You have an extensive family to get to know.'

Justin takes this in for a moment, then he asks, 'Do they know about my family?'

'They've always known. Our Sean even visited you once, when you were little. Took photos of Jack's mam and Walter and you to bring back.'

Justin frowns. 'He did?'

'Oh, he didn't make himself known,' Aisling says. 'Jack was mighty upset when he admitted it, I tell you. But there. What's done can't be undone.'

Jack says, 'I'm after thinking we should have a gathering in the summer for my birthday. I'll be eighty-five years old if I make it that far. If not, they'll all be at my wake,' he adds with a laugh. 'Will you both come over?'

'Sure, we will!' Justin answers, beaming.

40

HANNAH

I can't recall all the words that were spoken at that epic meeting, but Justin and Jack bonded as if they had known each other all their lives. Perhaps there's something in the genes after all, that passed from Justin's great-grandmother, to her son, to his grandson. Whatever happens now, in our future, I know that this meeting will have a profound effect on Justin's peace of mind. His granddad left to follow his heart, but it wasn't so much an act of cowardice as great bravery.

How strange that both Justin and I, in the space of just a few weeks, have discovered such complex family histories. I'd like to say it's life-changing, but whether this new knowledge will affect our future, who knows? Only time will tell.

When we arrive back at the hotel, we relate everything to Aine and Danny.

'I wish I could have been a fly on the wall in that house,' Aine sighs. 'So blooming sad and happy at the same time. All these years Jack was still alive and no one knew. But at the same time, you'd want to kill him, wouldn't you?'

She has a way of dispelling the gloom, but Justin makes the

sad observation that he doesn't know whether he will meet Jack again in this life.

'We can but hope,' I say, and he hugs me close.

Justin is silent on the drive home the next morning. Danny takes the road through Ballyvourney rather than negotiate the winding pass. We drift through a changing landscape of rich farmland through to the marginal, rugged hillsides that bound Roone Bay.

Danny drives straight up the slope to the hotel. 'Noel and Caitlin said you can stay at theirs,' he says to me as he parks. 'But we'd like you to spend the evening with us before we leave for England.'

'But—'

'And don't you worry about the cost. Justin and I have decided. Mark will probably still be up at the farm,' he says bluntly. 'Best to leave that conflict for another day.'

Justin says, 'It's been a strange few days, eh? It would be nice to simply chill for a bit. Get to know Aine and Danny a bit more.'

And get to know each other a bit more, I think. I gaze at my future husband, still hardly daring to believe that this wonderful, caring man has come into my life. I couldn't have imagined just a few weeks ago how happy my future could be.

At the reception desk, Grace takes one look at our faces and shows us straight into the dining room. 'Sit down and eat. Tomorrow will take care of itself.'

As we eat, Justin admits, 'It was strange, really. I've always thought of Jack the way Great-Gran and Granny Rose described him: a big man, over six feet tall, with broad shoulders, a placid manner and gently spoken, and he was this little old man, so frail a breath of air might blow him away. I thought for a moment that it was all wrong, that this couldn't possibly be Jack, but he just looked at me, and almost instantly I knew it was him.'

'He's a lovely man,' I say. 'The sort of man you just like the moment you meet him, even if you don't know why.'

'He is, but he was right to wonder how I'd react. I didn't know myself whether I'd be angry at his lifelong betrayal of my grandmother and my father, or be pleased to discover he hadn't been murdered by the rebels all those years ago.'

'Did he speak of the war? The First World War, I mean?' Danny asked.

'Not in so many words. Aisling said it had damaged him, so it sounded like it would be best not to ask,' I say.

Justin nods. 'He just said that he had spent a lifetime trying to forget it, and only death would achieve that. He said he'd made his peace with his mother and with God and now with me. He asked if I would keep his secret at least until he and Aisling had passed.'

'And will you?' Aine asks.

'I will. Aisling understood because she'd run in the hills with the IRA and seen a little of death, but my father would never understand.' He looks up wearily, but his eyes are level as he adds, 'I wanted to be angry with him, but he was younger than I am now when all this happened, and he'd already seen and done so much in his life. I get the impression he was losing the will to carry on when Aisling met him, and yes, I do think she saved him.'

'What will you tell your family?'

'I'll tell them I put a wreath on his grave. Maybe next year I'll be doing that for real. My father was never interested in knowing what had happened to his real father – it was old history to him. Dad is more like his stepfather, who was an accountant, and is a somewhat complacent character. I think that's why I gravitated towards Great-Grandma. She had a spark in her, like her son. It's strange to think that while I was growing up and she was telling me stories about what Jack was like as a child, she knew all the time that he wasn't dead.'

'It's amazing that she could keep that a secret all those years.'

'Yes, it is. But thinking back, I'm sure she enjoyed the subterfuge, in her own way. She would have liked Aisling. She always said Rose was just like the flower, pretty and scented with hidden thorns.'

I give a snort of laughter. 'But she was loyal to Rose all the same.'

'She was. And if she's up there looking down on us, I think she'd have a smug smile on her face. We've agreed to come back to Ireland in the summer, when it's Jack's birthday. He isn't sure he'll still be around, but I hope he will be. You can both come with us, if you wish.'

'Try to stop me!' Aine says. 'This is just so exciting!'

'And it isn't even your story,' Danny reminds her. He looks at me. 'So, have you decided what you're going to do?'

'She's going to marry me and come back to Somerset,' Justin says.

'I mean about the farm.'

'Mark can have the damn farm. I don't care.'

'Good,' Justin says. 'We can't take it with us to England, after all.'

Danny nods approval. 'Right, we have to set off quite early for the ferry tomorrow, so me and Aine need to go and pack.'

'Oh, the time has gone so quickly!'

'It has, but as you're coming to England, we're going to see more of each other. It won't be ten years next time.'

'Absolutely,' I agree.

'And you'd better not get married without inviting us!'

'Ditto,' I say, laughing.

'So, we'll see you in the morning before we leave.'

I stand and hug my sister and Danny.

'So,' Justin says after they've gone, 'maybe we ought to wander up to see Noel? He'll be itching to know how we got on.'

We walk up together and knock on the door, but there's no answer, so we slip around the side of the house to where I guess the kitchen door is situated. Through the glass doors, I see Noel in the easy chair, his head tipped back in sleep. The three dogs sitting at his feet glance up curiously.

I knock on the glass, and Noel jolts awake. There's a moment of confusion before he sees us and beckons. 'Hannah! Justin! Come in, come in. This is most opportune!'

We go in, and I pull the door shut behind us. With all the posh rooms at his disposal, I'm slightly amused that Noel chooses to sit in the kitchen. He's not so far from his poor-boy roots, after all he's been through.

'So,' he says eagerly, 'did you find anything at all?'

'We found out everything,' Justin says complacently and proceeds to explain.

Noel is as delighted as a child at Christmas. He keeps interspersing the narrative with exclamations, and when Justin winds to a halt, Caitlin arrives and he has to tell it all over again.

'And so,' she says finally, 'is that all?'

Noel looks confused, but Justin laughs. 'It takes a woman to see these things. I've asked Hannah if she'll marry me. She'll be coming back to England with me after all.'

'Oh my!' Noel exclaims, his gaze popping from Justin's face to mine. 'Oh my! Oh, grand! That's grand, so it is!'

He insists on hugging me and shaking Justin's hand until Caitlin tells him to desist before he pulls it right off. 'So, you have something to tell,' she then reminds Noel.

'Oh, absolutely, sure I do,' he says. 'A solicitor from Bantry was asking after you, asking for you to go in to meet him and Mark.'

'I don't want the farm any longer. I'm not going to contest Mark's claim. He can do what he wants with it.'

'Maybe,' Noel says, 'but there's something strange going on. It's not the solicitor you saw before, the one who wrote Adrian's will. It's a different one. I do wonder whether Adrian made another will after all, and it's just come to light.'

'I don't want to be bothered,' I say, grimacing.

'Well, perhaps we should go, just to find out what he's after?' Justin advises. 'I'll be there with you, and if anything upsets you, we can just leave.'

'All right,' I sigh. Whatever it is, best to get it over with so that I can get on with my life. At least now I have the support of people who care about me.

41

HANNAH

The solicitor's small, neat and functional room is painted a nondescript magnolia. It contains half a dozen chairs, a huge bookcase crammed with what I suppose are legal tomes and an enormous desk. Mark is already seated before the desk when we arrive, his arms crossed over his chest. He fills the space with his belligerent scowl.

'Brought the back-up team?' he sneers as Justin escorts me into the room. But his expression morphs into confused surprise as our neighbour, Mickey Hoolihan, follows us in, nodding a greeting.

Why is Mickey here? Something to do with the renting of the fields, I guess. I find I don't care very much in all honesty. He and Mark can sort it out between them. I'm going to marry Justin and go to England, and nothing else matters. I'm floating in my own little bubble of happiness, hoping that whatever is said today isn't going to burst it. I don't see what can. Justin and I have had all the surprises we can cope with, and life will never be the same, thank goodness.

I will leave Roone Bay with a clean slate. The farm is gone. Noel is going to add Old Grey to his collection of retired donkeys, and Mickey has already rescued my hens. There's nothing left here for me to worry about.

I wait as the solicitor puts his elbows on the table and steeples his fingers. 'Right. Now we're all present, there's no point in procrastinating. For the record, none of you need be here at all, but Mickey has asked that you be present so that there is no subsequent room for doubt.'

'Advised of what? What's Mickey Hoolihan got to do with it?' Mark growls.

The solicitor ignores him. 'Firstly, I would like to assure you, Hannah, that your father's last will and testament, as provided by Mark, is legal and valid.'

Mark sneers smugly in my direction.

Justin reaches for my hand and squeezes it in silent agreement that we no longer feel the need to contest it.

Then the solicitor throws a verbal bomb into the room. 'But subsequent to the drawing up of the will, Adrian Barry sold the farm, complete and in its entirety, to Mickey Hoolihan. So, although Mark legally inherits everything according to the terms of the will, there is, in fact, nothing to inherit.'

His words are greeted by a long, stunned silence.

Then Mark suddenly screeches his chair back with an oath. He stands with fists clenched, leaning towards the solicitor aggressively. 'No,' he snaps. 'That's not right. It's my farm! Dad left it to me!'

I flinch, but the solicitor's expression barely changes. 'Please sit down, Mark. I won't have that sort of behaviour in my office.'

Mark sits, slowly and reluctantly, sullen as a schoolboy, and the solicitor continues. 'Your father said, if I recall correctly, that he had no children worthy of inheriting. He said – excuse me, Hannah; I'm quoting – *the cripple my wife brought home from the hospital was more worthy than all of my own children combined.*' He casts a sidelong glance at Mark as he speaks. 'The agreement made with Mickey allowed that Mickey would not pay outright for the farm but provide Adrian with a weekly stipend until such time as Adrian passed. After that, Mickey would unconditionally pay the balance of the agreed sum to Hannah. Mickey is now ready to honour that stipulation. Mickey, Hannah and I will discuss the process once we have the room.'

I'm shocked speechless.

Mark, who had gone into an almost catatonic state after sitting, jolts to the awareness that he's been dismissed. He rises and casts a look of pure evil in my direction. He stabs a threatening finger in my direction. 'I'm going to contest this. It's my farm.'

'Don't waste your money,' the solicitor advises. 'There's nothing to contest.'

Mickey's stance tightens, but after a brittle moment Mark stamps out, slamming the door hard behind him.

The solicitor grimaces. 'I really thought he was going to hit me. I wasn't looking forward to that meeting.'

'But why on earth didn't we know about this before?' I ask, finally finding my voice.

'That was my fault,' Mickey admits. 'I was waiting to see if he intended to do right by you. I thought that being a married man with children, he might have grown a conscience, but once a langer, always a langer. When he arrived home, I watched him throw money over the bar trying to impress his mates. The only good thing he did for you was tell everyone in the bar, including Cathal Carrol, that you weren't getting anything.'

I flush faintly. Does everyone in Roone Bay know how daft I'd been? Or how desperate. 'He was hoping I'd contest the will, but I'm pretty sure he knows that we're finished.'

'It won't be long before people know I own the farm,' Mickey says, a slow smile creasing his cheeks. Then his gaze flicks between me and Justin. 'Hannah, I'm very pleased for you.'

So, that word got around quickly, too.

'Maybe Hannah and Mickey could discuss the payment?' the solicitor reminds us.

Justin's hand exerts a small supportive pressure. 'I'll leave you to work out the details. I'll be outside.'

'I feel a little sorry for Mark, actually,' I say.

'Save your energy,' Mickey says. 'He wouldn't have given you a penny. In the grand scheme of things, it's a very small inheritance. But it's up to you.'

'I'm not him. I was thinking about his children.'

'Well, don't do anything in a hurry,' the solicitor advises. 'Take your time, find out about his circumstances. And you can be sure, if you give him anything, he won't thank you for it.' A small smile tips the corners of his lips. 'I wasn't looking forward to this meeting, but there's a certain poetic symmetry to the events, don't you think?'

42

HANNAH

That night, Justin pulls me in front of him and puts his arms around me, holding me in a close embrace. The moon has risen, turning the Atlantic into an undulating sheet of mercury. The stars above are sprinkled thickly. 'It's beautiful, isn't it?'

So beautiful I almost want to cry. 'I'm going to miss Roone Bay.'

'I know. But you'll love West Somerset. It's not really the same as here,' he says softly. 'It's got big rolling hills that sweep down towards the sea. There are hedge boundaries centuries old, and woodlands that stretch into deep valleys with tumbling streams. Our children will be happy there. We can get a dog. And a cat.'

'And some chickens?'

'And chickens, of course! Just imagine. You won't be homesick, because when you wake up in the morning and look out over the sea, you'll know Ireland is just over the horizon. And we will visit often and show our children where you grew up. And visit your new family, of course.'

'How strange life is,' I muse. 'A couple of months ago, I felt so lonely, so abandoned, and now I have friends and family everywhere. It's weird, so it is.'

Before we leave Ireland, I harness Old Grey to the cart for the last time, and Justin joins me for a farewell jaunt. I pull the old donkey to a halt as we descend from the Big House towards the main road. The Atlantic stretches out into the bay and further into the unknown. I never tire of this view. Sometimes the sea is the colour of the sky sprinkled with glitter, sometimes it's black as the priest's frock and sometimes it's one of a million shades between.

I will miss my home.

I've seen this view when the storms are down, when the angry waves claw at the quay and reach for the houses straggled around the shoreline. Today the sea is a sheet of steel, with a faint winter breeze brushing the dark clouds. There's something uniquely magical about this rugged, battered coastline that doesn't need to be enhanced with myths. Our own legends, built on a gossamer gauze of truth, speak out from every peak and valley, from every grave marker and standing stone. I drink in the view and the scent of the sea, wondering if I'll find solace in Somerset.

As we trot along the road, people I don't recognise wave. They all know my story. They all know I'm leaving Roone Bay forever. Their expressions of satisfaction are not because I'm leaving but because I've found happiness, and that brings hope to people whose own problems lie hidden.

I can't stop beaming. I am loved, and my child will be loved.

I click my tongue. Old Grey plods on down the hill, through a narrowing arch of skeletal branches. Soon the tiny buds, presently nodding in the soft breeze, will swell and burst, and the boreens will sing with spring once again, whether I am here or not.

EPILOGUE

HANNAH

West Somerset is as beautiful as Justin said it was. We're locked in a silent embrace at the bedroom window of his – our – cottage, gazing out over the sea towards Ireland. The sea is not black and silver here, but stained in a brown fan by the mud that leaches out from the estuary on every tide. It smells the same, though, of salt and wet stones, and seagulls still wheel overhead with their endless scream for food. There's a small harbour at the foot of the road that smells of fish and lobster pots, and old fishermen gather in Sailors Bar in the evening and tell tall tales.

Below, on the front lawn, Glory, our rescued golden retriever, is presently barking wildly, bouncing around Paul on his hind legs, playing a game they seem to have invented between them. I have newly bought chickens in a run in the back yard, and occasionally I think of Old Grey and wonder whether he misses me and the old cart.

'I still feel sorry for Mark sometimes,' I muse.

'Not too sorry, I hope,' Justin says. 'He got more than he deserved. As the solicitor said, he wouldn't have given you anything at all.'

'I'm not him.'

Justin nuzzles my neck. 'I'm aware of that.'

My belly is beginning to weigh me down, and my legs are aching more every day. One of the sad things about polio is that although I can't use my legs, I still feel pain. I'll be glad when the baby is born. I'm a bit afraid of childbirth, but as Justin reminds me, I have a doctor close at hand, and he won't let anything bad happen to me. Everyone thinks the baby is his. *No need to start the little chap's life with prejudice and confusion*, he'd said.

'What if it's a girl?'

'I'll be happy out.'

I laugh. 'That's a very Irish expression!'

'I learned it from Great-Grandma. She's still with me, in here.' He puts a hand over his chest. 'And so are Jack and Aisling. I've decided to carry on with Great-Grandma's tradition of writing to them every month. By the time we go and visit, we'll have a little more understanding of everything that went on back in the day and how they lived after they got to Kerry. If any relatives come over to visit, we can say they descend from Great-Grandma. We won't be lying exactly.'

'So, you've decided not to tell Rose or Walter about Jack?'

'I promised Jack I wouldn't. They think he's long gone, and he soon will be, in truth.'

'So, we're starting our relationship with a bucketload of secrets?'

'Much the same as most married couples. Which reminds me, my love, we'd best get going. We don't want to be late for our own wedding.'

He grins as Aine yells up the stairs asking if we're ready. I hug him. 'Especially since nearly everyone in my real family has made the effort to come to England for the wedding, even though a few months ago they didn't even know I existed.'

'I think it's wonderful. They can't do enough for you.

Doesn't it give you faith in human nature? You had a bundle of bad experiences, but we have a lifetime ahead of us to make up for that.'

'Just think. So much good has come out of your granddad Jack's decision to go to Ireland. If he'd gone back to Rose, they both would have ended up unhappy, you would never have come to Ireland, and I might have married Cathal... Do you remember the priest in Macroom? You know what he would say?'

He lifts a brow. 'And what's that, then?'

'God had a plan after all.'

He's chortling as we descend the stairs together.

A LETTER FROM DAISY

Thank you so much for reading *The Irish Daughter*. I would love it if you kept up to date with all my novels and any other significant news from Bookouture, so do make sure to sign up at the following link. Your email address will never be shared, and you can unsubscribe at any time.

www.bookouture.com/daisy-oshea

At the time of writing, in Ireland alone there are still some 250,000 polio survivors, not only coping with their disabilities in daily life but discovering that polio can re-emerge as post-polio syndrome in later life.

While visiting a charity shop in Skibbereen, I met a lady who had contracted polio as a child in the 1950s epidemic. She has worn callipers since she was four years old and was surely the catalyst for Hannah's character. She told me of some of her experiences, such as being whisked away from her family in an ambulance and spending so long in hospital she didn't recognise her mother when her parents came to take her home. She underwent numerous painful operations that enabled her to walk, she endured bullying from other children because she was 'different' and when a local man asked for her hand, her father actually said, 'There must be something wrong with him if he wants to marry you.' I had a brief thought: what if the woman who had collected her from the hospital, who she didn't recognise, truly hadn't been her real mother…

A beta reader suggested that surely a mother would know her own child, but my own mother was in hospital with scarlet fever for several months as a three-year-old, and when Gran went to pick her daughter up, she truly didn't recognise her. Sickness can change a person's appearance, and fear can change a mother's perception.

One of my most gratifying experiences as an author is to know that readers enjoyed the novel and closed the last pages with a sigh of satisfaction, even maybe a little tear. If you did, then I'd be delighted if you would leave a review to let other readers know how much you enjoyed the story. Be sure, though, to dwell on the characterisation, the writing style and your own emotional responses, and don't give away any critical plot points.

I've lived in West Cork since early retirement, and it's been the most fulfilling time of my life. I love the wild countryside, the rocky seashores, the call of the sea, the scarred history, the underlying myths and legends, and most of all, the inclusive warmth of the dauntless Irish people. There's a wisp of fey here, in rural Ireland, that subtly underpins all our lives and which quietly infuses my stories. I do hope you're looking forward to my next book as much as I'm enjoying writing it.

All the best, Daisy

www.daisyoshea.com

facebook.com/DaisyOSheaAuthor
x.com/westcorkwriter

AUTHOR'S NOTES

DISCLAIMER

Roone Bay isn't a real town, and any individual homes and businesses mentioned are fabrications. There are many families in the area with the surnames I've chosen to use, but any similarity to real persons, alive or dead, is entirely coincidental. All views in the work are those of the characters, not the author.

OVERVIEW OF IRELAND

Ireland is divided into the four provinces: Connacht, Leinster, Munster and Ulster. There are cities, towns and townlands, but the term 'village' is not used. Within the provinces there are thirty-two counties containing around 64,000 townlands – historic areas that once might have been clan boundaries and which can be anything between one hundred to five hundred acres.

Roone Bay is set in Munster, on the southern coast of Ireland, in the mythical townland of Tírbeg, somewhere between Bantry and Skibbereen. (In Irish, *Tír* means place, *beg* means small.)

PRONUNCIATION

Aine: *Onya*
Aisling: *Ash-ling*

Caitlin: *Kathleen*
Cathal: *Ca-hal*
Eoghan: *Owen*
O'Shea: *Oh Shay*
Poitín: *po (as in pot)-cheen*
Turlough: *Ter-lock*

ACKNOWLEDGEMENTS

My thanks go first to my husband, Robin, who's believed in me in every way from the moment we met. A staunch supporter of my passion for writing, he's the first critic of my work, my best friend and also my 'til-death-us-do-part love. Thanks to my lovely mother, Alma Yea, one-time librarian and teacher, for encouraging me to read fiction when I was a child. Thanks to the whole team at Bookouture, who manage the process so efficiently. Thanks to Angela Snowden, editor extraordinaire, who points out my bloomers. Last, but certainly not least, thanks to all the readers who enjoy my fiction. Without you, my work would be pointless, so don't be afraid to reach out and provide me with much-needed reassurance.

PUBLISHING TEAM

Turning a manuscript into a book requires the efforts of many people. The publishing team at Bookouture would like to acknowledge everyone who contributed to this publication.

Commercial
Lauren Morrissette
Hannah Richmond
Imogen Allport

Cover design
Tim Barber

Data and analysis
Mark Alder
Mohamed Bussuri

Editorial
Kelsie Marsden
Lizzie Brien

Copyeditor
Angela Snowden

Proofreader
Laura Kincaid

Marketing
Alex Crow
Melanie Price
Occy Carr
Ciara Rosney
Martyna Młynarska

Operations and distribution
Marina Valles
Stephanie Straub
Joe Morris

Production
Hannah Snetsinger
Mandy Kullar
Ria Clare
Nadia Michael

Publicity
Kim Nash
Noelle Holten
Jess Readett
Sarah Hardy

Rights and contracts
Peta Nightingale
Richard King
Saidah Graham

Printed in Great Britain
by Amazon